THE FIFTH TWEET

Roy M. Burgess

This edition published by Mill Tower Books 2023

ISBN : 978-1-7394807-3-8

For Ruth, who encouraged me to start this journey
and in whose memory I completed it.
The strength (but not the dodgy book-keeping)
of the women in the book comes from her.
Ruth Burgess 1969-2018

When I started out, I knew nothing about writing a book. For inflicting early drafts on friends, I am genuinely sorry! Thanks to Morwenna, Keith, Mike and Kevin for feedback and encouragement. Most of all, thanks to Clare for the free consultancy, grammar lessons and total support. Thanks also to Pulp Studio for the cover design. Stand by - work on a follow-up starts now.

Please get in touch via:

Twitter - @royburgess40

Facebook @royburgess40

Sign up for the mailing list at RoyBurgess.com

Reviews are crucial to any author. If you get a minute, please add one to Amazon and Goodreads.

Anyway, hope you enjoy The Fifth Tweet.

Roy Burgess June 2021

1

Let's face it, 2016 didn't get off to a great start. David Bowie died. My musical hero - gone. Just like that. My girlfriend - gone. Just like that. Well, not quite just like that; she's still very much alive. But she's living with Brian now, not me. Still, with January out of the way, I could concentrate on February being crap.

I'd always pitied the old guys, sitting alone in the pub in the afternoon. Now I appeared to have joined them. Not joining them as in sitting with them and conversing. More sitting alone, with a pint, and feeling miserable. Not bad for thirty-seven. Thirty years ahead of schedule.

I was busy investigating what I took to be egg on my shirt and didn't notice the approaching barman.

'I wish you'd stop shredding beer mats. It doesn't count as a real hobby, you know.'

I looked down at the sorry, soggy mass of ex-beer mat on the table. 'Sorry, Ambrose. Bad day.'

'Any other type these days?'

'Suppose not. Give us another.'

Ambrose issued one of his looks, and I watched him while

he pulled another pint.

'You do realise you're starting to, like, kinda smell?'

'Cheers, mate.'

'I'm serious. You've sat there for the last four nights and most of the afternoons as well.' I moved my left arm and applied the sniff test. He was right. 'And you've had a face like a slapped arse all week. I don't want to sound like I care, but what's up?'

'Nowt.' I took a long drink from the new pint in front of me.

'Cheer up then, for god's sake. This place is miserable enough as it is on a Monday without you being a mardy-arse.'

'There's no other bugger here; why do I need to be cheerful?'

To prove me wrong, the front door opened. Bill and Jean shuffled in, shaking the rain from their matching coats. Nods were exchanged, and Ambrose went off to get their drinks without asking.

Ambrose was right, of course, but I was sulking. The whole point of sulking is that you don't have to admit when somebody else is right. There didn't have to be any logic attached. I didn't make the rules. I suppose, over the years, Ambrose had gradually become one of my best mates. Friends from school had drifted away, married, some had kids, one had two years for breaking and entering. Actually, I didn't mind losing contact with Billy. I bumped into him when he got out. I asked the obvious question, what are you doing these days?

'Last week I did a post office.' Time to move on.

A pint of mild and a gin and bitter lemon dispensed, Ambrose returned to try again.

'I'd heard Cheryl fucked off with Brian. Bit of a double whammy.' He took my grunt as encouragement. 'Shame.

Brian was a laugh.' He wiped the table. 'Cheryl had a canny arse as well.'

I couldn't help laughing, the first in four days.

'Bastard.'

Cheryl. I couldn't even say her name for a long time. For a while, I knew her as some unpleasant things. Now I recognise that I don't hate her. I hate what she did. She left me. She walked out and took with her my original copy of Ziggy Stardust, two grand from our savings account, the charger for my electric toothbrush, and my best mate and business partner. Technically, ex-best mate and ex-business partner, henceforth treacherous bastard Brian.

I took another drink.

'Bastard', I said again.

'That's more like it. Seriously though, we've all been dumped. Why wallow in it like this?'

'It's not just being dumped. Everything's such a bloody mess. I really thought Cheryl was the one.' I couldn't believe I put air quotes around the last bit. 'The business for a start. All the clients we had will go with him.' Ambrose was polishing glasses from the other end of the bar. He walked back towards me and grabbed a bag of crisps from the shelf, putting them in front of me. 'How can you be sure?'

'For a start, they included both his dad and Cheryl's new company. Somehow, he'd managed to get a foot in with the local council as well. I can't see them taking a risk with somebody totally new.'

'OK, you may have a point, but come on, fresh start and all that. Get more clients. I've never really understood. What do you do, exactly?'

'We build websites and manage social media.'

'So, most of the time, you dick around with Facebook and Twitter.'

'There's more to it than that.' I shuffled indignantly as

Ambrose raised his eyebrows. 'I dick around with Instagram as well.'

'There you go. Clients should be queuing outside the door by now.'

'Brian handled all that sort of stuff. I do – did the technical side. Well, me and Rupert. Rupert was a kind of intern. I think that's what they call it when you don't pay them anything. He was too good for Brian to lose, offered him a job at the same time as he offered me a payoff.'

'So you have cash to live on?'

I shuffled uneasily. This is where I knew I'd been a dick.

'Not really. I told him to "shove his money up his arse."'

'Doesn't that mean you still own half the company?' I was extremely uncomfortable at this point and simply shrugged. 'What does a shrug mean?'

'I sort of signed the papers, then wrote "shove your money up your arse" on the contract.'

'Prick.'

'Thanks.'

'OK, you fucked up. So go get a job in IT. There's a million companies out there. Start being positive.'

'I am positive.' To prove it, I picked up my phone and continued to sulk while pretending to read Facebook. Ambrose took the hint and went off to straighten his pork scratchings. I couldn't resist flicking to a photo of Cheryl. It was my favourite. She was sitting on the beach in Blackpool, just after we'd had fish and chips. The setting sun reflected in her face. She was wearing my fleece, and I'd been frozen but wouldn't admit it. How could it have got to this? I was less than three years from my forties, for Christ's sake. Everybody else had grown up by the time they reached forty. Not me, apparently.

Two minutes later, Ambrose was back. 'Playing with that won't help either. You need to talk to real people.'

'You're real people.'

'I don't count. I'm being paid to do this. Look, I've got an idea. I've got a challenge for you. Something I read about last week. Give me five days, and I bet things turn around. If not, you can carry on being a miserable git, and we'll just buy some air freshener.'

'Go on then, what's your big idea?'

'Not now. Back here tomorrow at 6 o'clock. I want you showered, presentable, and open-minded.'

'This isn't anything pervy, is it? Or one of your grandma's old Jamaican remedies?'

'No. Now fuck off home and stop drinking for the night.'

Strangely enough, that's precisely what I did.

I had tried to spend the day constructively, honestly, but I couldn't concentrate. The Muppets box-set just didn't do it, so I frittered the time away instead. Something about the conversation with Ambrose last night bothered me. What the hell was he going to suggest? It'd better not be some weird folk dancing thing. I said I'd never do that again. Having said that, for such a hefty bloke, Ambrose was very nifty. He looked like a heavyweight boxer but danced like James Brown on speed. Then there was the time his uncle was over from Jamaica, and we ended up being asked to leave the test match. Okay, we were thrown out, and I haven't touched rum since.

Probably safest not to turn up. That was it. I would avoid the pub and do something else instead. But what? After a good twenty minutes, I couldn't think of anything. I would go to the pub and face whatever he had in mind. Then again, it was probably just a big wind-up. Everybody would have a good laugh that Ambrose had got Frankie to get spruced up in his best tee-shirt and hoody just to sit in the corner of The Crown all night. Still, it was a cool tee-shirt with the yellow

Stax label and a picture of Steve Cropper on it.

The tee-shirt was a birthday present from Cheryl last year. That was before it came to light that I was immature, emotionally repressed, incapable of an adult relationship, and a bit boring. This was her view, not mine. Having said that, she may have had a point, not that I would admit it. Admitting it would be mature and require me to express emotion, a bit like being an adult. The bit about being boring was probably fair as well. Well, not boring as such. The truth is, I was content. I was happy to sit in our little flat and watch re-runs of Morse. Cheryl was everything I'd ever wanted. Almost. When I was a kid, I wanted to top the bill at the Harlem Apollo with James Brown supporting. Even then, as a pasty, ginger-haired, tone-deaf kid from a council estate in Bradford, I realised this was a long shot. I still couldn't believe she'd gone. Not only that, but she took with her my original copy of Ziggy Stardust, two grand from our savings account, and the charger for my electric toothbrush. Fair enough, I had drunkenly given the album to her as a token of my eternal love. Eternal until she legged it at any rate.

Technically, the two grand was already hers. The plan had been that we both paid a hundred pounds a month into the account. We were saving for our future. Just short of two years later, I still hadn't got around to setting up the standing order, and Cheryl took exception to my fecklessness (and two grand).

The toothbrush charger was another matter altogether — definitely not my fault. We'd bought matching toothbrushes. They sat side by side on the bathroom shelf. Cute. There was only one plug socket on the wall. Cheryl decided to 'tidy' one of the chargers into the bin. It turned out, nearly two years later, the binned one was mine. Now I had a toothbrush on borrowed time.

I was still muttering to myself when I realised I was at the back door of the pub. I shrugged and went inside, ducking slightly under the low beam. That beam was a real danger to anybody over six feet tall, but concussion was, thankfully, rare.

Brenda was working. She brought me a pint and a bag of smokey bacon crisps, handed over my change before returning to emptying the dishwasher. There was no sign of Ambrose. I saw my chance and retreated to the corner. Before I could get my phone out, Ambrose was beside me.

'Bloody hell. How did you do that?'

'Secret passage from the taproom.'

Like an idiot, I looked at the wall where he was pointing.

'Dick-head. I was sitting at the table by the door. You up for this then, Frankie, or are you scared?'

'I don't scare easily. Except earwigs. Shit scared of them.'

'Earwigs?'

'Yes, earwigs. Nasty little things.'

'Don't look so worried. A fresh start, remember?'

'Do you want a drink?' I was stalling.

'No thanks, I need to get behind the bar. Brenda needs to get off to feed her cats.'

'OK, if you haven't got time for this...'

'It'll only take five minutes, I promise. You've got your phone, I take it? Hand it over.'

Now I was worried, but did as he asked.

'The time is 18.03.' Ambrose showed me the clock on the locked screen. I nodded. 'At 18.05, I want you to open Twitter. Ignore anything that has already appeared in your feed. From that point, you have to act on one of the next five tweets. By act, I mean do something that results in you getting off your idle Yorkshire arse, and engaging with actual people.'

I must have looked as worried as I felt.

'Don't worry, son, I'll be there as your guide. Trust me.'

I said nothing. We both stared at the display on the phone.

I swallowed hard as 18.04 ticked around. What the hell was I getting myself into? What did he mean by 'engage,' and what would the god of everything shite throw into my feed? I tried to run through the sort of stuff that came up. Oh shit! I looked at Ambrose and was about to tell him to do one, but he held up a hand to cut me off. I was trapped.

18.05. Ambrose handed me the phone, and I entered my PIN. The app was already open. Ambrose took the phone and refreshed the screen.

'Five from now. When you pick one, you're committed.'

'What if I don't pick one?'

'Don't worry. I have a forfeit worked out. If you knew what it was, you would pick one of the five!'

I took the phone.

Was it my imagination, or had the pub gone quiet? I told myself to stop being stupid. The pub was always quiet at this time of night, except Friday. On Friday, it was like a Roman feast, thanks to free sandwiches and pork pies. I looked at Ambrose. He raised an eyebrow and nodded. Let's do it. I looked at the screen again — two new tweets. I swallowed hard and read the first.

It was from Susie Dent from Countdown.

'Clinophilia is the love of beds. It's also the word for the tendency to maintain a reclining position wherever possible.'

'There you go. A definite sign that I should go home for a lie-down.'

'Nice try. '

'How could that get me out and about?'

'Not sure. When do people recline in public?'

It was my turn to raise an eyebrow. Ambrose tried again.

'Yoga. You could go to a yoga class. I'm pretty sure some of that is done lying down.'

'I could get a job in a bed shop.'

'Now you're thinking.'

I thought. 'No. I'd be bored senseless. Next tweet.'

We both looked at the screen.

The National Lottery.

- Second slice of EuroMillions luck for Market Drayton pie syndicate.

'I see what they did there. Pie syndicate, slice of luck. Nice one. That settles it. I can go to the shop up the road and buy a tenner's worth of lottery tickets.'

'Hardly going to be life-changing, is it, man?'

'Would be if I won.'

'Go on then. Even though the odds are about ten gazillion to one, say you won ten million. What would you do differently?'

This is a game I had played before and knew the answer automatically.

'I'd give up work for a start.'

'What work? We're here because it gave up on you, dick-head.'

Ambrose had a point. I pondered. The second answer was always that we would go off to sit on an island somewhere and let it all sink in. Trouble is, the 'we' was Cheryl and me, and she, as Ambrose so succinctly put it, had fucked off with Brian. The third thing was to buy a house for my mum and dad. Brian was due a house as well, but he can swivel now. That made me feel better. Maybe there was something in this challenge. I would keep my winnings to myself and make them both jealous. Then the problem hit me: ten gazillion to one chance of winning. Besides, I would need to go to the cash machine first, then back to the shop. It all seemed a bit complicated. In short, I couldn't be arsed.

'Maybe the lottery is a long-term plan.'

'Good thinking, Batman. Next.'

I was about to refresh the screen, but panic set in. I only had three chances left. What if they were all non-starters? I needed a backup plan to wriggle out of Ambrose's forfeit. I could be up and out of the back door in three strides if it came to it, but the evil Geordie had blocked my exit. He could see what I was thinking and leaned across to refresh the screen again.

Brian Masters Web Design.

'Let us design your social media marketing campaign. The world can be yours.'

'Cheeky girlfriend-stealing bastard. He's started advertising again already. How does he expect to run a business when... what the f—' Ambrose cut me off.

'He got off his arse and started again, just like you're doing, remember?'

I drained my pint and tipped the glass towards Ambrose.

'You can have another when we've finished this. I take it that one is a pass?'

'I could punch his lights out. That would get me out and about and doing something useful.'

'True, but hardly a long-term plan for your future. Don't panic; still, two chances left. Something's bound to crop up.'

I was about to complain, but decided resistance was futile. We looked at the screen again. One new tweet. I refreshed the screen with my left hand and crossed the fingers of my other under the table.

'Bright Ideas Writing Workshops.

Still time to join our next workshop. No hassle, just support. A space and time to write. Tonight from 7.00pm.'

A picture of a woman sucking the end of a pencil gave details of the address. It was just up the road at the community centre. Ambrose pounced.

'Exactly the sort of thing; meet new people, do something outside your normal, dull life.'

'Meet a load of people that I have nothing in common with, most likely.'

'You'd be at the same workshop; that's one thing in common. You never know; they may be miserable gits as well. That'd be two things.'

'Besides, what do I know about writing?'

'You don't need to know owt. They'll help you get started.'

'What if I'm rubbish at it?'

'You probably will be rubbish, but that's not the point. This is tweet four of five. Feeling lucky on the last one?'

I have to confess to being quietly tempted. I'd always been quite good at school and had always fancied writing a book. Hadn't everybody? I could see a few things in favour. It would get Ambrose off my back tonight, day one of the challenges done. It was two hours, and I could be back in the pub at 9.30. I would have to walk past home to get to the community centre, so I could pick up my laptop. Besides, if I didn't go for this, I would be stuck with tweet five, which could be hideous.

'Okay. I'll go for it, but no taking the piss, mind. This is all an experiment. If anybody is weird, I'm coming straight back.'

'Final answer?'

'Yep. Let's do it.'

'I want a couple of pictures as proof you went, but well done. A first step. Do you want to see what you could've won?'

I felt relieved, but wanted to see what I'd missed. I nodded. Ambrose refreshed the screen. It was a re-tweet from my mate Bob.

Velvet Corner Gentleman's Lap Dancing Club. Introductory offer tonight only, all drinks £1 free admission.

Bollocks.

The community centre was at the top end of the village. Locals still call it a village, but these days it was more like two new estates clinging to the side of a traffic jam between Leeds and Bradford. There was still some of the old charm. It had two pubs, The Crown and Mary's Bar. The Crown dated back to 1760, apparently, as did half of the regulars. It was slightly past its sell-by date, and I loved it. Lots of small rooms and nothing much happening.

In contrast, Mary's Bar was like the saloon in an old western. I have no idea who Mary was, but the place is now run by an ex-wrestler called Norman. Like his previous profession, it was never too far from a fight. The main thing it had going for it was the proximity to the bus stop at the start of a night out in Leeds. All of that has nothing to do with why I was at the top end of the village.

I must have passed this place hundreds of times, but this was the first time I had even considered going inside. I was totally out of breath from climbing the small hill and, in truth, a bit nervous. I know that sounds a bit wimpy, but I have never liked walking into a room full of strangers. Suddenly, it felt like the first day at a new school. I decided to read the posters taped to the door. I was on the third read of the 'Bums and Tums' notice and almost leapt out of my skin.

'Sorry, didn't mean to make you jump. Do you think you could…'

The voice belonged to a woman, wearing a yellow raincoat and carrying the most enormous box of files I had ever seen. She was nodding at the door and smiling. Smiling at me. Wow! Another nod.

'Sorry, here, let me help.'

I reached for the door. It opened outwards, and I found myself standing to the left of it, right arm stretched, completely blocking her entry. She looked at me and thought about ducking under my arm. I apologised again and, somewhat awkwardly, moved out of the way. In a swish of yellow, she was through the door and gone. I was about to follow her when I felt a hand on my back.

'Ah. New blood!'

I turned to find myself looking down at a red-nosed woman with hair to match, a bit younger than me, but it was hard to tell. The baggy beige cardigan added to the picture. She blew her nose and pushed the used tissue into her sleeve.

'Sorry, lousy cold. Here for the writing workshop? Good, I'm Jen, welcome.'

She ushered me inside and across to a small desk by the window. Five minutes and one form later, I was signed up and instructed in the ways of the tea and coffee facilities (help yourself and make a voluntary donation in the cash jar).

Jen explained how the session worked.

'We believe the biggest barrier for would-be writers is time. This is a quiet area where you can devote two hours to your writing without fear of distraction. We used to spend the final half-hour discussing our work for the evening, but since Mrs Kemp, we decided that comments, however well-meant, didn't form part of our remit.'

I wondered if Mrs Kemp was still around.

Scanning the room, there was no sign of the yellow raincoat. She must've gone into one of the other rooms that led off the main corridor. I could see half a dozen people spread across various tables and easy chairs. All were diligently bent over laptops or notebooks—time to join them. I picked the table in the corner, unpacked my computer, and hung my jacket over the back of the chair. In no time, I had set up a new folder called Writer's Workshop. To be fair, it had been named and re-named many times already. Also, I couldn't decide about the apostrophe. Was it a workshop for multiple writers or just for me? I decided I could always change it later and was good to go.

Next decision: what to write? I created a document and stared at the blank screen. It was then I noticed that the laptop battery was almost flat. I pulled the power cable from my bag and searched under the desk for a place to plug it in. Nothing. I scanned the room again. Everybody was busy tapping or scribbling. I stood up, scraping the metal chair on the wooden floor. Everybody looked up.

'Sorry!' I whispered, bowing slightly for reasons that weren't apparent. Scribbling resumed, and I spotted a socket two seats away. Gathering my belongings, I shuffled silently towards it. Crash. The laptop's power pack hit the floor. All heads lifted.

'Sorry!' Again, the bow. Why? Where had this newfound love of bowing come from?

After carefully placing everything on the new desk, I retrieved the power pack from the middle of the floor. I crawled under the desk and plugged it in. Triumphantly, I stood up, only to crack my head on the desk.

'Fuck!' I bowed again and tried to decide which scribbler had tutted. Eventually, I was seated in front of the blank screen again. I wondered what the others were writing. Whatever it was, it wouldn't be as good as my masterpiece. I started.

'A novel by Frankie…'

That wasn't right. I needed a nom de plume. Fifteen minutes later, Mac De La Riviere was ready to compose. Well, just as soon as he had picked a font. The default was Arial. Not bad, but there must be others to jazz things up a bit. A convoluted test run whipped through many examples. Athelas, Big Caslon, Courier New, Courier (not sure what was wrong with the old one), Prime, Kifa, Typewriter, and Yuppy. Arial looked best. Time for a coffee. I managed to avoid scraping the chair and was quietly pleased to find the kettle was almost full and recently boiled. I helped myself to a Jaffa Cake and went to my pocket for some change. A trawl turned up exactly 11p in coins or a five-pound note. I looked around shiftily before dropping the coins in the jar. Well, a fiver for a coffee was a bit steep. For good measure, I grabbed two more biscuits and headed back to my seat.

Again, a blank page, except for the author's name, now centred in bold Italics. I remembered that Ambrose wanted photographic evidence that I had turned up. I tried various selfies with the coffee cup, my laptop, the tutters, and the room in general. As I looked through them, there she was, just in the corner of the last shot. The woman in the yellow raincoat just approaching the door. I spun around, but she had gone. Going after her was a bit futile. Besides, what would I say? Needing time to think, I sipped the coffee until my glasses steamed up. As the mist cleared, Jen was standing over me. She slipped a notebook and pen onto the desk.

'Try this,' she whispered.

I pulled the book towards me and closed the laptop. In the middle of the first page, I wrote:

'The novel that Yorkshire has waited for by Franklin Clancy De La Riviere.'

Turning the page, I looked again for signs of the beautiful woman in the yellow raincoat. Did I mention she was beautiful? I'd been beside her for less than twenty seconds but was struck by the smile. It made her face light up. Not in a weird Ready Brek way, just fresh, natural. I looked again. Nothing. I glanced at the clock on the wall. It was ten to eight. Where does the time go when you're so busy? Before long, I had doodled a Dali-style melting clock and a shocked face with a speech bubble.

'Where did the time go?' it asked.

I had always been good at drawing, and ten minutes later, a handsome face (Okay, it was me) was posing a question. 'Where is she going?' At the same time, the tail of a raincoat disappeared through a doorway. I looked at the cartoon, which wasn't bad.

'I wonder what's through the door?' The bearded beret wearer looked at me from behind his pencil as I said this aloud. I hurriedly looked away and bent to my task again.

When I eventually looked up, I was surprised to see the room was almost empty. Jen leaned over my shoulder.

'Sometimes easier without the technology, isn't it?'

'Not exactly the great novel, though.'

'We all start somewhere. May I?'

I handed over the notebook, expecting to be told to sling my hook, and never darken their door again.

'Hmm. I think you're onto something here.'

'But it's just a few scribbles. Hardly writing at all.'

'I disagree. People have been telling stories for thousands of years. Nobody said it has to start Once Upon A Time and deliver 300,000 words in small print. You grabbed me from the start. I wanted to know what was behind the door. Once I saw it, I wanted to know what happens next. You pulled me, the reader, in. Now comes the tricky bit.'

'You mean turn the pictures into words?'

'No. Finish it. See you next week?'

'OK, great.'

Jen handed me the notebook and went to get her coat. I packed the laptop into my bag, a beaming smile on my face. She liked it!

Time for a pint.

2

When I left the community centre last night, I had fully intended to go to the pub. On the way there, I was thinking hard about what Jen had said. So hard that I walked straight past the pub and found myself at my front door. I figured an early night would do me no harm and let myself in. The trouble was, I couldn't relax. After opening a bottle of Malbec, I settled down with my headphones on and grabbed the notebook. At least I had Ziggy on my phone, even if the LP had gone walkies.

By Wednesday at 6pm something strange had happened. I had spent most of the night, and all day, filling the notebook with sketches. I must have fallen asleep at about four in the morning, and then had a trip out at lunchtime to buy a proper artist's pad. Now it was time to report back to Ambrose.

I ducked under the low beam and ordered a pint at the bar. Ambrose joined me at the corner table, and I explained what had happened.

'Bloody hell, man, we've created a monster!'

'I wouldn't go that far, but it felt really good to do

something different.'

'So what are you gonna do with it now?'

'What do you mean?'

'Well, writing it is just the start. What about getting it published?'

'Nobody would publish it. It's just a few crap drawings, and a bit of a story.'

'Graphic novel mate. That's what they call 'em these days. You should tout it round publishers. Better still, publish it yourself. Shouldn't be too hard for a techie like you. Back in a minute.'

He went off to serve another arrival. I downed half the pint at one go, feeling really pleased with myself. Before long, Ambrose was back with another pint.

'That's on me, in recognition of you getting off your arse and framing yourself.'

'Cheers.'

'Come on then. Day two.'

I was hoping he had forgotten about the challenge.

'Do we need to carry on? I think you've proved your point, and I'm not being miserable. Job done, surely?'

'Dream on. Get your phone out.' The display said it was 6.13pm.

'Okay. Same as yesterday. As soon as it gets to 6.15 you refresh the feed, and the first five tweets from then.'

I wondered just how bad the forfeit could be, and shuddered. Easier to look at the tweets.

'Los Lobos Tattoos

- Let us change your look. Free consultation. All work spellchecked.'

Reassuring as it was that all of their work was spellchecked, I think I could safely pass on this. Taking my shirt off in public meant answering lots of questions or just a lot of embarrassing stares. It's something I've avoided since, well, for years. Apart from that, I had never understood doing something permanent to your body in the name of fashion. Besides, it hurts. Ambrose, on the other hand, thought it would be highly amusing.

'Go on, you could have Love and Eight on your knuckles. Spellchecker wouldn't pick that bugger up. Or Cheryl 4 Ever across your thigh.'

'Fuck off.'

'Okay. Too soon?'

'Yes, too soon. Move on.'

'Were you mis-sold PPI? Let us check for you.'

'For crying out loud. When are they going to stop trying to flog this particular dead horse? It was bad enough trying to sell the stuff in the first place.'

'I take it that's a pass?'

I nodded.

'Northern Soul Tonight 7 to 11.30, Brighton Mods Club.'

I looked at my watch.

'How long to drive to Brighton?'

'About 6 hours at a guess.'

'Not gonna happen really, is it?'

'No.'

Shit. On to number four. One more after this. I hit refresh, but nothing new appeared. I took that as a sign that a bag of crisps was called for. Ambrose gave me a look, and I tried again.

'The Vinyl Cellar

- Yorkshire's biggest selection of second-hand records, books and magazines. Open daily 10-6pm.'

'Yes! I can look for a replacement Ziggy. No forfeit for me pal, I take this one!'

I knew roughly where the shop was, no more than two miles away. It would be a nice trip out tomorrow. I downed the second pint in celebration, and Ambrose went off to pull another one.

I couldn't resist looking at number five.

Velvet Corner Gentleman's Lap Dancing Club. Introductory offer tonight only, all drinks £1 free admission.

Double bollocks.

The record shop didn't look overly promising. A steep flight of stone stairs led to a dimly lit cellar. I suspected the smell came from the leather-jacketed character, leaning back in the chair, feet up on the desk. It looked like Ian McShane in Deadwood and didn't move its eyes from its newspaper. He took the pen from his mouth and filled in another crossword clue. From the bottom step, I scanned the room. It was vast. My dad would love this place.

Although I was born in the CD era, my dad had always collected vinyl, a collection I had hoped to inherit one day. I remember seaside holidays as a kid always included several trips to places like this—a chance for Dad to search out that elusive import or white label. I would tag along and blow my paper-round money, often with Dad nudging me in my choice or stepping in to drive a deal with the shopkeeper. Those excursions still influenced my love of music from the sixties onwards. The vinyl fix had taken a back seat over the last few years, but now I was on a quest.

Actually, I thought about the future a lot last night. What did I want out of my life? A bit deep? Maybe, but I couldn't sleep, and one thought led to another. I'd realised that if I could achieve one thing in my life, it would be to make things right with my dad. I know, logically, he didn't blame me. He was just so sad. I couldn't bear it and withdrew from their lives. There's still the odd phone call. There'd been no major falling out. When they retired to Bridlington, I just saw them less and less. It would be nice to change that.

The place was deserted apart from leather jacket, eerily

silent and very, very impressive. I walked past rack upon rack of Northern Soul singles, twitching to flick through. I knew if I weakened, I would be there for hours. There would be time for that on another day. This was a mission. Discipline was required. Everything to my left appeared to be singles. I turned right and walked through Country, Folk and Jazz until I reached the vast swathes of Rock. I was relieved to find the albums arranged alphabetically rather than in a million sub-genres that nobody understood. Familiar covers tried to tempt me: AC/DC; America; Argent; Blondie. As I closed in on the B section, something magical happened. The vast speakers burst into life. 'Five Years' filled the room—the first track from Ziggy. I looked back at the desk, but leather jacket was nowhere to be seen. Slightly freaked by the coincidence, I reached the Bowie section and began my search.

'Is this what you're after?'

Shit. Where did he come from? It was McShane. But he spoke like Christopher Biggins. Trying to calm my racing heart, I looked around. A copy of 'The Rise And Fall Of Ziggy Stardust And The Spiders From Mars' was in his hands.

'How the hell did you know that?'

'Been in this business most of my life. Call it a sixth sense. I'm Joe.' He reached out a slightly grubby hand. After the handshake, I took a step back, out of reach of the breath.

'I'm Frankie. How much do you want for it?'

'Forty five quid, perfect condition.'

My dad always tells me the tale of buying the album for two quid and getting a life-sized poster thrown in.

'That's a lot more than I wanted to pay.'

'Got plenty of Rolf Harris albums for a pound each, if you'd rather. If you want the best, you're not gonna get it for any less.'

I was warming to my new acquaintance.

'Go on, I'll take it.' We made our way to the cash desk.

Again, the racks of singles tempted me. 'Joe, I don't suppose you have a copy of *Malnutrition* by James Fountain?'

'Peachtree Records, 1970, *Seven Day Lover* on the B-side.'

'Bloody hell, you're good. Have you got it?'

'Nah. Rare as rocking-horse shit, mate. Would you be interested if I could lay my hands on it? Not cheap, mind. Four, five hundred quid, maybe.'

'Ouch. Only if I win the lottery. Worth a try.' I was about to hand over two twenty-pound notes when I spotted the display of tee-shirts. In particular, the black one with the Tamla Motown logo in gold letters. I pulled out another twenty. Joe looked very pleased. I left the shop with a smile on my face, then remembered that I have no job and I'd just blown sixty-five quid. I'd also given my phone number to Joe, just in case James Fountain turned up.

I had always had a simple theory when it came to not having enough cash. You can cut your spending to a level that matches your income or increase your income. Strictly speaking, I had no income. So, unless I wanted to give up eating (and spending sixty-five quid a time in record shops), option one was not really viable. I had to make some money. But how? That was why, as I settled into my window seat at See You Latte, I did an audit of my skills. This is always preferable to going out and finding a job. One large Americano later, the list looked like this:

Web programmer;
Social media manager;
Call centre operative selling PPI;
Pizza deliverer;
Washer up in a Spanish bar;
Two hundred metres breaststroke certificate;
Would-be novelist;
Quite handy with a camera.

Admittedly, by the time I got to the swimming certificate, I was struggling. I wasn't sure how I could make a living from it, anyway. The PPI job was one I didn't admit to very often. It had been in the call centre of the well-known bank where I met Cheryl. To be fair, they became a lot better known due to me and my mates selling shedloads of insurance policies to people who didn't understand it. Come to think of it, nobody understood it. I hated that job with a passion. That script was like torture, day after day. Still, seemed to turn out okay in the end.

I think I can rule out a return to the heady world of pizza delivery, particularly at the place I used to work. Let's just say I resigned in a somewhat flamboyant fashion. The recipients of my final drop probably don't eat pizza anymore, anyway. I had to face it; the only thing I have ever been good at was creating websites. That's why I started the business with Brian. I loved that job. Actually, it never felt like a job. We turned up at the office (the corner of the living room of my flat), drank coffee, and pissed ourselves laughing all day. Somehow, he landed enough clients for us to make a living. We even got enough work to take on staff. I say, staff, Rupert sort of counted.

Little did I know that while I was working my magic on code until late in the evening, Brian was waving his wand around with Cheryl back at his place. Bastard. Bastard for taking Cheryl, but, I had to admit, bigger bastard for ruining the business and the comfortable life I had. Actually, the final bastard must've been out loud rather than in my head. The two women at the neighbouring table were staring at me. Probably time to go.

I was gathering my jacket and the bag from Joe's shop when the woman in the yellow raincoat walked in front of the window. I had thought about her a lot since last night. Not just because she was gorgeous (which she was), but I had made her the central character in my fledgeling novel. I needed to talk to her, get to know her. I grabbed my stuff and headed for the door, narrowly avoiding the tray of drinks being carried to the table, where the two women were still staring at me.

As I emerged into the drizzle, I looked up the street, searching for the yellow coat. Nothing. I broke into a brisk walk and headed up the hill, checking shop windows and side streets as I went. After a couple of minutes, I was a bit red in the face and sweaty, hardly attractive if I caught up with her. I decided to abandon my search and head for the bus stop. Two seconds later, the bus passed me on the opposite side of the road.

Bollocks.

Sitting halfway back, reading her phone, was the woman in the yellow raincoat—double bollocks.

Later, on the bus home, I thought about Cheryl. We'd been together about five years. We met when I worked in the call centre at the bank. She was on the same floor of the massive office block, but in the IT department. I say met. She actually hit me with a door and caused a concussion. We always joked that I saw stars when our eyes met. Our team leader had the great idea that we should have a 'stand up meeting' every morning in the lifts' area to talk about our performance. The idiot thought it was good for morale. On that fateful morning, I was late and more than a bit hungover. I crept in at the back, hoping he wouldn't notice me. After a few minutes, my attention wandered, and I yawned. Loudly. The team leader gave me a withering look. To stay awake, I had a good scratch and a stretch. My neck cracked as I leaned back. At this exact second, a tornado in a blue suit burst through the door. Apparently, the crack of the wood meeting my skull was enough to bring a second withering look from the boss. I was unaware of this as I slumped to the floor.

I remember opening my eyes and thinking I had died and gone to heaven. This beautiful creature was cradling my head gently and saying, 'Oh shit' over and over again. At first sight of the blood trickling from my skull, she fainted, right on top of me. Now I knew I was in heaven.

Half an hour later, we were both at the local A&E. The paramedics wanted Cheryl to get checked out after the fainting, and I got three stitches in my head. She apologised for the hundredth time.

'Don't worry about it. It happens all the time.'

'Really? You get whacked on the noggin with a door regularly?'

'Well, not regularly. It happened once before, at school. I dropped a 10p by the front door just as the bell sounded. I got flattened that time, and at least you picked me up.'

'Then I fainted on you. Sorry again.'

'Don't worry, that was the nicest bit. In some countries, we'd have to get married now.'

'Slow down a bit, tiger. You could at least take me for a drink first.'

'Okay. What are you doing tonight?'

And that was how it started. A couple of months later, we got a flat together, and everything was great. Cheryl even convinced me I could do better than the call centre and helped me to get onto a programming course at the local college. She also introduced me to Brian, the backstabbing bastard. To be fair, at the time, he was just Brian. He was a business analyst, whatever that was, in Cheryl's team. We got on really well from the start, and he became a regular at the flat. We drank beer, listened to music, watched the telly: all the standard stuff. After one particularly long night in the pub, we decided to pack in our jobs and start a web design company. Just like that.

* * *

When I reached home, I changed into my new tee-shirt and played Ziggy. I'm not one for delayed gratification. After listening to the whole of side one, I turned the volume to just below 'door rattling' for side two and began flicking through my sketches.

I have to admit, presented as a comic strip, the story was better than I remembered. It opened with a drawing of the mysterious woman in a yellow raincoat, struggling with a massive box of papers. She goes through a door at the community centre. As the door closes, an envelope falls from the top of the box without her noticing. Our hero, knees weak after she smiled at him, runs down the corridor and retrieves the bulky, sealed envelope. He tries the door, but it is locked. Knocking gets no reply. He rejoins his writing class in the main hall but chooses a seat where the door is visible. But, two hours later, she hasn't emerged. He asks around, but nobody knows anything about the woman, or the mysterious door, except that she often arrived around 7pm. He decides to return the following night and reunite the envelope and mysterious woman in the yellow raincoat. Simple. At home that night, he starts to wonder, what is in the envelope? What lies behind the locked door? His mind races through the possibilities before curiosity gets the better of him, and he steams open the envelope. It is stuffed with £20 notes. I had already decided that episode two would show them meeting and revealing what was behind the door. Our hero would be drawn into the mysterious world of the 'woman in the yellow raincoat'.

All of that seemed like quite hard work from where I was sitting. Playing with technology would be a lot more fun use of the afternoon. I started by scanning the sketches into an art app on my Mac. By six o'clock, I had registered a web address, designed a rudimentary site, and pulled together some code to present the sketches in an online comic style.

Half an hour later, I had Facebook and Twitter pages set up, and I was ready to go. A flashy logo and a few targeted tweets later, and the site was launched. Time for a quick shower, then to the pub. The only bad news was that the toothbrush finally died less than thirty seconds in. I decided that would do and chucked it in the bin, useless without its charger. Tomorrow, I needed to trawl through the 'holiday drawer'. Cheryl was bound to have bought travel toothbrushes at some point. Old-fashioned manual would have to do for now.

'What time do you call this?'

'Good evening to you too. Pint of bitter, since you ask.'

Ambrose reached for the glass. 'I thought you'd bottled it tonight.'

'Been busy.'

'Oh yes? Spill the beans.'

I showed him the website on my phone.

'Bugger me. You actually got off your arse and did it! Well done, mate. Can I send myself the link?'

'Be my guest.'

He fiddled with my phone for a few seconds before handing it back, returning to pulling my pint. 'I'll read that later. What else have you been up to?'

'I went to that record shop. It's like Aladdin's cave down there. One copy of Ziggy and this little beauty,' I said, pointing at the tee-shirt.

'Very smart. I'll have a half. Thanks for asking.'

I grinned and feigned surprise. It was still a tradition in these parts to buy the barman a drink. To be fair, he bought them for me regularly. I handed over a tenner. Brenda emerged from the taproom and took over behind the bar. Ambrose joined me at the corner table just as my phone said it was 7.14.

'OK, when it hits 7.15, we look at Twitter.'

A tall, dark-skinned woman pulled out a stool next to us. Ambrose kissed her on the cheek.

'Hello, love, we're just about to start.'

Stella was Ambrose's wife and often joined us in The Crown.

'Hi, Frankie. I was sorry to hear about Cheryl. You two seemed good together. I was so shocked when I heard.'

'A bit of a surprise for me too, if I'm honest.' I smiled to try to make her think I was okay.

Ambrose cut in.

'We were just about to do day three of the challenge.'

'Great, I wanted to see this. I think you're fearless, Frankie. Especially knowing what the forfeit is.'

'You know?' I was alarmed. 'Just how bad is it?'

'Oh, it's not that bad, really.' She grinned at me. 'Come on, let's do this.'

I refreshed the screen, and we were off. The first tweet was from the writer, Danny Kelly.

Well done, Aston Villa fans. Sticking two fingers up to the Shitehawk Of Adversity.

We all got the giggles, but Stella spoke first.

'What a brilliant phrase. I have to remember that.'

'Could be the next bestseller.' I offered, "Harry Potter and The Shitehawk Of Adversity."

Ambrose came back with "Star Wars Episode 10 - Revenge Of The Shitehawk Of Adversity."

Several more followed before Ambrose drew us back to the task at hand. We never watched the video clip of Villa fans celebrating winning a corner.

The following tweet was from somebody in Texas.

'Just read the first episode of The Woman In The Yellow Raincoat. Immediate fan. Keep up the good work. #TheWomanInTheYellowRaincoat'

'Fuck me', both Ambrose and I said together before apologising in unison to Stella.

'Somebody has actually read my stuff in the first hour it's been online.'

'Not only that, they love it.'

We high-fived before realising we weren't twelve and sheepishly took a drink.

'What's all this?' asked Stella.

'Frankie posted his first story. Looks like he has a fan. We can have a proper look later. I take it you're not proposing to go to Texas to meet your groupie?'

'I should. Mind you, it would cost a fortune. Besides, I'm busy building a publishing empire. What's next?'

Tweet three was from the Community Centre.

'Join our camera club from 8pm tonight. Want to know how to light your portraits? New members welcome.'

'That sounds good. You told me you were into photography.'

'I am, but the Community Centre two nights this week? Could be viewed as a bit sad.' Then I realised - the woman in the yellow raincoat might just put in an appearance. 'On the other hand - let's do it. Even got time for another pint. Cheers.'

Ambrose returned with a refill.

'By the way, it's my night off tomorrow. I'm taking Stella for a meal.'

'Very nice too. Hope you have a lovely time.'

'Ta. I'm only telling you because it means you get a night off from the challenges. We start again on Saturday.'

'OK, Saturday it is.'

I risked a look at the fifth tweet.

'Need booze quick? Quality beers and wines delivered to your door in under an hour.'

Bugger.

* * *

It was Jen that greeted me at the community centre. The discreet tissue tucked into the sleeve had been dropped in favour of carrying a large box of them.

'No better then?'

'Doe. I beel derrible. But you bust be a glutton for punishment, here again.'

'Just trying to broaden my horizons. How come you're here again, anyway? I didn't know you ran the camera club and the writer's group.'

'I don't. I'm just filling in at short dotice. We help each other out where we can.' Jen grabbed a tissue and sneezed loudly.

'By the way, thanks for your help the other night.'

I'm sure she blushed at this point, although difficult to tell, what with the red nose and eyes.

'My pleasure, always happy to help.'

Another form filled in, and I was a provisional member of the camera club. Having nodded to one or two other members, I unpacked my trusty Pentax. Now, I think I know my way around a camera, but some of these people had kit — a lot of it. As the evening went on, it was apparent that half of them didn't know what any of it did. After a couple of minutes, everybody found a seat, and our host for the evening (I missed his name) got to his feet. For thirty minutes, he ran us through the theory of how to light portraits for the best effect. I think he could have done it in two minutes and still had time to put the kettle on. It was only when our model for the evening arrived that my interest peaked. Taking off her yellow raincoat, she was introduced as Robbie and positioned herself on the stool at the front of the room. She was dressed simply, black, loose-fitting trousers and a white silk shirt. She almost glowed and looked terrific.

We set the lights for the first batch of shots, and a scrum

formed. There was a fair amount of jostling for position, and getting a clear picture was almost impossible. I decided to move to the side for a quick sulk. It was then that something magical happened. Robbie turned her head and looked over her shoulder at me. She smiled, and I melted. I say I melted. It was more like everybody else in the room melted. They disappeared, and there was only Robbie, her blue eyes locked onto the lens. Her smile lit up the room more than the array of lights. I was mesmerised, and then, what seemed like seconds later, it was all over.

'Thanks, everybody, thanks, Robbie. A round of applause for our model. Now please take your seats.'

I glanced at the camera. Three hundred and twelve shots! I looked up just in time to see a flash of yellow raincoat at the door. My heart sank. Then she turned, and I'm pretty sure mouthed the words, 'Foam pee'. As I still had the camera in my hands, I snapped a quick shot as the yellow raincoat left the building.

The rest of the session ranged between dull and deadly dull. Our nameless host asked for a volunteer to share their work on the big screen. Still, after he confirmed that part of the deal with Robbie was that we could publish the photos, I had lost interest. I'd got what I needed from the session, the pictures. Besides, the presenter was very dull.

My mind wandered back to what Robbie had said as she left the building. 'Foam pee' was a bit unlikely, but you never knew. What if it was a need to go to the loo, and she has some strange condition that made it foamy? The last thing she would want is some lunatic phoning her mid-flow. Actually, it could have been 'phone me'. Shit. More to the point, if it was 'Phone me', how the hell would I do that? I didn't have her number. I had some detective work to do, so I decided to slip out unnoticed and silently gathered my stuff. As another unremarkable image lit up the screen, I deftly rose from my seat. Half-crouching, I set off for the door, only to trip over a carefully placed backpack and crash to the floor.

'Shit!'

Every pair of eyes in the room turned to me as I regained my feet, camera still clasped safely in both hands. I did one of my famous bows and left quickly, never to return. Once in the corridor, I almost clattered into Jen.

'Hello again, what on earth have you been up to?'

I raised a confused eyebrow.

'Photography workshop,' I offered.

'I didn't mean that. What about the blood?'

'What blood?'

'The blood trickling from your nose and top lip.' That was news to me. 'Come on, let me clean it up for you.'

I followed Jen towards the office. She produced a green plastic first aid kit and pointed to a seat in front of the desk. I slipped the bag off my shoulder, put the camera on the desk, and sat down.

'Ow!'

'Shut up, and hold still.' Whatever was on the cotton wool stung like hell. 'Now be a brave soldier, and you can have a sweetie when it's all done.' I laughed and winced again. The smell of the anti-sceptic mixed with menthol was strangely comforting. Her hair smelt lovely, too. 'There you go, all done. How did you manage to do it?'

'I was making a graceful exit from the photography workshop and went arse over end.'

'I really should enter it in the accident book.'

' Not exactly my finest moment. Can't we just forget it?'

'I suppose there was no real damage done. Except to your dignity.'

'Dignity? I lost that the other night at the writer's workshop when I cracked my head on the table and generally made an arse of myself. I seem to make a habit of being clumsy in this building.'

'How's the writing going?'

'Actually, something exciting has happened.' I told her about the website and the fan in Texas.

'Wow. That's brilliant. What happens next?'

'Well, that was why I was here tonight. I was playing with the idea of having a composite of photos and sketches to make up the illustrations. Sounds a bit crap when I say it out loud, but I can see it in my head. Almost like an old black and white gangster movie. Stylised bad guys, and stunningly good-looking women.'

'They say that glamour sells.'

'Exactly.'

'Is that where Robbie comes into it?'

'You know her?'

'Oh yes. We were at school together. In fact, they lived next door to us until we were about fifteen. We were best friends for years.'

'Were? Not now?'

'Not so much, no.'

'How come?'

'We just drifted apart, I suppose, after they moved house. My dad fell out with her dad, which made it awkward.'

'Why the falling out?' Jen gave me a look. 'Sorry, just nosey.'

'I don't really want to go into detail. It was complicated. Dad wouldn't talk about it, just said that making money had turned his head. They moved off the estate to a big house by the river. She's still there now. They converted one of the outbuildings into an apartment for her. Still works for her dad.'

'What does her dad do?'

'What doesn't he do? He started with a shop, then a warehouse, trucks, importing, storage. Operates from the industrial estate. Dexters Logistics. Anyway, she seems to have made a big impression on you.'

'I hardly know her.'

'Yes, but you've spent the evening taking pictures of her, and you made her the star of your graphic novel. I think you're smitten.'

I actually blushed. 'OK, I admit to a certain attraction. If I wanted to get in touch, how would I go about it?'

'Easy. Her dad's company rents a small office here. It's where she works most days.'

So much for the detective work!

3

Thanks to Jen, I now had a phone number for Robbie and knew a bit about her. As a confident adult, I could now call her and confidently arrange a date. As a confident adult, we would chat, find out we had lots of things in common, and meet on Monday. I'd take her for a drink on Tuesday, and by Wednesday, I'd be looking forward to the rest of the week and a chance to chill on Sunday. Life would be good. But I'm not confident, and I'm no Craig David.

If I had to define myself, it would be as average. Not overly tall, but not short. Not exceptionally bright, but not thick. Five-ten, dark hair, cheeky grin, glasses on days when I can't face contact lenses. I suppose if I was a place, I'd be Long Eaton. More or less in the middle, nobody hates it, but nobody's favourite and difficult to point at on a map. If only I were more confident.

I remember at school, there was a kid who wasn't exactly blessed in the looks department. It was as if the creator knew what a face should look like but had run out of parts. A sort of face that was made late on Friday afternoon, just before home-time. Anyway, he didn't give a toss. He just waded in.

Rejection meant nothing to him. He ended up with a succession of gorgeous girlfriends. I envied him so much. Not the face, obviously. It was the confidence. Me? At the first sign of rejection, I would take to my bedroom for two weeks and hide.

It was difficult then, but got significantly worse after the fire. It was difficult being some sort of love machine while keeping your shirt on. Over the years, it just seemed easier not to get too close to anybody. Then I met Cheryl, and somehow she meant more to me than keeping my scars hidden. She'd been wonderful when she found out. We both cried the first time we went to bed together. She'd gently traced her fingers across the ridges that run diagonally from my left shoulder to my right hip. Now she's left me. No more gently applying moisturiser on the bits I can't reach. No more telling me not to worry about people seeing it. I'm not sure why I'm telling you this. I never tell anybody as a rule. Oh yes, I was talking about confidence. I simply don't have it when it comes to women, I suppose.

I can see it now. I'll call and hang up quickly because I can't think of what to say. Even worse, I'll speak to her, and she'll be horrified that I'm stalking her, or she'll not be able to hear what I'm mumbling. What would a proper adult do in this situation? Have a cup of tea and three chocolate Hob-Nobs, that's what. I was just about to go for a fourth biscuit when I realised I had to come up with a plan. I reasoned that I needed to be disciplined with writing, growing the website audience, and seeing where this thing went. It was nearly half-past nine now. I would write until one o'clock, then call Robbie straight after lunch. My reward for working all morning would be a successful chat with the famous woman in the yellow raincoat.

I reached for another biscuit before realising my cup was now empty. OK, another cup of tea, work until one, then call

Robbie. I put the kettle on again. Actually, writing until one wouldn't leave time to post updates on the website and generate social media entries. Right, new plan: write until twelve, update website, post stuff on social media, lunch, call Robbie. Sorted, I would take my tea to my office, then start work. Just as soon as I'd been to the loo.

As I said before, I call it my office, but, officially, it's the far corner of the living room. Actually, the far corner makes it sound grander than it is. Two strides from anywhere in the room, and I'm at work. At least I can afford the rent. As I took my seat at the desk, I started to worry about money. Yes, I could afford the rent for a couple of months, but without an income, that could very quickly become a problem. Shit. I clicked play on Ziggy and started writing.

Otis Blue followed Ziggy, Talking Book, The Boatman's Call and Stanley Road. A busy morning. I pushed back from the desk, and my neck cracked alarmingly. I rubbed my eyes and looked out of the window. It was dark. How did that happen? I looked at my watch. It was just short of eight o'clock. Almost ten hours had flown by. The desk was covered in paper; sketches, post-its, to-do lists. What the hell had just happened here?

For a start, I had been so absorbed that I had forgotten to eat, and that never happens. Ever. Apart from two beers and something small and brown, the fridge was empty. I opened a beer and drank half of it while I inspected the brown thing. I decided it was probably half a lime and closed the fridge door.

After I had ordered an Indian takeaway, I realised something else. I had forgotten all about calling Robbie. Too late now. I only had her office number. Would she work on a Saturday? What if she didn't? That would make it Monday before I could ring. Four days after, she told me to call (if that is what she'd said). Shit. She'll think I am playing it cool. Not good. I'm not cool. Why the hell didn't I call this morning? Idiot. So much for Craig David. Met her on a Monday, didn't call her for four days. That wasn't a hit single!

I calmed myself by getting the last beer from the fridge. When the food arrived, I automatically switched on the TV but couldn't settle. Fifteen minutes later, I licked my fingers, burped loudly, and stood up to stretch my legs — time to get to work on the photos from last night.

I started the upload from the camera. While it was running, I checked the Twitter account for TheWomanInTheYellowRaincoat. I was excited to see that I now had a proud total of twenty-eight followers. Impressive. Hardly taking over the world but, with minimal effort on promotion, it was a start.

The photos had finished uploading. I hunched over the small PC screen, thinking how much I missed my Mac. I say my Mac. Technically, Cheryl bought it and walked out with it when 'negotiations' ended. She'd shouted several words that I didn't realise she even knew, then stormed out. Well, not quite stormed out. She couldn't open the door with the massive screen in her arms, so it lost the dramatic effect when I had to squeeze past her to open it. Then I'd meekly followed her out to the car and opened the back door for her.

Anyway, the PC would have to do. In the first few pictures, you could tell I was out of practice. After that, things improved dramatically. Robbie looked natural and very much at home in front of the camera. Lots of eye contact and that smile — wow! I was feeling quietly pleased with myself and slightly terrified at the prospect of calling this woman and asking her for a date. Then I saw the last photograph. It was perfect. Framed by the door, looking back over her shoulder, and pouting slightly. The camera had somehow captured the movement, the light step, shoulder-length blonde hair covering part of her face — best of all, the bright yellow coat.

Against the dark background, the colour shone like a light. This was precisely what I needed for the website, and thanks to the nameless bloke at the workshop, I had Robbie's permission to use it.

I spent the rest of the evening designing a front page for the website centred around the photo. It was basically a book cover, and I was extremely pleased with myself. I resisted the urge to publish it straight away, as I wanted Robbie's agreement. I didn't want to do anything to blow my chance with her.

It was still dark when I woke up on Saturday morning. I'd had a very restless night. I looked across at the clock - it wasn't even seven yet. The only time I'd seen seven o'clock on Saturday morning was coming home from a party at Brian's last summer. Usually, I would just go back to sleep, but I knew there was no chance of that today. I had to admit to myself that I hadn't felt like this before. I was looking forward to getting back to my desk because I was desperate to write. By two o'clock this morning, I had sketched out The Woman In The Yellow Raincoat's next episode and produced most of the drawings for it. With a big push, I could have it finished and published by tomorrow night.

Once I'd made coffee, I slumped in my armchair. My phone was still on the left arm from last night. The right arm being reserved for the TV remote, obviously. As I switched on the sports news, I picked up the phone. I had a text from Joe at the record shop. He'd sent it at 4 o'clock this morning, somebody else who couldn't sleep.

No James Fountain single, but I have something that may interest you. Call in soon and bring money!

Sounded interesting, if expensive. I could go this morning and restock the fridge as part of the same trip. I checked Joe's website for opening times. Ten o'clock suited me. I could do an hour knocking the sketches into shape, quick shower, fried breakfast at See You Latte, and be on his doorstep when he opened.

When I reached the shop, the door was already open. Before I was halfway down the stairs, I heard an excited voice coming towards me, greeting me like a long-lost friend.

'Frankie! Come in, come in. Good to see you.'

'I thought you didn't open until 10.'

'Stuff to do, money to make. Once I'm here, I may as well be open. Always crosswords to do, even if no bugger turns up to buy stuff.'

'I got your text. Couldn't sleep?'

'I'll sleep in the office later, for a couple of hours, anyway. Sent the text on the way between clubs. Felt fabulous, but getting too old for all-nighters.' An all-night clubbing spree probably accounted for the transformation from the surly character I'd first encountered. 'Now, come through, I've got something to show you.'

We walked through the rows of CDs and LPs to a back room behind a red velvet curtain. Joe saw me look at the two wall-mounted screens.

'CCTV. Thieving bastards'll nick anything round here. Have a seat.' He reached into a desk drawer and produced, complete with a theatrical flourish, a red tee-shirt. I'm not sure what I'd expected, but this wasn't it. 'What do you think?' he said excitedly.

I reached out and took the shirt.

'Wow.' I was truly impressed. The design was a reproduction of the label from *Malnutrition* by James Fountain — the single I'd asked about last time. The red was the same colour as the label, Peachtree Records, with the label's address at the top. William Bell's name as the writer under the title. I turned the shirt over. Sure enough, it showed the B-side, *Seven Day Lover*. 'How on earth did you get this?'

'A mate of mine supplied the images. He's the only person I know with a copy of the single. He paid twelve hundred quid for it last year, apparently. I printed the shirt here. See for yourself.'

He led me around a corner, and more of the cellar opened up. It contained a small tee-shirt printing factory.

'Bloody hell. I had no idea you had this down here.'

'Not something I tend to advertise to the locals, but it is a very profitable part of my business empire. Especially at £30 a pop.'

'Thirty? The Motown one was twenty-five.'

'Ah, but this is bespoke, special. Tell you what, £25 to you.'

'OK, done.' A small idea was forming. 'Can you print any image?'

'Within reason. I'm not usually too keen on testing copyright laws but, in theory, yes. Not just tee-shirts, either. I can do hoodies, mugs, key-rings.'

'Look, I'm not in a position to go for it yet, but would you be interested in a partnership for a range of tee-shirts and stuff?'

'Always interested in making money. What do you have in mind?'

I told him the story so far about coming up with the idea for The Woman In The Yellow Raincoat and the level of interest I was getting. If this thing took off, tee-shirts would be a natural opportunity. Coming up with designs wouldn't be a problem, and Robbie would be a superb model for more pictures.

'I take it Robbie is a woman?'

'Of course. I'm hoping to get her to have a night out with me.'

'Wouldn't be Robbie Dexter, would it?'

'Yes, I think that's her name.' Joe frowned.

'What is it? Do you know her?'

'Oh, I know her alright. She's fine, very nice, in fact. Not as keen on her dad, but I don't suppose you're asking him out.'

'I hadn't intended to ask him as well. Nah, probably not my type. It would be a bit weird, too. Would you like to go for a meal? Oh, and bring your dad as well.'

'Fair enough, but you be careful. Nasty piece of work, that bloke.'

'What do you mean? How do you know him?'

'You get to know everybody when you run a business as long as I have. Look, I've said too much. You'll be fine.' Just then, the door beeped. 'Customer, got to go.'

I followed Joe out to the shop and gave him £25. We shook hands, and I set off for the supermarket.

I've always had a thing about using the phone to arrange dates. I'm crap at it. Actually, it's not just the phone. As the Americans would say: I'm crap, period.

When I was thirteen, after weeks of chickening out, I finally plucked up the courage to phone Veronica Maples. She was, according to my male classmates, the third-best-looking girl at my school. My plan was to take her to see *Home Alone* at the Odeon. I'd considered *Graffiti Bridge* because Prince was in it, but everybody was talking about Macaulay Culkin that Christmas. It threw me when her younger brother answered the phone, but I managed to convince him to get her. When she finally answered, I blurted out my script. Her reply etched on my memory forever — 'No. Seen it.' Phone down. Boom! An impressive mic drop for a thirteen-year-old. I was devastated, and I never really recovered.

The supposedly adult me was mentally preparing. Beads of sweat were already forming on my forehead. I couldn't believe how nervous I was. I took a sip of water, but it went down the wrong way, and I coughed violently — more water, this time drunk like a normal human being, with no choking.

Then I needed the loo. I tried to convince myself it was all in my head, but, no; it was real. When I got back, my throat was dry again. After another drink, I remembered the old exercise I had been taught for this situation. Standing up straight, I raised, then dropped my shoulders, shook my hands and, out loud, repeated the phrase 'I am the very model of a modern major general.' After five reps, I felt better and picked up the phone. It was answered on the second ring.

'Dexters, how can I help?' Shit. Male voice, unless Robbie had a rich baritone. No, she didn't. I spoke to her at the writer's workshop, didn't I? 'Hello, can you hear me?'

'Oh, err, hello.' Good start. 'I'd like to speak to Robbie, please.'

'Who can I say is calling?'

'Robbie. Sorry, no. Frankie, I'm Frankie.'

'Where are you calling from?'

'Erm, home. The sofa, oh, I see what you mean. It's a personal call.'

Whoever had answered the phone held it away from his mouth, but I still heard clearly his following sentence.

'Robbie, there's some idiot on the phone for you.' Rude, but probably accurate. I heard a hand being placed on the handset, followed by a muffled conversation.

'Hello, this is Robbie. '

'Hi, Robbie. Erm, this is Frankie, from the photography club. I'm hoping you meant for me to call you.'

'Right, Frankie, hi. Look, just ignore my dad. Nothing personal, he's just an arsehole with everybody.'

'A kind of equal opportunities arsehole.' She laughed. She only chuffing laughed!

'I'm glad you called. I'd quite like to see some of the photos from the other night. Are they any good?'

'Good? They're grrrreeeat.' Where the hell did Tony, the bloody Tiger come from – idiot. But she laughed again. I was on a roll. 'Maybe we could meet up for a drink one night, and I could show you them on my iPad?' I hope it wasn't apparent that I had my eyes closed and fingers crossed.

'That sounds great. The only problem is, I'm off to Spain tonight with my mum and dad for a few days.' Bugger. 'I don't suppose you could meet later today? YEEEESSSSS. I tried for calm.

'That would be great. '

'Okay, I finish here in about an hour. I need to pack, but then I could get Dad to pick me up on his way to the airport.' There was something inaudible and probably offensive said in the background. 'Ignore him. He'd love to pick me up. Where do you normally drink?'

'The Crown.'

'I know it. See you there about five?'

'Perfect. See you later.' She hung up, and I stared at the phone. I'd done it. Things were looking up. Time to copy the pictures to the iPad and make myself presentable. I had the very tee-shirt!

I limited myself to the best twenty photos. I spent some time 'tarting them up' in Photoshop and was quietly pleased with myself as I copied the selected shots to my iPad. When I'd finished, I still had time to spend an hour reading the results of my labours on Friday. Then I planned a quick shower and set off to The Crown to see the football results before Robbie got there.

Five minutes later, the confidence and excitement I'd felt all day was in danger of disappearing altogether. I went back to the beginning and read again, but this only confirmed my fears. It was rubbish. Well, not rubbish exactly, but not as good as I'd thought last night. The dialogue didn't work, sounding clunky and unnatural. Two characters had changed names, and one didn't seem to have any purpose at all. I had no idea why I had introduced him. Then there were the illustrations. The sketches were reasonable, but there was no consistency in how much text went with each one. I seemed to go into great detail for some scenes, then make a giant leap in the storyline with no explanation.

This was bad. Last night, I convinced myself that it was only a matter of time before the awards started rolling in. Now, a job pushing trolleys around a supermarket car park was beckoning. I went back and reread the stuff I'd written at the start of the week. Hang on a minute. This was miles better. The characters were natural, even funny. The action flowed, setting up later scenes with subtle hints. How can the two bits be so different? Shit! Look at the time. Forget about it for now. This could all wait. I urgently needed to move myself, as I had a hot date with a woman in a yellow raincoat.

By half-past four, I was entering The Crown's back door, slightly stooped as usual to avoid the low beam. Ambrose greeted me with open arms, a pint on the bar in front of him.

'Here's the very bloke.' I looked quizzically at him. He leaned in close as I got to the bar and said, in a whisper, 'New tee-shirt, in here early doors. I sense a date with a real-life woman.'

'How the hell did you guess that?'

'She's in there,' he nodded towards the snug. 'Watching the football scores, and told me to let you know she was there.'

That sparked a minor panic as I paid for the beer. Robbie was early. No chance to sit and compose myself. On the plus side, she wanted to see the football scores. Oh my god! What if she was a Man United fan? There's no way I'm having a deep and meaningful relationship with a Red. On the other hand, she could be a Leeds diehard, which would be perfect. Of course, round here, it could be Bradford City. I could live with that. Just.

I picked up my pint, drank the top inch, then walked down the short corridor to the snug. I opened the door, and there she was. She looked as perfect as I remembered her, blonde hair shining and the yellow raincoat neatly folded on the seat beside her.

'Frankie, hi. Good to see you.' She smiled and stood up, hand outstretched. A handshake? Was that good or bad? Bit formal? I supposed it was easier. A kiss on the cheek is always fraught with danger. One cheek or two? Left or right? The whole nose-clash thing. This was safer. 'I'm a bit early but thought I would take the chance to catch up with the scores.' I laughed.

'Don't worry. I was doing exactly the same.' We sat down at right angles to each other, scanning the TV screen on the opposite wall. Leeds were one-nil down, a poor start to the night. Man United were one-nil up. Even worse.

'Bugger. Leeds are one down. Oops, sorry. I meant to say…'

'Don't worry. Working with my dad, I've heard worse. Anyway, my lot are one up.' I reached for my pint again as consolation.

'Don't tell me you're a Man United fan.'

'Get lost. Do I look stupid?'

'No. You look lovely, actually.' Smooth or what?

'Thank you.'

'So, who do you support then?' I took a mouthful of beer.

'The mighty Rochdale.' I laughed hard. This is not advisable with a mouthful of beer, which shot from my mouth and nose in a fine spray towards the television. I started choking, unable to catch my breath. Robbie slapped me, hard, between the shoulders, and I breathed again. 'Serves you right for laughing.' She grinned at me, then picked up her glass.

'Sorry. But Rochdale? Of all the teams you could pick. I

mean Rochdale! How come?'

'When I was a kid, my dad used to take me in the truck to a warehouse in Rochdale. We passed the ground one afternoon, and the floodlights were on. It looked magical.'

'Obviously.'

'I was fascinated and nagged my dad all the way home. Eventually, he gave in and said he'd take me to the next game. He did, and we've gone together ever since.'

'Actually, that's a heart-warming story and a noble reason to support them.' I raised my glass, and we chinked gently.

'Is it just you and your dad that go to the games?'

'Yes. My mum's just glad to have him out of the way for a few hours, and my brother is a bit of a geek.'

'Does your brother work in the family firm as well?'

'No. Dad wants him to, but he works for some crappy little software company. They seem to spend all day farting around with Facebook, from what I can see. How about you? Which team?'

'Leeds.'

'Predictable round here, I suppose. What was your epiphany?'

'When I was nine, a kid at school said he would kick the crap out of me if I didn't support Leeds. No contest.'

'That's a lovely heart-warming story, too.' We laughed. It was going well! 'Another pint? I need a few more gins before I get on that plane later. Never been a great flyer.'

'Me neither. It makes my arms ache.'

'Idiot.'

She laughed again before picking up her empty glass.

'Here, let me get them.'

'That's alright, you can get the next ones.' With perfect timing, Ambrose appeared behind the bar. He'd been listening, and he already had a pint, together with a gin and slimline tonic. The man is a genius. 'Impressive. Get yourself one. Cheers.' Robbie returned and put the drinks on the table. 'Come on then. Show us what you've got.'

I resisted the smutty reply and opened the cover on the iPad. She leaned in close. So close that I could feel the heat from her, smell her perfume, and just a hint of gin. I snapped back into the room and opened the folder.

'Wow. Is that really me? You're good.'

'Thanks. You're a very natural model.'

'Ta. Actually, I did some modelling when I first left school.'

'What made you stop?'

'Let's just say one photographer had a slightly different career path in mind for me. I slapped him so hard his glasses flew to the other side of the room. I grabbed my stuff and left. Never looked back and worked for my dad ever since.'

'Do you regret it?'

'Nah. I have a great job.'

'So what is it you do?'

'Just about everything, to be honest. Dad has several businesses, and I do all the finance type stuff. Keeping the books straight, that sort of thing. What about you?'

I told her about the business with Brian and the mad idea to try to make money from the story. She seemed interested, especially when I told her about The Woman In The Yellow Raincoat.

'Is that based on me?' Had I offended her? Was I about to get slapped?

'Yeah, sort of. Actually, quite a bit. It was seeing you the other night, at the community centre, that gave me the idea. Hope you don't mind.'

'Mind? I think it's brilliant. What happens in the story?'

'Well, I'm not entirely sure at the moment. I've just come from reading the stuff that I wrote. The first session was great, the second, not so great.' We chatted naturally as we drank. The TV confirmed a defeat for Leeds and a win for Rochdale.

I plucked up the courage to ask my question. 'Would you mind if I used this photo on the website?' I pointed at the one I took as she left the room.

'Feel free — fame at last. By the time I get back from Spain, I expect plenty to read. Hell — look at the time. My dad will be here any second to go to the airport.'

'Can we meet up when you get back?'

'Course we can. I want to hear all about the woman in the yellow raincoat.' With that, she picked up the raincoat, kissed me on the cheek, and made for the door. 'Hang on a minute. Give me your phone.' I handed it over, and she tapped away at it. 'That's my number. Text me.'

With that, she'd gone. Short and sweet, but I had another date in prospect. Time for another swift one, I think.

Magically, Ambrose reappeared behind the bar with a pint.

'How the hell do you do that?'

'Anticipation. Separates mere bar-men from professionals like me. Works with driving and midfielders too.'

'Well, I am eternally grateful. Cheers.'

'Don't get too pissed. It's day four of your challenge when I get my break.'

'Bugger. I was quite hoping you'd forgotten that.'

'No chance, mate. About ten minutes, I reckon, before we get busy.'

'Terrific.' I really had hoped he would forget this. As far as I'm concerned, it'd worked. I'd got off my backside and changed things. I'd been lucky so far, but sensed that may not last. Still, I was developing a gentle, comfortable buzz because of the beer. The date with Robbie had gone well, and it was still early. What could possibly go wrong? I started to flick through the pictures on the iPad. I had to admit, I was falling for Robbie. That smile was something special. Not only that, she wanted me to text her. I was feeling good. I must've been looking for a while, as Ambrose was suddenly sitting beside me. He had a mug of tea, which looked tiny in his massive hand.

'Right, sunshine. Are you ready?'

'Actually, I need a pee. Here, have a look at the photos I took, and I'll be back in a minute.'

I handed Ambrose the iPad and set off back down the corridor. The gents was over by the door where I came in. I wandered back through the bar and realised I was ever so slightly wobbly already. I ducked under the low beam and turned right into the gents, making for the left-hand urinal, as usual. I was always amused by the mechanism installed to hang a small plastic football on a wire in the target area, complete with a set of goalposts. With perfect aim, it was possible to get the ball to hit the back of the net. Small things like that had been keeping drunks amused for ages, me included. Having scored twice, I zipped up and turned to wash my hands. I couldn't resist doing the *Match Of The Day* post-match interview in the mirror. A few seconds in, a flush came from the cubicle. Shit, I didn't know there was anybody in there! To avoid further embarrassment, I quickly dried my hands on the back of my jeans and left. Ambrose was waiting in the snug. He put the iPad on the table.

'Great photos. You certainly have a good eye.'

'Having a good model helps.'

'Now, can we do this?'

'Yes. All sorted.' I pulled my phone from my pocket. 'You sure we have to do it?'

'No. There's always the forfeit, if you'd rather.' The smile on his face caused instant panic.

'OK. Let's do it.' I opened Twitter and refreshed the feed.

It was Susie Dent again.

Spuddle (1600) - to attend to trivial matters as if they are of great importance.

'Ha. You'd never catch me doing that.'

'Really? How many goals did you score when you went to pee?' He had a point.

'Two.'

'Post-match interview?'

He was good.

'OK, you win. Next.' I scrolled so I could only see the following Tweet.

It was in Italian. I don't speak a word of Italian. Not true; I suppose pizza and pasta are both Italian, but you get my drift. It was an advertisement for a sports channel. Still, beyond that, I had no idea what it was selling or why the gods of the internet thought I would be interested.

'I take it that's two down?'

'Yes. Struggling a bit with that one.' We looked again at the screen. The next Tweet was from a mate that I used to work with.

Great weekend in Budapest. Just cracked the last clue to get us all out of the escape room. What a hero. Time for a pint.

'Typical of him, to like that sort of thing.'

'Why not give it a go?'

'Long way to Budapest at this time of night. Anyway, I think I'd rather do your forfeit.' Ambrose rubbed his hands together and laughed. 'Hold on. I've got two left yet.'

'Seriously, why not go for the escape room?'

'You're joking. I'm getting panicky just thinking about it. I have visions of not understanding the clues and being locked in there forever. I'm sure that's what happened to that Lord that vanished. His mates suggested it, and nobody's seen him since. No chance. Number four.'

Band looking for lead singer. Influences Marilyn Manson, Slipknot, Tiny Tim. No weirdos. Tampa area.

Ambrose almost wet himself. 'How can they list influences like that and not want weirdos?'

'I could audition. See what they think.'

'Sounds like a plan apart from the Tampa thing. I reckon that's about four thousand miles. Not exactly convenient for the community centre!'

'OK. Isn't it about time you went back to work? I could do with another pint.'

'Nice try. Last one coming up. Feeling lucky? Go ahead, make my day…'

'Not funny.'

Here goes. It was from our local Italian restaurant.

Make that romantic gesture. Bring your loved one to Aldo's on Valentine's Day. We'll do the rest.

'Yes. Back of the net. I take that one. I'll give them a ring now.'

'You jammy sod. I take it your date went well?'

'Oh yes. Now, I can set myself up as a romantic hero and whisk her off to Aldo's for a slap-up do.'

'OK, but remember, I need photographic evidence.'

Ambrose picked up my empty glass and went to get me a fresh drink. It was only then I panicked. What date was it? I checked on my phone. Valentine's day was Wednesday. Would Robbie be back from Spain? I wracked my brains for a clue. She'd said 'a few days'. That could mean anything. Then the doubts set in. Valentine's day was a bit of a statement for a second date. What if I'd misread things? Besides, the challenge didn't specify a particular date, just that I had to act on the Tweet. I quickly called Aldo's and made a booking for next Saturday, getting Valentine's day out of the equation. Also, giving me another couple of days to make sure my date was actually in the country.

With a fresh pint in front of me, I sat back and surveyed the empty room. My mind went back to the tweet about the escape room. Not my cup of tea, but a lot of people loved solving clues, overcoming challenges. Cracking the case. I sat bolt upright. That's it! Make the website genuinely interactive. Each instalment of The Woman In The Yellow Raincoat having several clues or tasks. Solve the clue, get access to the next instalment. I could even make some clues really hard and buy myself more time for writing. My mind was buzzing now. What if it was just the beer thinking? I've had nights like that before when brilliant ideas after a skinful turn out to be rubbish in the morning. Even worse, they get forgotten amidst the hangover. I need to write this down. Grabbing the iPad, I started to tap away, ensuring I explained everything for tomorrow. I was on a roll and started to map out clues and tasks. This could work. Plenty of programming for me, but that is what I'm good at.

I must have been busy for a while. When I looked around, the pub had filled up.

'Mind if I join you?' It was Stella. 'Ambrose finishes at ten, so I thought I'd drop in for the last hour with him.'

'Of course. Sit down. What can I get you?' Obviously, Ambrose then appeared with a glass of white wine and a pint. He waved away my tenner, kissed Stella on the cheek, and disappeared back to the bar.

'Sorry, I broke you off. You looked really busy.'

'That's OK. I needed a break anyway.'

'Anything interesting?'

I told her about the latest idea.

'That sounds great. Clever idea. I'd certainly have a go.'

'The really clever bit would be to monetise it,' I said.

'There must be loads of stuff you can do. Think of the merchandising if it takes off.'

'Sounds like it would take a lot of time. I've been struggling to keep up the quality of the writing.'

'Concentrate on what you're good at. Get help. There are always people to shoulder some of the work. You need to keep the ideas coming.'

'Is that an offer?'

'Sorry. No. I would love to, but my job keeps me fully occupied.'

'I know it's something financial, but what do you do exactly?'

'I'm an accountant. Don't look at me like that. You'll be very grateful for one when the millions roll in.'

'So you look after the money?'

'Sort of. I tend to concentrate on finding it when somebody has been a bit naughty! I piece together the story after a major fraud has taken place. Sounds exciting, but tends to involve lots of pokey offices, and weeks on end in faceless hotels.'

'That explains why you're away so often.'

'Yes. Novelty wears off sometimes, but somebody has to do it.'

'What does Ambrose think of you being away?'

'He's fine. He tried the corporate world and didn't like it.'

'How come I don't know that? What did he do?'

'He was a solicitor for the same company. That's how we met. He hated every minute, apart from meeting me, obviously. That's why he's here. He loves this job.'

'He's very good at it, too. Always seems to arrive with a pint when you need one.'

'That is a special talent, I grant you. Talk of the devil.'

More drinks appeared. This time, Ambrose pulled up a stool and sat with us. It must mean it was ten o'clock. It hit me that with logic like that, I would make a brilliant detective. This gave me the giggles. Ambrose looked at me as he took a drink.

'What's up with you?'

'Nothing, mate. Just a bit pissed!'

'I'm not surprised. You started early, and you've not been hanging around.'

'Feel like celebrating!' I hiccupped.

'Steady Francis, don't want any accidents.'

'I'm fine, Ambrose. Actually, point of order. First, I feel great cos Robbie likes me, and — b — two, whatever, it's not Francis.'

'Sorry, I just assumed Frankie was from Francis.'

'Nah. S'Frankie Valli. My mum was besotted with Frankie Valli. It's on my birth certificate and everything.'

Stella laughed. 'Just like Ambrose!'

'What, was your mum a fan of Curtley Ambrose?' Stella laughed again, and Ambrose put his hands to his face. Eventually, he spoke.

'Slade. She was a big fan of Slade, right back to when they were Ambrose Slade.'

'No way.'

'All true, I promise.'

'Tell me your middle name is Noddy.'

'Fuck off. No, it's not.' He took a drink. 'My dad put his foot down, and she settled for Don.'

I hiccupped again. 'If you will excuse me, I need to avail myself of the facilities.' So saying, I gingerly stood up and tottered off to the loo. I was just about to duck under the beam above the door when Brenda called from behind the bar.

'Ambrose wants to know if you want crisps?'

'Yes, please. Prawn cocktail.' I turned and walked smack into the low beam. The next thing I knew, I was flat on my back, looking at the pub ceiling.

'You seem to make a habit of this.'

I concentrated very hard on the face, peering down at me. The red hair and big smile gave it away. It was Jen from the community centre.

'Hello. Fancy seeing you here!'

'You gave yourself a right crack. Are you OK?'

'I'm fine. Honest. Cured my hiccups anyway.' I giggled

uncontrollably and tried in vain to stand up. Two giant hands grabbed me under the armpits and hauled me upright. I was glad to see the hands belonged to Ambrose and not Jen, which set me off giggling again. A seat was found for me, and Jen pressed ice, wrapped in a towel, to my forehead.

'That's going to hurt in the morning,' said Jen.

'Stings a bit now, if I'm honest. I think I'll live. Amazing how quickly you can sober up.'

Once they'd made sure I wasn't in danger, I was allowed to continue my journey to the toilet. When I returned, I ducked theatrically under the beam and got a round of applause from everybody in the bar. I looked around for Jen to thank her, but she appeared to have gone. I went back to join the others, and Jen was already there. It was Ambrose who spoke.

'I thought it best that Jen joined us in case you need any more first aid. She tells me this is becoming a habit.'

'Ha-bloody-ha. Jen, thank you for the ice. I feel such an idiot.'

'You are an idiot.' This brought a dig in the ribs for Ambrose from Stella's elbow.

'Now, play nicely, you two. Tell Jen what you were telling me earlier.'

I explained how I had developed the idea for *The Woman In The Yellow Raincoat*, but felt the most recent stuff I'd written wasn't the same standard.

'It often happens when the first burst of words evaporates. It just takes time. You need to work at it, craft the ideas, refine the language. It'll come. You proved that you have a talent. All you need now is to find consistency. Failing that, you could cheat.'

'Cheat? How do you mean?'

'Well, not cheat, really. Think about the best comedy shows or soaps on TV. It's usually not one writer. There's a team involved. They kick ideas around, write parts while somebody else writes another part. A third person might re-write, make changes etc. It's more like a committee, but it gets results.'

'You're a genius. But where would I find somebody who can write and understands what I want to do?'

It was Ambrose who broke in. 'You know, for a clever bloke, you can be really thick. Jen, would you be prepared to help this idiot write his story?'

'I thought he would never ask.'

'Technically, I haven't yet. But would you? It would be fantastic if you would.'

'Send me what you have so far. Come to the workshop on Tuesday, and I'll see what I can do by then.'

We swapped email addresses and voted that it was my round. I somehow negotiated my way to the bar and back, with all four drinks upright. I sat back feeling lovely and drunk and couldn't resist a big grin — what a belting night.

4

Have you ever become conscious and, in the seconds before your eyes open, realised that this is going to hurt? My tongue was stuck to the top of my mouth. I could feel my neck was at a peculiar angle. Oh, and the headache. Don't forget the headache. I felt like I had drunk my own weight in beer, then walked into a thick wooden beam. Hang on, that's exactly what I'd done. I felt sick and tried to bring myself upright. The world spun, and I held on to the headboard. After a while, I tried again, this time making it to my feet.

I followed the trail of devastation towards the bathroom. Jeans, tee-shirt and one sock littered the floor. Its partner was, more or less, still on my foot. As I reached the bathroom door, I noticed the takeaway bag on the hall table. I suspected that was a curry, though I couldn't be too sure. At least it was intact, which meant I didn't have to worry about food later. The thought of chicken tikka and keema was almost too much for my insides. I lurched into the bathroom and sat down.

I must have fallen asleep. My phone was ringing in the bedroom; its urgent tone triggered a flight response. I stood up. I fell down. My legs were completely numb, and yet again, I found myself on the floor.

'Bugger the phone,' I muttered and decided a shower was in order.

Twenty minutes later, I had coffee and toast. The recovery could begin. Remembering the missed call, I pulled the phone from the pocket of my shorts. Two missed calls — both from Ambrose. I tapped the screen to call back and took my first mouthful of caffeine.

'It's alive.' Ambrose sounded ridiculously healthy.

'How come you sound okay?'

'I didn't start drinking at 4.30 and then try to demolish the pub with my head.'

'That would probably do it.'

'Stella made me call to check you were still alive. She was worrying when you didn't answer the second time. I told her you'd be fine, and even if you weren't, you must be used to hangovers.'

'Your concern is touching. Hang on. What time is it?'

'Almost two.' Wow! I must have been asleep on the loo for a couple of hours. 'Listen. We sort of made plans to meet up tonight to do your last challenge, but you don't sound as if you'd be any use. Why don't we put it on hold till you've recovered? I'll see you later in the week.'

'Cheers, mate. Sounds like a good idea.'

As I ended the call, I noticed the email alert. Apparently, I'd emailed myself at 3.15 this morning. This should be good. As expected, the message was barely legible, but the thoughts came back to me after a while. I remember my brain going into overdrive, mapping out the story, and building an app to allow progress through the clues. I'll come back to that later, I thought. Toast and coffee were much more urgent at the moment.

My phone had barely touched the chair arm when it lit up

again — a text from Robbie.

'Arrived safely. Hot n sunny. Enjoyed drinks. Let's do it again when I get back xx.'

Two kisses! Wait, was that just her standard text end, or would that be just one kiss? I typed my reply. 'Really enjoyed it. Stayed on when you left. Now got the hangover from hell. When u back? xx' Two kisses. Safe. Just doing the same as she did.

'Back Wed. PM. Drink Thu?? Xxx'

Three kisses! She's upped the ante.

'Sounds gr8. Meet Crown at 7.30? Xxxx' I see your three kisses and raise you one. No, wait. Too keen? I removed a kiss and pressed send. Just then, another text, this time from Joe at the record shop.

'May have something coming into stock you'd be interested in. Call in next Sat.'

Okay, will do xxx.'

I hit send. Shit! Three kisses. What the hell are you doing?

'Very friendly all of a sudden? xxx'

'Oops. Sorry. Habit.'

'Now I'm hurt xxx Don't fret, pulling your plonker. See you next week.'

I sat back and had another mouthful of coffee. Robbie was responding.

'Read first instalment this AM. Luv it. Get writing!!! x'

Only one kiss? What the hell did that mean? Is she cooling things already? Did she somehow know I'd upped to four, then gone back to three? Texting was just as difficult as real life. After a pause, I settled on a blushing face emoji and went off to make more toast.

As I settled again, I struck a deal with myself. Just watch one 30 Rock, then start coding the new app. It was halfway through the second episode that I remembered the promise to email the stuff to Jen. I set a reminder on my phone and raised the footrest on my armchair.

When I woke up, it was dark. On the plus side, the headache was bearable. I grabbed a glass of water from the kitchen and moved across to my desk. The reminder flashed on my phone, and I set about pulling together the documents to send to Jen. Having done that, I leaned back in my big office chair and surveyed my empire. On the wall by the desk was a large whiteboard. Screwing it to the wall accounted for one hundred per cent of the 'improvements' I had made to the flat since I moved in. It was still covered in diagrams and notes from the last session working with Brian, the git. I grabbed the cloth from the floor underneath it and cleaned the lot. Then, using Post-it notes, I mapped out ideas for the new app. Down the left was a column for each feature I wanted to build, one post-it per idea. I used a simple colour code: Green was a feature for the app; Yellow was the ideas for content; Blue was for skills I didn't have but would need or stuff that would take too much time. These represented people I would need to rope in if this was going to work.

After a couple of hours, I was just about out of space on the left with dozens of Post-its arranged in neat rows. I was good at this bit. More coffee and toast needed. As I ate, I scanned the list of Post-its before selecting one. It read 'build member sign up module.' That was my first task. I stuck the green label to the top of my screen and opened the code editor.

It was almost midnight when I pushed back from the desk. I peeled off the green note and moved it back to the whiteboard, this time on the right-hand side — done! I scanned the left-hand list and selected the next task, sticking it to the screen again. As I sat down, my neck cracked loudly. It was then I realised how tired I was. This could wait until tomorrow. After a poor start, this had been a none too shabby day. A beer and another 30 Rock before bedtime was called for. It was then I remembered the uneaten curry from last night. Result! Microwave, here I come.

5

After a restless night, I gave in and got out of bed at around six. Even when I was working for a living, this would've been way too early. I pulled on a fleece and shorts before making my way to the kitchen in search of coffee. It was cold and dark. The light from the street gave the kitchen an eerie yellow glow. As I waited for the kettle to boil, I stared at the blue light. A wave of sadness washed over me. I missed Cheryl. I missed Brian and constantly laughing as we worked. In truth, I missed my old life. Most of all, I missed Cheryl. The click of the kettle snapped me out of it.

'Don't be an idiot,' I said out loud. 'They betrayed you. Fuck 'em. Mainly, fuck you, Cheryl, for not showing me how to override the timer to get the heating on when I get up early.' I actually laughed. That's better, but it is bloody cold in here.

I made a mental note to work out how the heating controls worked. Sounded like the sort of thing I should know, now that I was fully independent for the first time in my life — also, the kind of thing to be tackled in daylight. I grabbed my coat from the hall and took my coffee over to the desk. I read the Post-it note stuck to the top of the screen and opened up the editor. This is what I loved. Losing myself in coding. Somebody once said to me that coders were never happier than when they had an enormous pile of poo to shovel. I think she was right. But, for me, it was more than shovelling. It was building something from scratch. Like a builder who can point to the house and say, 'I built that,' it was the same with a system. A thing of beauty. Until a bug showed up. Then it was a pain in the arse and very frustrating.

By the time it was getting light outside, another Post-it had made its way to the right-hand column. Even the heating had come on with a satisfying click. I made another coffee and sat by the window, soaking up the early-morning winter sun. I tried to work out why I had felt so miserable this morning. It was fine now, but I had missed Cheryl so much. Or had I? Had I just been missing having somebody there? Yes, it had been good with Cheryl, but, in the end, she'd buggered off with my best mate. Besides, look at Robbie. She's great fun to be with and, for reasons known only to herself, she seems to like me. Then there was the business.

I say business. We were basically doing okay, not making a fortune, but enough to live on. We didn't even pay Rupert and sold it to him as valuable experience, and he seemed fine with that. I was actually quite excited that I had the prospect of building something based on The Woman In The Yellow Raincoat. So, if it wasn't really Cheryl or work, what was it? There was a minor niggle at the back of my mind, I suppose. How long could I last on the money in the bank? I only had a vague idea of how much I had and absolutely no clue how much I needed each month just to pay bills. Cheryl had looked after all of that. What money I had left had come from mum and dad. At first, when I told them I wasn't going to university, they went apeshit. Later, when I showed them I was building a business with Brian, they gave me what they called my college fund. At some point, I would have to tell them what had happened. Not just yet, though. One thing at a time and today was the timer for the heating — later, anyway. I stifled a yawn and was just wondering about sneaking back to bed for a couple of hours when the phone rang. I answered without looking at who was calling.

'Hello.'

'Hi, Frankie. It's Dom.' Dom? Who the buggery bollocks was Dom? 'Dom, Rupert, from work?'

'Rupert! Hi, sorry about that. Still can't see you as a Dom. You've always been Rupert. '

'Don't worry, I'm used to it. How're things?'

I was a bit thrown. We'd never really done social chats, particularly at this hour of the morning. I think I'd only ever spoken to Rupert about the jobs we had on, or how to tackle the latest problem. 'I'm great, thanks. How's life with Brian?'

'Oh, you know. Okay, I suppose.'

'Doesn't sound okay.'

'It's just, I don't know, different?'

'You're missing me, aren't you?'

'Yeah, I suppose. It's Brian. He's just being, I don't know, sort of…'

'A twat?'

'Yeah. A twat.' I sensed Rupert relax. 'Don't get me wrong. I'm really grateful to him. He's even started paying me.'

'What a twat!'

'Exactly. But he's changed. So serious. I'm not sure things are going too well at home. Seems to be lots of rows.'

'Excellent! I mean, shit. That must be difficult for you if there's an atmosphere.'

'He's piling the work on. That's why I'm calling so early, so much work later. He doesn't seem to understand that I'm not you. I take longer to do stuff, and when I get stuck, you're not there to ask.'

I suddenly felt responsible for him. Almost paternal.

'Just tell him to fuck off.'

'Not sure how that would go down. Look, the reason I'm calling is, I need a favour.' Here it comes. A friend in need is a pain in the arse etc. 'We have a rush job on, I'm snowed under. The trouble is, my dad needs me to do some website changes for him. He's bought another business and wants to get it merged and onto the same site. There's a fair chunk of work, but it needs doing in the next couple of days. I could just about do it, but Brian would go mental. Could you do it?'

Shit. It sounded like a lot of hassle. How do I tell him to do one?

'He's willing to pay a grand to get it done.'

'Course I can. Anything to help a mate. I'll have it done by tomorrow night.' Well, a grand is a grand, very useful.

'Wow, thanks, Frankie. I'll email you the details and the source files. Before he left, he wrote a fairly decent description of what he wants. I thought you could do the work, and I'd test it, and then load it up onto Dad's site.'

'Brilliant. I'll get started straight away.' I hung up, feeling pleased with myself. The day was looking up already. Think I'll have that couple of hours back in bed now.

When the alarm went, I was flummoxed. I don't do alarms. It was very insistent, so I opened my eyes and realised it was daylight. Then I remembered the cheeky return to bed. Time to get up. There's money to be earned from Rupert's dad. I was intrigued to see what I'd let myself in for. Within minutes, I was at my desk. I placed the coffee cup next to the empty one from this morning and checked for emails. There was a link from Rupert to access the files I needed. I clicked on the one called specification and read. It looked pretty interesting. Apparently, Rupert's dad already had a storage company and had just bought another, with two sites. He wanted customers and staff to access an online layout of the new facility and reserve any empty units. The system already worked. It just needed the new sites' arrangements to be added and the websites to point at the amended code. Proverbial piece of!

I clicked on the current site. I needed a picture in my head of how it worked now. It was basic, but seemed to work okay. I made a few notes of improvements that would be easy enough to implement if I could tease more money out of Rupert's dad. This could be an excellent little side project if I played my cards right. Then it hit me. The logo on the website. Dexter's Storage. That can't be right. Dexter's is where Robbie worked. Holy shit! Hang on. That means Rupert is Robbie's brother. Holy shit! I wonder if he knows? Obviously, he knows he is her brother. But does he know that I'm planning to, you know, given half a chance? Holy shit!!

I pushed back from the desk and blew out my cheeks. My heart was pounding. Music, need music. Two clicks later, and Ziggy filled the room. Why was I panicking? Nothing's happened with Robbie. Yet. Even if it had, it's got nothing to do with Rupert or his dad. Actually, this could have an upside. More work from this would mean an excuse to spend time in the office with Robbie. Not to mention the extra cash, so I could afford to take her somewhere classy. No, this is a good thing. Do a good job, make an impression, definitely a good thing. With that thought, I got back to work and, by six o'clock, I'd broken the back of the changes.

I was just taking a beer from the recently restocked fridge when Robbie called from Spain. She was keen! We chatted for ten minutes or so but, for some reason, I didn't mention Rupert or the work. It just felt like something to talk about in person. She reminded me about drinks on Thursday, and I mentioned booking the table at Aldo's for Saturday. She laughed at me 'being enthusiastic' but said she was looking forward to it. It was official — three dates in a week. I wondered if she knew about the theory, about what happens after the third date? I bloody hope so!

It was difficult to settle back to work after the phone call, so I opened Twitter. I had two more messages asking when I was publishing more of The Woman In The Yellow Raincoat, now officially shortened by both of them to TWITYR. For the first time, I noticed it almost spelt Twitter. That's an omen if ever I saw one. I needed to let people know that more was coming. I fired up Photoshop and created a banner. A brilliant yellow slash of colour diagonally across the page. I applied an effect to make it look like the top corner was peeling, then superimposed it over the website's text. Coming soon. The full story! Nothing like a bit of pressure to concentrate the mind. Having said that, I was hungry. I ordered a pizza and settled down in front of the telly to watch the football.

6

On Tuesday, I busied myself checking the work for Rupert's dad. When I was finally happy, I emailed him and switched my attention to TWITYR (as I now thought of her!). As the Post-its gradually transferred from left to right on the whiteboard, the site's plan became more precise in my mind. This could work. At 6.30, the reminder popped up on my screen — time to get ready to go to the community centre and week two of the writing workshop. I was looking forward to seeing what Jen had come up with.

In the shower, I took stock. I couldn't believe how much had changed in the space of a week. I'd gone from being really entirely down in the dumps to absolutely flying in just a few days. There was even money on its way once Rupert got back to me. Things were going well.

Still buzzing, I arrived at the community centre early. Well, early for me. The writer's session had started about five minutes before I arrived. This time, I managed to slip in quietly and set up my laptop without disaster. I was just getting started when I felt a tap on my shoulder. It was Jen, holding a big green first-aid kit. She had a finger to her lips to keep me quiet, then tapped the box, smirked, and walked away. Very funny. Everybody is a comedian. You walk into one wall. Okay, one wall, after falling over in a community centre and suddenly a first-aid kit, is hilarious. Actually, it was pretty funny. I smiled and watched her walk away to peer over the shoulder of another member. At least the cold seemed to have gone, and the nose returned to a regulation colour.

Five minutes later, Jen was back. She placed a small wad of paper on the table in front of me and slid silently back to the front of the room. There was a note on top.

'Can you spare some time after the session for a chat? Really enjoyed doing this. Have a read and see what you think.' There must have been twenty pages of text here. Neatly typed and double spaced. I pushed my laptop aside and started to read. Basically, she'd picked up where my initial effort ended and re-written the stuff I'd added later. Reading through, I could see where my words had seemed limp and uninspired. Somehow, she'd changed things and brought them to life. The dialogue now seemed natural, where mine was stilted. In short, she could write. Coffee time. This time I even put a pound in the box and only took two biscuits. I was just about to return to my seat when Jen appeared. An elegant green dress had replaced the beige cardigan of last week.

'Nice touch with the first-aid kit.'

She smiled.

'I thought you would appreciate me being ready, just in case.'

'Don't worry, I'm planning on staying safe tonight. Listen, thanks for the stuff you've written. It must've taken hours.'

'No problem, I enjoyed it. It was nice to have something to get my teeth into. What did you think?'

'You're kidding. I think it's great. When can we talk about

it?'

'I could stay on here for an hour if you like, then I need to get away.'

'Okay, sounds good.'

When I got back to my seat, I pulled the laptop closer and set about mocking up a couple of pages of the new site, using Jen's text and some of the photographs from last week. By the time I had something that was starting to look good, there was a general scraping of chairs, and people were drifting towards the door. I watched Jen wave the last one-off. She walked back towards me and magically produced two cans of diet coke.

'Not sure you heard the last bit. Next week we are moving to Monday night. They need the room for something or other. Thought you might need sustenance. I've never seen anybody so engrossed in what they were doing.'

'Thanks. I need that.'

I took the offered can and opened it, half expecting it to spray everywhere or injure me in some bizarre fashion, but, no, I did it just like an adult.

'I love what you've written. It tells the same story as I was trying to do, but yours is so much more readable,' I said.

'Believe me, you did the hard bit coming up with the storyline. I struggle with that, but I'm quite good at the nuts and bolts of making it work on paper. It's my training, I suppose.'

'Training?'

'Yes. I was a journalist.'

'Was?'

'Then Charley arrived. Charlotte. She's three. That's why I need to be back in about an hour. My mum is babysitting again. She looked after her on Saturday night, so I could go for a drink with Sue that I used to work with. It was the first time I'd been out in months. Anyway, she was making eyes at a bloke in the pub so, when you decided to throw yourself on the floor, she made her move. Thanks to your mate Ambrose, I got to sit with you guys rather than play gooseberry with Sue. Anyway, I decided not to go back to work after my maternity leave. The plan was to write the great northern novel, become a millionaire, and retire to an island somewhere with a reliable bloke.'

'How's that going?'

'Not so good, if I'm honest. I just can't seem to get the storylines right. That's why I loved doing this. You provided the story like a skeleton. I was just adding the flesh and clothes.'

'I suppose I've always enjoyed making stuff up. Look, I know you need to get off, but I wanted to show you this.' I slid the laptop across. 'It's still a bit rough, and none of the functionality works, but I think the look of it is starting to take shape.' I felt very nervous as Jen scanned the page.

'Wow. It looks great. I love the black and white photos, with just the coat in yellow. The way you've used different close-ups of the same shot looks great. When you said graphic novel, I pictured something like Viz.'

'Me too at first, if I'm honest, but I wanted something that allows the text to stand up on its own but use the photos to make it really pop. You can also use them to hide things in plain sight.' Jen looked puzzled. 'Okay. This is my plan. It's changing all the time but, as of 9.45pm on Tuesday, this is it. Most people my age have an attention span of about ten minutes, even shorter for the next generation. A lot of people give up on books because they take too long. What if we could serve up a book in ten-minute chunks, then give them something else to do? Distract them with shiny things, then back for another ten minutes? We have a story that gradually unfolds, looking stunning on a laptop or tablet, and offers things to do other than just read. Get people involved. I want to set puzzles within the story, clues that the characters come up against, or something in the picture that points readers a certain way. We could add some sort of lock at the end of each chapter with a password. Solve the clue to get the password. Enter the password correctly, and move to the next chapter. It's a bit like the escape rooms, but you're not locked in some sweaty room. The puzzles themselves could be interactive. We could attract advertising, sponsorship, give prizes, sell stuff directly.'

'That's a hell of a plan. I could never have come up with that.'

'I think you could, but I know you can write. We could work together and make this work.'

'But what about setting clues and stuff?'

'That's detail. We can figure it out later. We need to map the storyline, then start to flesh it out, but I'm more convinced than ever that I can't do this alone. I need you to work with me.'

'What, work for you? Like a job?'

'Better than that, mainly because I can't afford to pay you, granted, but a partnership. We make a success of this, we both benefit.'

'What about the techie stuff, making it all work?'

'Leave that to me. I love that sort of thing. Come on, what have you got to lose?'

'So long as you understand that Charley comes first. Spare time can be taken up by this, but I'm a mum, first and foremost. '

'Done. What about a 50-50 split?'

'No. That's way too generous. You're going to be doing most of the work. I'll do it for fifteen per cent. Like an agent. Make it work, and we both make money.'

'Twenty-five per cent, and that's my final offer.'

'I'll drink to that.' We clinked coke cans. We were in

business.

7

On Wednesday morning, I woke up early. Partly, this was down to excitement about progressing the website and app. The rest was down to fear. Not fear exactly, more like worry. It sounds a bit strange, but I was worried about what to wear on Saturday. Drinks in the pub with Robbie was one thing, tee-shirt and jeans were perfect, but Aldo's, on Saturday night, was more of a statement. Robbie was classy. Her family obviously had money. She wouldn't be impressed with a scruffy little bugger like me turning up, charming and handsome as I am. A quick scan of the wardrobe and washing basket confirmed my worst fears. I was going to have to go shopping. I scooped up the pile of tee-shirts and underwear that was now on the bedroom floor and pushed them into the machine. Just before I pressed the button, I remembered the new red tee-shirt. Having previously used something similar to turn all of Cheryl's worktops pink, I was learning. I pulled the potential offender out of the washing machine. A quick sniff convinced me I could actually get away with wearing it again today — result!

If there is one thing I really hate doing, it is shopping for clothes. I had spent much of my adult life shuffling around record shops, and I can happily spend all day there. Clothing is another matter entirely. I treated clothes shopping like a military manoeuvre. I knew exactly which shop I would target; just one, not a range. Having got off the bus, I arrived at the shop at 10.08. By 10.19, I emerged with a very smart (for me) fine checked shirt (blue), chinos (black), and boxer shorts (red x 1, blue x 1 and black x1). Technically, the undies were an extravagance, but you never knew. If I was to be called into action at the weekend, I wanted to look my best. Anything that would boost the confidence was welcome.

I was only two streets away from Joe's record shop. Being so close, it would be rude not to call in to see my new friend. Besides, I wanted to know what he was getting in stock that he thought I would be interested in.

'Frankie! How wonderful to have a regular visitor.' Joe strode towards me, and I thought he was about to hug me for one horrible moment. Instead, he ushered me to take a seat next to his desk. 'Tee-shirt looking good. Tell me about your exotic and wonderful life! How did it go with the fragrant La Dexter?'

'Robbie was great, actually. She's fantastic company. Makes me feel better just being with her, and that smile just lights up the room. She even holds her own talking football. '

'So, I take it further meetings are planned?'

'Tomorrow night, as a matter of fact.'

'Ah, so it's a new tee-shirt you're after to impress her?'

'Not exactly.' I pointed to the bag at my feet. 'Gone a bit more upmarket for this week.'

'I'll have you know my shirts are of the utmost quality,' he said in mock indignation.

'They are. This one went down very nicely on Saturday.' I did a little twirl to show it off. 'I'm still serious about selling shirts through my new website, too.'

'How's that going?'

I told him all about the meeting with Jen, the role she was going to play, and the idea of setting clues, attracting sponsorship, and selling merchandise.

'This could be where you come in. I know you're keen on crosswords. Would you be willing to help out with a few fiendish clues?'

'How exciting! I would love to.'

'Need to start easy and gradually make them harder. I won't be able to pay you much, at least until it starts to make money.'

'You'll pay me precisely nothing. Happy to help. I love the idea of setting challenges.' Joe actually clapped his hands together. 'Even better, I want to be your first advertiser. I could make the first clue music related to tie in with the shop.' Joe pulled a notepad towards him and started scribbling notes as he spoke. 'How much to advertise?' This threw me.

'I've got absolutely no idea. We don't even have any readers yet.'

'Yes, but you will, and you could do with the cash injection, I suspect.'

'That's certainly true.'

'How does £100 sound?'

'Fantastic. Are you sure?'

'Yes, of course, I'm sure. As long as you promise to keep me involved when you're making millions.'

'Done.' We shook hands, and Joe pulled a wad of £20 notes from his pocket. He peeled off five and pushed them into my hand. 'You'll need to send me an invoice, or my accountant will rip me a new wotsit, but I'm happy to pay upfront.'

'Joe, this is really generous of you.'

'Nonsense. Look, a friend of my mum's did something similar for me when I was setting up this place. I've never forgotten it, and it would be good to make a difference.'

'What do you want the ad to look like? What should it say?'

'Oh, I'll leave that bollocks to you. Just point people at the website and say how fabulous I am. That sort of thing.'

'Okay. Leave it with me. You mentioned, in your text, that you were getting something in that I might be interested in.'

'Yes, I am, but you can't afford it yet. I'll keep it for you until the business is up and running. Then you can buy it.'

'What is it?'

'Too expensive for starving new business owners like you. Trust me. You'll want it. Just not yet. Okay?'

'Okay. Not even a clue?'

'No, I've got enough on trying to come up with clues for this website thingy. Now bugger off and get to work. You've got an empire to build.'

Twenty minutes later, as I got off the bus, I got a text from Joe.

'What about this for the first clue? Slade waved her off. But who took the time, 15 years later, to work out what she wanted? (6-5). Let me know what you think.'

I walked down the hill towards home and started to mull over the clue. Strange he should mention Slade after the thing about Ambrose the other night. So, before I was born, but what songs did I know by Slade? There was the Christmas one. Nothing about waving in that. You wave when you say goodbye! Goodbye t' Jane. That must've been the early seventies. So the second part was the mid to late eighties. Baby Jane by Rod Stewart? Too early and doesn't fit the six and five letters bit. Jane Wiedlin, Rush Hour, The Go-Gos? None of that fit. Then the light went on — Understanding Jane by Icicle Works, six and five. Get in! I texted the words 'Icicle Works. Nice one.' To Joe and let myself into my apartment.

I went straight to my desk. Coffee could wait. I scanned the list of Post-its in the left-hand column and selected 'Create clue answer module.' The adrenaline was flowing, and I worked quickly. A few hours later, with only two coffee breaks and one toilet visit, I had a working module. It displayed the clue and responded with a series of comments if you entered the wrong answer. A correct answer showed a somewhat clunky animation of a vault opening. Inside the vault was a TV screen. As the screen got more prominent, the ad for Joe's shop appeared on it, with a website link. The instructions included another question that could only be answered by visiting Joe's site. In this case, it was the phone number prominently displayed on his home page. Entering the number opened another vault containing the next instalment of The Woman In The Yellow Raincoat. I needed to work on the animation and the rest of the graphics, but the code worked.

It was getting dark outside when I got another text. This time, it was Rupert. 'Testing finished. I've uploaded the changes. Dad is happy. Send him the invoice to get paid. Cheers.'

Two invoice requests in one day! I knew I had a template somewhere but was a bit vague on what I should be putting on it. Brian had done all of that sort of thing. Right, chippy first, then look, for example, invoices online to copy.

8

Nuts!

There was a flashing light on the washing machine. I'd forgotten to empty it yesterday. I opened the door and dragged the contents out. A quick sniff confirmed my fears that it hadn't reacted well to being left overnight. I shoved everything back in and started again.

Not a great start to the day. Especially one that includes drinks with Robbie. We'd spoken briefly last night when she was on her way from the airport. She wanted to hear all about the progress with the website and was looking forward to seeing me. After a couple of minutes, I could detect her dad in the background, but couldn't make out what he said. She told me to ignore him, but that just confirmed that he'd said something unpleasant. I almost told her about the Rupert situation but decided face-to-face was better.

I took my coffee to the desk and had to push aside the two cups from yesterday to make room. More Post-its had made their way across to the right, but there was still plenty to go at. I picked one at random, read what it was, and picked a different one. I also needed music. Icicle Works had been on my mind since the text from Joe, so it was the Best Of that belted out as I worked.

At just after nine, I noticed a text come through. It was from Jen.

'U free 4 coffee partner? Lots to discuss.'

That seemed better than sitting at the desk for the day. The local greasy spoon did a wonderful bacon butty and was handy for both of us. I suggested we meet there in about half an hour.

Jen waved from the corner when I arrived.

'I took a chance and ordered you a bacon butty. Hope that's okay.'

'Are you psychic?'

'A bit, yes, from my mum. Mainly just hungry, and I didn't have the nerve to just order one for myself. The nice lady behind the counter says you drink black coffee.'

Just then, the coffee was plonked in front of me by the nice lady — Ildiko. She ruffled my hair and called back over her shoulder as she went back behind the counter.

'Bacon butties ready in a minute, love.'

Jen laughed. 'You seem well known around here.'

'What can I say, once seen and all that?'

'I've been giving the structure some thought. I hope you don't mind.'

'Certainly not. We're partners. Besides, I'm a bit worried I may have bitten off more than I can chew.' Right on cue, the butties arrived. 'Tell me what you've been thinking.'

Jen carefully cut her sandwich into four pieces.

'Okay. Based on what you said about the ten-minute attention span, I reckon each instalment should be around a thousand words. We need to make them fairly self-contained, but push the story forward, and finish on a cliff-hanger, hook them in so that they want to solve the clue.' I nodded and spread tomato sauce on my sandwich. 'We need to decide where the overall story is going, how things develop.'

'I'm with you. I've knocked up a basic shared workspace and I'll email you a link so that you can access it. The idea is we mimic a series of post-its stuck to a wall. I could map out a basic story with each instalment on a separate Post-it. You develop the text for each, and I then load it to the website.'

'Sounds great. What about the story itself?'

'Well, so far, we have the envelope full of money and the locked door. I think the money should hint at her being very successful. She's good at what she does, even though we aren't too sure yet what that is. She's well rewarded and likes the finer things in life. I want the woman to be a strong character. We develop her as a sort of really hot Miss Marple, Lara Croft, writing wrongs and generally being an all-round clever bugger. She's bound to have dealings with thugs and drug dealers, but I think she would be just as comfortable with them as she would be at a royal garden party. Does that make sense?'

'I'll go for that. It's all about creating a believable character and putting her in situations that seem impossible to get out of. Then we get her out of it.' Jen tapped her chin. I was just about to take another bite when she laughed. 'Your chin: tomato sauce.' She handed me a napkin. 'Actually, it's down your shirt as well.'

'Bollocks. Oh, sorry.' I rubbed at the offending blob, but only succeeded in moving it around a bit.

'Don't worry. I just noticed I've got a bit of sick on my jumper. Not mine before you ask. Charley decided to explode just as I dropped her at my mum's.'

'Nice.'

'I felt guilty leaving her and getting my mum to clean her up, but she insisted. Need to get back soon, though. What about the clues?'

'Ah. I roped in my mate Joe. He's come up with the first

one. Tell you what. When I get home, I'll create a mirror site that only we have access to, and you'll be able to see what I've done so far. Oh, and he's become our first advertiser or sponsor, whichever it is. We're off and running.'

'Almost. Calling her The Woman In The Yellow Raincoat all the time seems a bit of a mouthful. Shouldn't we give her a name?'

'That's a fair point. I suppose I was getting a bit carried away and forgot that. Any suggestions?'

'Well, when the picture of her comes into my head, I think of a flower standing out against the background. Could we call her Buttercup?' The look on my face betrayed me. 'How about Daisy?'

'That I like. Let's call her Daisy.'

Ten minutes later, we had split the bill, and I was making my way back home with even more tasks on my list!

When I got in, I decided more coffee was not what I needed. I set about creating the dummy site and compiling an email for Jen with all the relevant links. Again, it was dark by the time I'd finished. I stretched and decided to get ready to meet Robbie. Bob Marley accompanied me as I cleared the desk of cups and put them in the dishwasher. It was then I spotted the flashing light on the washing machine again.

Bugger.

I needed a clean tee-shirt for tonight. I fished everything out and sniffed. The second wash had worked, and all smelt fine. Just needed to get a shirt dry for tonight. Quickly, I scattered the damp clothes across the radiators throughout the apartment. Spreading things neatly, as previously instructed, many times. I selected the Stax shirt for special treatment. Cheryl had left behind a hairdryer, perfect for tee-shirt drying. Twenty minutes later, I had a perfectly acceptable tee-shirt. Ten minutes after that, I was showered and on my way to The Crown.

* * *

I navigated the low beam successfully and made my way to the snug. Robbie was sitting in the same seat as at the weekend. A slight tan made her look even more gorgeous, if that was possible. She smiled and lit up the room. I leaned in and kissed her on the cheek.

'You look great. The sunshine obviously agrees with you.'

'Are you saying I looked pasty on Saturday?'

'No. I …'

'Don't worry, I'm messing with you. It's been great, but glad to be back.'

'I'm glad you're back too, on balance.' Just then, Brenda appeared with a pint for me.

'I said you'd pay,' laughed Robbie. She took a sip of wine. I handed over a £20 note.

'Get one yourself, Brenda.'

'Anyway, I hear you've come into money,' said Robbie.

'Me? What makes you say that?'

'I've just spent the afternoon with my darling brother, going over some changes to our site.'

'Ah. He told you then?'

'I kind of worked it out, from his description of the bloke he used to work with.'

'I was going to tell you tonight. I didn't realise myself until a couple of days ago. What description?'

'Never you mind. Actually, he looks up to you. Says you taught him quite a bit. You must be outstanding if you can teach that idiot. Before I forget, you made a good impression on my dad.'

'I thought he took an instant dislike to me.'

'He did. He does that with everybody. Says it just saves time. He still thinks you're an idiot, but you did a good job with the coding. In fact, he wants you to take on another job.'

'Really, That's great. What would you think? Us seeing

each other and me working for your dad.'

'So, we're seeing each other, are we?' Oh, bugger! I must've looked crestfallen. 'Cheer up, you dopey bugger. It's too easy to wind you up. I'm looking forward to some decent food on Saturday. Let's take it from there, shall we?'

'Sounds like a plan to me.'

'I must warn you, I'm not up for a full session tonight.' I nearly choked on my beer. 'Steady on, I only meant I'm tired after the flight and need an early night rather than a skin-full.'

'Actually, that suits me too. Not that it wouldn't be great to have a skin-full with you. I just have a lot to do tomorrow.'

'You do, cos my dad wants to see you. He suggests 10 o'clock at the office.'

'I think that should be okay.'

'Good, his suggestions don't tend to be suggestions, more like commandments. Don't look so worried. You'll be fine. Tell me what you've been up to while I've been away.'

I told her all about my week.

'So, Jen. Is that the Jen I was at school with?'

'Yes, she said she knew you.'

'I've not spoken to her for years. How is she?'

'She's good. She's like Super-Mum. She has a three-year-old daughter called Charley.'

'Married?'

'No. At least, I don't think so. She never mentioned a husband.'

Brenda appeared behind the bar with a fresh supply of nuts on a cardboard picture of a smiling brunette. I took the opportunity to order another round. When I sat down again, Robbie snuggled up really close.

'This is nice,' she said.

'Yes. Very nice.' We clinked glasses, and I leaned in for a kiss.

'Oy! Get a room, you two.' Brenda, subtle as ever. The moment sort of went as we laughed, but she stayed snuggled up really close. This was nice, very nice. We stayed in the same position for another hour before Robbie tactfully pointed out she needed to go. I offered to walk her home, but she pointed to her shoes.

'Walk in these things? Think again. I'll order a cab. Do you need one?'

'No, I only live around the corner.'

'Interesting. Handy for next time.' With that, she smiled, kissed me on the cheek, and set off for the ladies.

When Robbie returned, her cab was already outside. I followed her out to the car park and leaned in for another kiss. I intended to make this one last. The driver stuck his head out of the car window.

'Put him down, love. I've got an airport run after this and need to get off.' We laughed, and I opened the door for her. As I waved her off, I turned to walk back into the pub. Then I decided against it. A lot to do tomorrow. Was I growing up? I hoped not, but set off towards home, nevertheless. It was only then that I remembered the photography workshop would have been tonight. Fuck it. I didn't need any other model.

9

Should I wear a suit? More accurately, should I wear *my* suit, as I only had one? I bought it for a friend's wedding two years ago. The wedding got called off with a week to go, so the suit went into the wardrobe, never to leave. I had to get this right. Not only was I meeting somebody who could provide a much-needed income, but also my girlfriend's dad. Girlfriend! I was confident after last night that this was the case. I savoured the sound of it, even saying out loud, 'this is my girlfriend, Robbie'. Fair enough, it was only to the rubber plant, but it felt good. I could tell the rubber plant was dead impressed.

I decided the suit would be too much. I wasn't applying for a job. He wanted to buy my professional services as an IT expert. Maybe not an expert, but close enough. As for prospective father-in-law (yes, I'd already got to that stage), Robbie knew I lived in jeans and tee-shirts, and she was happy. I pulled the 'Nod's As Good As A Wink' tee-shirt off the shelf. Perfect. I knew I had the musical taste of a 60-year-old, but I was okay with that. 'Proper' music, as my dad used to say. I'm not saying all modern music is crap; far from it. I still loved discovering new bands but auto-tuned karaoke wannabes — no thanks.

I zipped up my hoodie and set off towards the community centre again, this time to the Dexter's office. When I got there, the door was propped open. I could see Robbie with the phone cradled on her shoulder. She waved and motioned for me to sit by her desk. She said her goodbyes and replaced the handset.

'Hello, fancy seeing you here! Dad is on his way. He likes to check in at a couple of the other offices, keep them on their toes.'

'Offices?'

'Yeah. He has a few. The main one is at the original warehouse, sorry — distribution centre, as he likes to call it now. This is just a convenient place for me to be housed. It means I can stay apart from the managers on the various sites, and I do the top-level admin. It works well.'

'So he has lots of different businesses?' She nodded.

'And before you ask, yes, he's loaded!' That was good to know. 'Coffee?'

I nodded. Robbie stood, came around the desk and kissed me. I almost panicked. What if her dad came in? Jesus, am I twelve? I must be a bit nervous. Robbie poured the coffees from a glass jug, sitting on a fancy machine.

'There you go. Oh, and here he is. Dad, this is Frankie.'

I turned in my seat and saw the massive frame of my potential client. He must have been six-foot-four and was almost as wide as he was tall. The picture was completed by a nose that pointed, ever so slightly, towards his left shoulder. I stood and took the outstretched hand.

'Frankie. Call me Dex; everybody else does. Have a seat.' He sat on a small filing cabinet next to Robbie. 'So, you're the lad who's shagging my daughter?' Every muscle in my bum tightened.

'Dad. Behave.'

'I'm only messing with the lad. I'm sure we'll get along fine.' He leaned forward so that his face was inches from mine and almost whispered. 'Seriously, hurt her, and I'll hurt you more.' He laughed, as if this was hilarious, and slapped me on the back, so hard my eyes watered a bit. 'Roberta tells me you're a bit of a whizz kid with the computers.'

'I'm pretty good, yes, even if I say so myself.' I cleared my throat nervously, as that had come out as a bit of a squeak.

'Good. And she told you, I wanted you to take on work for me?'

'Yes. It sounds interesting. What is it, exactly, that you want me to do?'

'Well, I own several companies, and they all rely on computers to some degree. We have a firm that maintains and develops stuff at the moment, but they take forever to get anything done. They document every change in triplicate and it is signed off by fifteen bloody managers before some bod in India does the actual change. The business has moved on by the time it gets done, and it has cost me a fortune. I want somebody on hand who can turn things around quickly and get stuff done. You impressed me with the changes last week, but don't get big-headed. Does it sound like something you can handle?'

'No problem, sounds good.'

'But there is a problem, isn't there?' Shit. Does he mean Robbie? Is he warning me off? 'Roberta tells me you have another business idea that you're trying to get off the ground. Surely that's going to take up all of your time?'

'Well, it will be tricky, but I work hard. Obviously, your stuff would come first, and I would work every hour to keep up.'

'Cut the bollocks. Everybody promises that, but you'll burn out and make a mess of everything. I can't afford that.' My heart sank. He was going to blow me out already. 'Listen. A bit of advice I learned this the hard way. You can't do everything. Do the stuff you have to and employ good people to do the rest; much more productive than chasing your own arse for a living.'

'The trouble is, I can't afford to employ anybody. It's just been me in my flat, so far.'

'How much would you need?' I shuffled in my seat, trying to think. 'If you were to employ somebody, you'd need an office. Computer equipment, pay their wages. What else?'

'Well. At the moment, everything is PC based. I'd need to buy a Mac so that we can make compatible versions.' Dex shrugged his shoulders as if I was speaking a different language. 'There's some software I need, server space.'

'Would twenty-five grand get you started?' Shit. Much more than that, and I'd be doing a runner to the Bahamas. I stroked my chin as if I was calculating. 'Okay, make it thirty. I don't want a stake in the business. What I'm offering is a loan. I have two conditions.' Here it comes. I knew it had to be too good to be true. 'First, anything urgent for my business takes priority.' I nodded. 'Second, you employ my idiot son, Dominic, and keep him occupied.' Is that it? Working with Rupert again wouldn't be a problem, and it would piss off Brian as well. Result.

'Are you sure? Just like that, thirty grand?'

'Believe me. It's worth it, just to stop my wife fretting about Dom. Actually, there is a third condition.' Oh god, no. 'You tell me where you got your tee-shirt. I love The Faces, and that's my favourite album.' He held out his hand again, and I shook it firmly. The deal was done.

After the financial future was seemingly assured, two unexpected things happened. Number one was Dex (as I now called him), giving Robbie the afternoon off. Second, instead of the pub, we went back to my place.

'That was fun,' I said as I pulled my tee-shirt over my head. The room was dark, with the heavy curtains closed tight.

'Fun? Not wonderful or amazing?'

'Hey, don't knock fun. It's what I live for. Actually, it was wonderful and amazing fun. How's that?'

'Better.' She threw the pillow at me as I left for the en-suite bathroom. Actually, I had to admit to myself, it was more than fun. My legs were a bit wobbly, so I opted to reflect on life whilst sitting on the throne—what a difference in a couple of weeks. I still couldn't believe my luck that a beautiful woman was currently sitting up in my bed, and I hadn't made a complete arse of myself. I hadn't even made a comment about one-nil to the Yorkshireman. However, I had thought it immediately after the moment. I decided on a quick shower.

Afterwards, I wrapped the towel around my waist and headed towards the bedroom. Robbie was sitting on the bed, wearing only my hoodie. She'd switched on the bedside lamp. I panicked and made a dash for the bathroom, where my tee-shirt still lay on the floor. Sheepishly, I re-entered the bedroom.

'Looks better on you than me.'

'You're a bit of a smoothie on the quiet, aren't you?'

'I can turn on the charm when needed.'

'Good, you can buy me a drink and charm me all over again. Do you mind if I take a shower?'

'No, of course not. It always amazes me in films or on the telly that people leap out of bed, get dressed, and go straight to work. Dirty sods. They must hum a bit by the end of the day.'

'They never need a poo either.'

'Different sort of film altogether if they did.'

'Suppose so.' With that, she scooped up her clothes from the floor, kissed me, and made her way to the bathroom.

I finished getting dressed and sat on the end of the bed. When Robbie returned, she was still damp; the towel wrapped around her like a toga. She sat beside me and took my hand. Her question froze me to the bone.

'You saw?'

'Sorry, couldn't help it when you put the bathroom light on. I sensed you were trying to keep covered. You didn't want me to see?'

'What do you think? I suspect hideous scars are a bit of a turnoff for most women.'

'I'm not most women. Besides, there's nothing hideous. They're part of you, somebody I happen to enjoy spending time with.' There was silence for a moment while I processed. It was Robbie who spoke first, very gently.

' Show me.'

'But—'

'No buts. If we're adult enough to do what we've just done, we're adult enough to discuss what happened, don't you think?'

I took a deep breath. Robbie was smiling at me but had a tear in her eye. I turned side on and pulled my shirt off. I felt her cool fingers on my back. She leaned close and kissed each line in turn. Barely touching the skin.

'Does it hurt?'

'Not any more. The skin dries out a bit if I don't moisturise with cream, but mainly, it's okay.'

'Would you like me to put some cream on for you? I'll be gentle, I promise.'

I reached across to the bedside table and took the E45 from the drawer. She motioned for me to lie face down. Tenderly, she applied the soothing cream.

'Is that okay?'

'Perfect.'

'Do you mind me asking what happened?'

I took another deep breath.

'I was thirteen. It was just before Christmas. The boiler at school had broken down. The place was freezing, so they sent us home early. I'd gone straight to dad's music room. I loved it in there. It had wall to wall records and a great hi-fi, huge floor standing speakers, the business. I was obsessed with the new R.E.M. album at the time, and the empty house meant I could play it loud. I remember going into the kitchen to make a sandwich, singing *Everybody Hurts* at the top of my voice. Like most kids at that age, I thought the song was about me. Anyway, it was weird. The music cut out, left me singing by myself. I assumed Mum had got home and turned the sound down. I mopped up the egg yolk from the plate and was just about to take my cup of tea back to the other room when I smelled smoke.'

Robbie finished with the cream and lay down beside me. We were almost nose to nose.

'All I could think of were the records. As I ran to the music room and could see the flames. I just started grabbing as many records as I could. I suppose opening the front door made things worse. The draught fanned the flames. I dropped the records on the lawn. Mrs Green from next door was on her drive, and I shouted for her to call 999. I think I was on the third trip to grab more records when the ceiling collapsed on me. That's what they told me afterwards. I don't remember that bit. The firemen dragged me out. Said I was lucky to be alive. It didn't feel like it. I was in the hospital for months. Dad gave me a right bollocking for going back in. The worst thing is, it was all pretty much pointless. The records I saved were ruined by the water and dozens of heavy boots. I suppose they were concentrating on the fire rather than the Motown Chartbusters series.'

'You're still here. That's the important thing.'

'Dad was never the same after that. I just assumed he blamed me. His pride and joy went up in flames.'

'I'm sure he wouldn't have blamed you. Didn't you talk about it?'

'No. By the time I got out of hospital, I had assumed the role of a surly teenager. I'd destroyed the one thing that had made my dad happy. Don't get me wrong, I still see him, but there's always that distance now.'

Robbie shuffled onto her back and held her arm out for me to snuggle closer, head against the top of the towel, and wept. She kissed the top of my head and held on to me. We lay like that for ages. Then she shivered.

'You're cold.'

'I can think of a way to warm up,' she giggled.

We could have another shower later.

Ambrose had a pint and a glass of white wine on the bar when we arrived.

'How the hell do you do that?'

'My grandmother was a remarkable woman and had certain powers that she passed on to me. Swore me to secrecy. Sorry.' He winked at Robbie and held his hand out for payment. She rumbled him.

'You didn't see us walking up the road then?'

'It's a fair cop. I got here thirty seconds before you and could see you from the car park. You both seem very cosy. I take it things are going well?'

Robbie squeezed my waist and said, 'very well, thanks.'

'I'm pleased for you. Look after him, though. He's a bit thick when it comes to affairs of the heart.'

'I'm still here, you know.'

'Don't worry, I intend to look after him,' said Robbie.

Ambrose moved down the bar to serve somebody else, and

we took our usual seats. Robbie looked at her phone.

'Problem?'

'No. Just a text from Dad. He's had a contract drawn up for the loan and paying you a retainer.'

'Blimey, he's keen.'

'Doesn't hang around when he decides on something. You must've made a good impression. He says I should take you through the details tomorrow in the office and get you to sign. Then you need to talk to Dom and tell him the good news.'

'Actually, I've got loads to do. Need to keep a clear head tonight.'

'True. I've got plans for you.' Excellent! I thought it best to protest a bit.

'I've got plans to make. Stuff to buy.'

'Don't I fit into the plan?'

'Suppose I can squeeze you in. Ow! You've got very sharp elbows, you know. I suppose planning can wait until tomorrow.'

'I may be able to help. I was thinking earlier. How would you feel about me doing the admin for you? You'll need a bank account, an accounting system, somebody to pay the bills. It's the stuff I do all day and every day. I could do it from the office. Nobody need know, not that my dad would care, so long as his stuff gets done.'

'That would be great.' At this rate, there would be nothing for me to actually do.

We chatted easily for the next couple of hours until Robbie drained her glass decisively.

'Come on. I'm hungry.'

'Free pork pies and sandwiches here in about ten minutes; it's Friday.'

Robbie pulled a face. 'I don't suppose you've got any food in?'

'I have actually, but I really fancy a pizza.'

'Pizza it is then. After that, an early night.'

Ambrose spotted us making for the exit.

'Just where do you two think you're going? I thought we were doing day five of your challenge?'

'Sorry mate, something came up.' I lied.

'Don't think I'm going to forget this and let you off the hook.'

Robbie laughed.

'Don't worry, Ambrose, I'll make sure he doesn't chicken out. You can have him next week. Right now, he's mine.'

'Fair enough. See you later.'

10

On Saturday morning, we woke up early but didn't head out to the cafe until nearly ten. Ildiko raised an eyebrow when I arrived with a different woman. I just grinned at her and ordered my bacon butty. I looked at Robbie, who shrugged and asked for a full English, fried bread, black pudding and toast.

'Don't look at me like that. I've worked up an appetite, thanks to you.' She took a sip of cappuccino. 'So boss, what's the plan?'

'Well, I intend to have my butty and a second coffee. Then we go to your office, sort out the paperwork, and then work out exactly what we need to do to get up and running. I have to admit I had a bit of a wobble this morning.'

'Blimey, aren't I enough for you?' she smirked.

'Not like that. No complaints on that front. No, I just got worried about borrowing so much money. It's an enormous risk. What if I fall flat on my face and lose it all?'

'My dad'll break your legs.' She saw the look of panic on my face. 'Joke. Look, he's not daft, at least when it comes to money. He wouldn't lend it to you if he didn't think it would work out. Besides, he's offering you regular work. In effect, you're starting two businesses. You've got the website and a software company. Relax, enjoy it. You get to spend somebody else's cash on all the techie stuff you can't wait to get your hands on, and you get to lord it over my brother, which is a bonus.'

'Does he know he's part of the deal?'

'Don't let on, but it was his idea. He looks up to you.'

'Wow, sad bastard. So, if you were me, you'd accept the cash and take the risk.'

'Do you have a plan B?'

'Not so as you'd notice. You're right. What have I got to lose, apart from my legs? I'll do it on one condition.'

'What's that?'

'I get one of those pieces of toast.'

'No chance. Get your own.'

'That's not very romantic, is it?'

'I'll give you romantic.' She leaned in very close so that her hair tickled my face and whispered in my ear. I blushed and ordered more toast.

When we got to the office, Robbie placed the contract neatly on the desk. She sat opposite me as I read it. I made what I took to be thoughtful noises and stroked my chin. She threw a screwed-up piece of paper at me.

'Do you understand all that legal stuff?'

'Not a fucking clue. Maybe I should get a solicitor to check it over.'

'Look, most of it is just standard bollocks that he puts into all contracts. A solicitor would just make you wait a week and charge you three hundred quid for the privilege. This is the important bit.' She leaned forward and used her pen to point at the relevant bits. 'Basically, he is advancing you thirty grand against you doing IT work for the company. You invoice him at slightly different rates for your time and

Dom's for the hours you put in. Once you've paid back the loan, he pays you cash.'

'What about leg-breaking? Anything in there about breaking any bit of me?'

'Only a bit, but it's dressed up in legal mumbo jumbo.'

'Where do I sign?' She handed over the pen, and I had thirty grand burning a hole in my back pocket. 'What happens now?'

'Now, my little sex bomb, you go away and start doing whatever it is you do. In the meantime, I will fill in forms to get you a bank account. I'll work my magic in the accounting software, so we keep records right from the start. I'll see you tonight at Aldo's for very pricey cocktails and something soaked in garlic. Don't be late.'

In fact, for once in my life, I was early. They greeted me like an old friend, even though I'd only been twice before. Maybe I'd made an impression, dropping a very sticky spare rib on the front of my shirt; not my finest moment, and yet there are so many from which to choose. Tonight I felt good — new clothes from head to foot and the confidence that I now had two business ventures. I perched on a stool and accepted the offer of two outsized menus. A gin and tonic soon followed, and I relaxed.

'Who do you have to sleep with to get a drink around here?' It was Robbie. She looked stunning. A silky red dress that came to just above her knees. The dress shimmered in the candlelight, but Robbie outshone it. She glowed. That was the only way to describe it. I was inordinately pleased when I realised that every pair of eyes in the bar were on her. She kissed me on the cheek and sat down next to me. 'Hope I'm not late. I've actually been here a while but needed to powder my nose. God, I sound like my mum. I needed a pee! Is that better?'

The waiter arrived just in time to hear the latter, and two more gins soon followed.

'By the way, Dom came to the office this afternoon. I hope you don't mind, but I recruited him for you. He starts tomorrow.'

'But tomorrow's Sunday. Whoever heard of starting a new job on a Sunday?'

'I thought you had a lot to do?'

'I do. We do. Fair point. Thanks for taking the initiative. It would probably have taken me a week to do that.'

'He's coming to your place tomorrow morning. Make sure you pile up the work. Dad says he's a lazy little toe-rag, who will do no more than what you put in front of him.'

'A glowing reference.'

'Indeed, but he is cheap. I made sure of that.'

The waiter was back and guided us through the crowded restaurant to our table. It was the one in the bay window. I'd wanted this table both times I'd been before, but was told it was reserved. In the summer, it had great views of the river. Tonight it felt all cosy thanks to the candles. I panicked when I saw the champagne in a silver ice bucket. Surely this was somebody else's table, and they would shove us in the corner next to the kitchen door. The waiter lifted the bottle, wrapping a towel around the base in one movement.

'With our compliments, sir.' He poured two glasses and glided away. Robbie was grinning.

'Let's just say Dad knows people. Cheers!'

'Cheers!' I could get used to this. We posed for the traditional selfie, which I sent to Ambrose as proof of completing the task.

By the end of the main courses, we were talking about TWITYR.

'Would you do some more photos with me?'

'So long as it is kit on. I'm a good girl me.' She grinned and lifted her glass. 'Maybe the odd nipple if you get me drunk first!' The champagne was long gone, but I'd splashed out on a rather spectacular Barolo, and we were both a bit giggly.

'They'll be very tasteful, naturally. I want to use them to set the clues. I was thinking some answers could be linked to what you're carrying in the photos, books, magazines, that sort of thing. Even what music is playing on your phone.'

'Sounds good. I saw this film once where spies were using a special code. The only way to crack the code was for the other person to have the same book. Not sure how it worked beyond that, but that's your department.'

'Good idea. Particularly if we make the codes harder as we go along. The book could be a first edition or something tricky to get hold of.'

'You got any first editions?'

'Probably not, but I have some quite rare albums with sleeve notes. You tend not to get the notes on CDs; not enough space on the covers.' I pulled my phone from my pocket.

'Bored with me already?'

'Sorry. No, of course not. I just need to send myself a note. Another glass of this, and I won't remember any of it tomorrow.' Robbie drained the rest of the bottle into my glass. I really, really like this woman.

I woke up at about 8 o'clock on Sunday morning, and the world had gone yellow, or so I thought. There was a post-it stuck to my forehead, covering my eyes.

Stuff to do. Don't forget, Dom's coming at 9.30. See you tonight. R x

Bugger. That changed my plan for the start of the morning. I crawled out of bed and headed for the bathroom. I'd forgotten that we'd arranged for Rupert to come to the flat to get started. It felt too early. I shivered in the cold air and decided I really must sort out the timer for the heating. As if by magic, I heard the slight click as it came on. Sorted.

I celebrated it being Sunday by making a pot of proper coffee before settling down to watch the end of the Match Of The Day re-run. Once that finished, the promise of an interview with the Prime Minister made me instantly switch off the telly and think about what to do first. Rupert would need somewhere to work. My desk was a decent size, but well over half of it was covered in crap. That would be a start. Five minutes later, the crap had been pushed into a more or less neat pile in the corner of the room. I pulled the desk away from the wall and angled it slightly before dragging one of my two dining chairs to the other side of it. Perfect. I now had a two-person desk. This management lark was easy.

Rupert arrived bang on 9.37.

'You're late.'

'Sorry, I got lost.'

'I don't pay you to be late and get lost.'

'To be fair, you don't pay me at all yet.'

'Fair point. Your sister is going to sort that out. Come in. It's bloody freezing out there.'

'Cheers. Bit of a turn-up, you and Robbie. Never saw that coming. You're not her usual sort of bloke.'

'What do you mean?'

'Well. My sister normally goes for them a bit, you know. A bit more…'

'A bit what?'

'You know. Physical.'

'I'm fucking physical. Aren't I?' This came as a bit of a shock. I looked down and sucked in my gut. Maybe in all this newfound wealth, I could join a gym. Or not.

'Look, she seems happy enough. Wouldn't shut up about you yesterday afternoon.'

That was more like it. We walked through to the kitchen,

and I showed Rupert where the essentials were. Coffee making would tend to be his job.

'By the way. How did Brian take it when you told him you were leaving to come and work here?'

'Ah. Technically, I haven't told him yet. '

'Coward.'

'No. Well, yes, but I thought we needed to formalise things a bit at this end first.'

'Formalise?'

'Well, at least explain what I'm gonna be doing.'

'OK. Come with me.'

I spent the next half-hour showing him what I had so far. The online card system to map out the story and the facility for Jen to upload text. The website and the start of the android app — finally, the animated clue and password module. I even impressed myself.

'You've been busy. This looks great.'

'It's a start. I want it to look fantastic. There's all that functionality to go.' I pointed to the whiteboard. 'We need to do that lot before we can launch. I'm relying on you for the Apple version of the app as well.'

'Wow. There must be a couple of month's work there.'

'We've got a week. By then, we need to be submitting the apps for approval and maybe launching just on the website. I want to get launched while there is still a bit of interest from the first post.'

'Better get cracking then.'

He picked the first Post-it from the left column and slipped into my seat.

'Nice try. You're on the dining chair. I presume you've brought your MacBook? Excellent. As a special concession, you get to pick the first album.'

'James Vincent McMorrow - Post Tropical.'

'Done. Nice and chilled' I picked up my phone, and

'Cavalier' filled the room. We had work to do.

11

On Monday, I slept until mid-morning. It had been a late one. I picked my way through the discarded pizza boxes and empty beer bottles. Rupert had left at about three o'clock, I think. The left-hand column of Post-it notes was about the same size as the right-hand column. We were halfway there. After James Vincent McMorrow, I remember choosing Ziggy, and insisting that we go through Aladdin Sane, Pin Ups and Diamond Dogs. There'd then been a short, high-volume discussion before we compromised on Fantastic Negrito, The Waterboys and Nine Inch Nails. Productivity nose-dived with Tindersticks, then picked up again with Kings Of Leon (when the beers came out). If I'm honest, I suspect we were well past productive by then. I'd almost forgotten how much I enjoyed working with Rupert and had to disagree with his dad about the lazy bit. He certainly put in a shift yesterday. By the time he left, he was all for going straight round to Brian's to tell him what he could do with his job. I think I persuaded him to do it more professionally after a night's sleep. Then again, it would be pretty funny to hear about the look on his face if he had.

While I was waiting for the kettle to boil, I had a quick tidy round and rescued the last piece of pizza from a box. Breakfast sorted, I sat at the desk to review what we'd actually done. This was all looking very exciting. I clicked on the card index to see what Jen had been doing. Another two instalments were waiting for me. I felt like a footballer, settling down to read his autobiography for the first time.

To say I was impressed was an understatement. Jen had taken the scruffy, half-baked ideas I'd come up with and turned them into beautifully written, self-contained stories. Each one left you hooked in, wanting to read the next. There wasn't even a spelling mistake. She was good. I wondered why she was doing this rather than writing her own book? I didn't really believe that she couldn't come up with ideas. She wrote so engagingly, she could regurgitate the phone book, and it would sound good. Maybe it was just timing. Charley was her priority. I got that. I decided not to look a gift horse in the arse, or whatever the phrase was, and make sure that we made a success of this.

I filled in another few cards to move the story on, even introducing Ambrose as a character. It occurred to me I hadn't seen him for a few days. I shouldn't abandon him just because Robbie's on the scene now. He did so much to jolt me out of my misery. The challenges had worked. I hoped he would forget all about the last one. Knowing him, he'll bring it up when I least expect it. Well, tonight was the writers' workshop, so I could call for a pint afterwards. Robbie's doing something mysterious, anyway. It's funny, but I was actually looking forward to the workshop. I could devote time to working out more of the story and setting more clues. That meant I could spend today working on the website. Rupert was due back at some hazily defined 'not stupid o'clock'.

Right; to work. Motown soundtrack to start with, then

maybe introduce Rupert to Kathryn Williams later. I decided to spend the morning getting to grips with the animation I wanted to achieve for the vault-opening module. By the time Rupert arrived at 11.15, I had watched a dozen tutorials but got absolutely nowhere. Everything was pointing to needing some quite costly software and a reasonably powerful machine to run it on. Then again, we had start-up cash on its way for just such investments. I texted Robbie.

'Free for lunch?' Thirty seconds later.

'About one for an hour?'

'Picnic in the park? I'll bring all.'

It's freezing.'

'Wear a vest. Nice n sunny, it will be fun. Meet by lake xxx'

'OK, but you'd better have a plan to keep me warm. xxx'

I was just settling into my seat when a deafening air horn sounded two feet away from me.

'You fucking idiot! I nearly shat myself.' I threw my pen at Rupert, who ducked just in time. 'What is the purpose of that, you arsehole?'

'I thought it would be good for morale. We sound it each time we move a Post-it across.'

'Can't we do it with something quieter?'

'I just thought it would be a laugh.'

'Give it here; let me have a look.' He handed over the bright red toy, and I immediately blasted him from close range. Six times. 'Actually, it's quite good.'

'You're supposed to sound it once,' he said, rubbing his ears.

'Yes, but I did loads of stuff before you brought the horn. Just catching up. Anyway, I'm going out for a couple of hours. I need to see your sister.'

'Get a room, please.'

'I've got a room. You're sitting in it.' I looked across at the sofa but decided not to say any more. 'Anyway, this is business. I need to get my hands on some of your dad's lovely cash to buy new toys for us.'

'In that case, you have my blessing. Can I change the music?'

'No, you fucking can't. This is the genius that is Smokey Robinson. Listen and learn. I'll be asking questions when I get back.'

I stepped outside into one of those days that makes you feel glad to be alive. It was cold, yes, but the sun shone out of a brilliant blue sky. I felt like a character from a Dickens novel as I strode down the street, wishing a hearty 'good morning' to everyone I passed. If I had a cap, I'm pretty sure doffing would've been on the agenda. I felt alive and, for the first time in ages, happy. I had two stops to make before meeting Robbie. After the first, I spotted an essential in a charity shop window. A third stop would mean having to hurry, but it would be worth it.

I was relieved to see that the bench I had in mind was unoccupied as I arrived at the park, with five minutes to spare. Carefully placing my shopping on the ground, I sat back to enjoy the sun.

'Anybody sitting here, mister?' I was just about to tell the newcomer to do one when I realised she'd tricked me again. 'You're too easy,' she laughed.

'It's one of my best traits.'

'I must be crackers. It's freezing.' She snuggled close.

'Don't panic. I am prepared.' I reached down and produced my charity shop purchase.

'A travel rug! Seriously? How old do you think I am?' I was crushed and went to return it to the bag. 'Don't be daft. Give it here. It's just what I've always wanted.' We covered our legs and tucked the sides underneath us. Robbie turned and kissed me. 'My hero. What have we got to eat?'

'Right. For my next trick, voila.' I produced the M&S carrier bag. 'Chicken and bacon, or prawn mayo?' Robbie grabbed the prawn mayo and opened the pack. 'Madame also has a choice of side dishes. Sausage roll or pork pie.'

'Which is the biggest?' I looked in the bag.

'Sausage roll.'

'Hand it over. I'm starving.' She took a bite of the sausage roll and scattered pastry everywhere. 'Shame we haven't got anything hot.' My triumph was complete as I produced the cardboard carrier with two cups of hot soup.

'Courtesy of Ildiko at the cafe. Tomato, okay?'

'Fanbloodytastic. This is the best thing ever!' She kissed me again before going back to the prawns. We sat for almost ten minutes in companionable silence, with just the odd comment about the ducks or the people passing, as we enjoyed our picnic.

'Come on then. Where is it?' She looked at me and grinned.

'What?'

'For somebody who's being so perfect, there must be pudding. Where is it?' I attempted my best eye roll before producing the bar of chocolate from my coat pocket.

'Perfect. I'm in love!' My heart was pounding. She'd used the 'l' word.

'I love you too!' She looked at me as if I'd taken a dump on the bench.

'I meant, I'm in love with Belgian chocolate.'

'Oh. Shit. Of course. Sorry.'

'Don't look like that, please. It's just a bit soon for pledging eternal love, isn't it?'

Soon? I already had names for our first three kids. I was besotted, but I'd fucked up.

'Yeah, you're right, sorry.' I tried not to sound sulky; honestly, I did.

'Look, I'm not saying never. You've made a bloody good

start. I'm having a great time. Yes, that too. I just think you've got a lot to do, with the business to run, without putting labels on what we're doing. Now hand over the chocolate, you numpty.' She smiled as she held her hand out, and I couldn't sulk anymore. 'Don't suppose you've got coffee too?'

We laughed, and we were back to normal.

'Listen, I've got something for you too.' She handed me a key. 'I've arranged to rent an office for you. It's all yours if you want it. Don't worry, I got an outstanding deal. You need to look at it this afternoon.'

'Where is it?'

'Upstairs at the community centre, right above my office.'

'I didn't know there were offices up there.'

'Technically, there aren't. It's a junk room at the moment. Got it very cheap if we, that is, you and Dom, clean it out. I've pulled in a few favours, and we can have broadband installed before the end of the week. I just need your approval.'

'Cool. I'll come back with you when we've finished here.'

'Oh. You also need to call in at the bank. They want a sample signature and some form of I.D. I put us both as signatories. They already have all my details, so just you to add.'

'Wow. This is fantastic. It must be taking up loads of your time.'

'It is, but Dad hasn't noticed. Besides, nothing's too much for my man.'

She was taking the piss, but I felt great again.

I turned the key and stepped into our potential new office. What a dump! Every inch of floor space was covered in boxes, broken chairs, bin liners and assorted tat. There was a strange smell that I couldn't quite place. I flicked the light switch, and a single, pathetic fluorescent tube flickered. Having said that, the room was huge, covering most of the roof space of the building. There was plenty of headroom in the middle, although the roof sloped at the edges — plenty of scope for banging my head.

'It's brilliant. We'll take it. What do we do with all the crap?'

'The agent says to just bin it all. I'll get a skip for tomorrow.'

'What a great find. Come here, you.' A long, lingering kiss sparked thoughts of locking the door and celebrating in style.

'You'll have to do something about that smell.' Ah well. Another time, maybe. 'Come on. I've got work to do, and you need to get to the bank before they shut.'

'You're right, and I need to see what Rupert's been up to.'

'I've meant to ask. Why do you call him Rupert?' I told her about his first day at work. 'So he gets a name change just because he once wore a red jumper? I'll never understand men. Not like normal human beings. Having said that, I like the name, so Rupert it is.'

I locked the door and went to give the key to Robbie.

'Keep it. I'll confirm things and get a copy of the lease for you to sign tomorrow.'

'Great. While we're on the subject of spending, I need to order some kit. Any idea when we'll get the bank cards through?'

'Probably next week. In the meantime, send me a list of what you need, and I'll take care of it. It's what I'm here for, after all.'

I decided I could get used to this management lark.

I was on the bus, coming back from the bank, when my phone vibrated in my pocket.

'Jen. Hi. I didn't hear it ring but then got the vibration in my jeans.'

'I'm not sure what to say in response to that. Anyway, I'm

just ringing round to cancel tomorrow's workshop. I'm needed at home.'

'Nothing serious, I hope.'

'It's Charley. She's off colour and wants her mum. Thought it best to give everyone some notice. Sorry to mess you about.'

'Don't be daft. Like you said, Charley comes first. While you're on. I loved the stuff you uploaded. You're a genius. '

'I don't know about that, but thanks. I'll work on more tonight when I get Charley to bed.'

'Things are moving at this end, too.'

I explained about the software company. Jen was still happy with our arrangement. Robbie would keep the two businesses totally separate as far as the books were concerned.

'I reckon we could launch within the next couple of weeks. Choose an outfit. I think we should have a big party to celebrate.'

'I'll see what I've got without sick down the front. Sorry, got to go. I'll see you next week.'

I walked into the flat to be met by the speakers turned up to eleven.

'What's this shite?'

'It's not shite. It's Vampire Weekend'

'Well, turn it down a bit. I need to tell you stuff.' The music reduced to just loud. I realised I'd just turned into my dad and felt terrible because I actually loved this album. 'Have you told Brian where to stick his job yet?'

'I have formally resigned, if that's what you mean.'

'How did he take it?'

'Like a twat, basically. He reckoned he was rethinking his business anyway and was going to let me go soon.'

'So he sulked, then?'

'Big time. So what have you been up to?'

'I have had a meeting with your sister, who has done a deal for us to move into luxury offices. So, tomorrow we are going on a staff outing.'

'Alton Towers?'

'Not quite. Operation Shit Shovelling starts at 10 o'clock sharp. Dress casual.'

'You mean it's a dump, and we have to clear up?'

'Always knew you were bright. Tell you what. Let's go for a pint, and you can tell me what I've achieved today!'

I ducked under the beam at The Crown. Rupert clipped the top of his head.

'What the f—'

'Mind your head. The beam's a bit low. Evening Ambrose, this is Rupert, and he wants to buy me a beer.'

'That's nice of him, hi Rupert, I'm Ambrose,' he said, thrusting out a huge hand. 'Remember to mind your head on the beam. Some clowns have been known to give themselves a right whack. What can I get you?'

'I'll have a pint of lager, please, and whatever you want. Suppose I should get one for the boss, as well.'

'Boss, eh? Things are moving forward then?'

I nodded. 'They certainly are, mate. We move into a new office tomorrow.'

'Sounds exciting. I'm not doing anything tomorrow; if you need an extra pair of hands, I'm quite good at carrying desks and stuff.'

'Thanks, Ambrose, another pair of hands would be very welcome. The community centre at 10. A few beers on me, back here afterwards.' Little did he know there was forty years of accumulated crap to get rid of, not to mention that smell. Ambrose took the £20 note from Rupert and extracted change from the till.

'How come you're not with that gorgeous girlfriend of yours? I'm surprised you have the strength to lift your pint.'

'Ambrose. Before you say any more, let me once more introduce Rupert, Robbie's brother.'

'Ah, right. Sorry, mate.'

'No problem. Cheers.' Ambrose muttered something about changing the bitter and disappeared into the cellar.

'So, while I was in my high-powered meeting, what were you up to?'

'I made a start on the code to create the Apple app and finished another couple of modules to do with social media. We can now get people to sign up for a newsletter and follow us on just about every platform you can imagine.'

'Sounds like a good day.'

'Much better than working with Brian. He used to be such a laugh. Now he's just a twat.'

'Guilty conscience, I suspect.' How pleasing!

'Oh, before I forget. My dad is talking about more work for us. He's being a bit cagey about what's happening, so I expect he's swallowing up another of his competitors. As usual, when it comes, he'll expect us to jump to it.'

'Better make sure we have the TWITYR stuff ready to go, then. You should have an early night. Big day tomorrow.'

'Yes, boss.'

We eventually left just after eleven, completely pissed, but with a comprehensive plan for taking over the world. If we could remember it tomorrow. We were on our way to greatness! Small steps, small steps.

12

It was just before ten when I arrived at the community centre. The skip had arrived and was almost half-full. Maybe Rupert had come in early and made a start? That didn't seem likely. I knew how hungover I felt, so he would be a right mess. I called in to see Robbie.

'Look at the state of you.'

'Thank you. You look lovely.' I went to kiss her, but she waved me away.

'No offence, but you stink of booze.' I was about to protest but realised I may throw up if I did. 'You need to get a move on. Skip's law has already struck. Order a skip round here, and it mysteriously fills up almost immediately. I've booked for it to be changed at lunchtime, so chop-chop.'

I saluted feebly and made my way upstairs. As I opened the door, there seemed to be even more rubbish than yesterday. What was that smell? I picked up a black bin bag that was just inside the door. It split immediately, and the contents hit the floor by my feet; not a good start. A wave of nausea swept over me, and I decided I needed a rest. I picked my way to the window, and, thankfully, it opened without a fight. I sat on the sill and glanced down at the street. Ambrose and Rupert were arriving from opposite directions. I sat until I pictured they would be halfway up the stairs, then got to my feet and looked busy.

'Morning, gentlemen. Oh dear, are you okay, Rupert?'

'I suspect he'll be fine once we get started.' Ambrose looked disgustingly healthy, as usual.

'How about we get started? In half an hour or so, I'll go and get coffees and bacon butties. Most stuff goes in the skip, but anything we can use gets rescued.'

Rupert nodded and picked up a black bag. The bottom fell out of that one too. Never had anybody looked more in need of a sit-down. I gave him a short motivational speech, and it motivated him to give me the finger. We were off and running.

'Frankie, give me a hand with this.' Ambrose had found a small sideboard with a leg missing (the sideboard, not Ambrose). I lifted my end of the cumbersome piece of furniture. As we approached the door, one cupboard fell open and dozens of old magazines fell to the floor. So far, we had got nothing in the skip and three lots of rubbish on the floor. This was not a promising start. At least the load was lighter now, and shortly afterwards, we were throwing it in the skip. Two seconds later, a bin bag crashed onto the sideboard from above, inches from my head. I looked up and saw Rupert grinning from the window.

'Sorry.'

'Be careful, you mad git. You could've killed me.' By the time we got upstairs, several more bags had taken the quick route from the first-floor window. A small patch of floor was now visible, which was more than could be said for Rupert. We found him when we lifted the small wardrobe in the corner. He crashed through the door and fell at our feet, almost helpless with laughter.

'I was going to carry the coat hangers from inside,' he explained as we edged the former coat cupboard out of the door. Once it was safely in the skip, Ambrose climbed the stairs again. I was about to set off on the butty run when Robbie appeared with a tray of takeaway cups and a carrier bag full of sandwiches.

'I thought you might appreciate these.'

'You are not only beautiful, but an absolute star.'

'And you, while slightly grubby, owe me fifteen quid.'

'Fair enough.' We sat on the bench outside the centre in the winter sunshine and tucked in. It was Ambrose who asked if we should let Rupert know that his breakfast had arrived. I was just about to shout for him to join us when he appeared carrying a high-backed swivel chair.

'I thought I could smell bacon. Just what I need.' He was just about to throw the chair in the skip when he realised there was no more room on the bench. 'Actually, this is quite comfy. It just needs a new wheelie thing on the bottom.'

'In that case, darling brother, I will order a new wheelie thing, and you have your first bit of office furniture. I'll finish this inside. I've got a call in a minute.' She passed her coffee to me and winked before turning and spinning Rupert's seat several times. We all got splashed with coffee but considered it worthwhile, as it was one of the funniest things we'd ever seen. She bowed, took her coffee, and returned to her office.

'Nutcase, that woman.'

'You're just upset that you didn't think of it.'

'I stink of coffee now.'

'It's better than what you smelled of ten minutes ago,' said Ambrose.

'It's the lager from last night. Always has this effect.'

'Remind me to only sell you orange juice next time. Oh, in the name of all things Marley, he's done it again. You really need to see a doctor.' We left Rupert laughing maniacally and moved back inside. It was Ambrose that stopped me and gestured towards the chair. I understood immediately; we both rushed back and gave the Rupert and chair combo, a push that the Jamaican bobsleigh team would've been proud of. There was another spray of coffee to match the swear words, and Rupert careered down the street. After twenty yards, a combination of gravity and a missing wheel catapulted Rupert skywards. We ran towards him, thinking we'd killed him. He just lay there, helpless with laughter.

'Bastards. Help me up and rescue my chair before it escapes.' We picked him up, and I agreed he could keep the chair.

Fully refreshed, we returned to the task at hand. Over the next two hours, we filled the first skip, made a good start on the second, and found Matilda. She became Matilda a few seconds after being unearthed, a mannequin, complete with wig and tartan dress, that Rupert waltzed around the room. Hence Matilda. A battered sofa turned up next. We also found two birds. One we named Wol, the stuffed owl, we allowed to stay. The dead pigeon was not, as it explained, at least in part, the smell. It must've got in somewhere and met its demise. We gave it a formal burial in the skip. Throwing things from the window was banned after a near miss involving a passing Yorkshire Terrier, and the discovery of a bag of 1970s dirty magazines briefly suspended operations. When Robbie brought tea and biscuits late in the afternoon, she insisted we get rid of them. Rupert was strangely insistent that he would carry them down to the skip.

Just before five, Robbie appeared again, carrying two floor-standing lamps, which meant we could switch off the overhead tube. She'd also managed to borrow Henry the hoover from the cleaner, and Rupert was elected chief operator. By six, the place looked habitable. Wol, Matilda, the two chairs, and a basketball hoop had all been rescued. The lights looked great, and the place was clean. All we needed now were a couple of desks, and our new computers. Then we could move in. Time for the pub, but this time we made Rupert drink Guinness until he pointed out that was worse than lager.

As we settled into the corner of The Crown, Robbie handed over a sparkly silver gift bag.

'You've worked hard today. I thought you deserved a present.'

'I would say you shouldn't have, but you definitely should. Thank you.' I peered inside. Excellent: an electric toothbrush.

'It's got extra plaque removing action, whatever that is.'

'I love it. Thanks again.' I kissed her on the cheek just as Rupert arrived with the drinks.

'Leave it out, you two. We'll have no physical displays while I'm drinking. Thank you very much.' He raised his glass. 'To our new office. God bless her and all who sail in her.'

We all cheered and drank a toast. Ambrose and Rupert went off to the jukebox. Robbie looked at me.

'You need an early night tonight.'

'Oh yes. You're insatiable.'

'Calm down. All I meant was that my dad has a big job for you. You're going to be busy, busy, busy. Early start too, your broadband stuff is being installed at 8.30.' Thoughts of an early night with Robbie receded. She could see the disappointment. 'I'm not saying you need to become a monk. We'll have an hour with this lot, then sneak off for a bite to eat and see where that leads.'

'You'll do for me.'

13

By half-past nine the following morning, we had broadband. I finished setting up the network just as Rupert arrived.

'Morning, boss.'

Rupert, morning, just the bloke I needed.'

'Something technical or a brew?'

'Brew.'

'I'm on it. Hang on a minute. We don't have a kettle. We don't have water, come to think of it.'

'Robbie says we can use theirs downstairs.'

'I'll be back in a jiffy.'

Two minutes later, I got a text. It was Rupert.

'Need help. Big box to carry.' How much coffee was he making? I went downstairs, and, sure enough, there was a big box with two coffees perched on top. I picked up the coffees and looked at Rupert.

'Executive privilege. Come on, put your back into it!' He was swearing at me when two big blokes arrived, with new desks for us.

We soon had the box unpacked, and the shiny new Mac installed on one desk. Together with the monitors for our laptops, it was starting to look like mission control.

'I suppose your executive privilege means you get to use the new machine?'

'Would I pull rank on a thing like that?'

'Yes.'

'You're right, normally I would. In this case, I thought coding is okayK on our laptops, and we use the Mac as a shared machine. Whenever you need something with a bit of power, like the animation, we use it.'

'Sounds like a plan.'

'It's also got a big fuck-off disk, so we can put loads of music on it!'

'I think I might just like working here.'

We sat back and enjoyed our first coffee, looking out over our new empire.

'You lazy sods got nothing to do?' It was Robbie at the door.

'Just taking a moment, my dear.'

'Well, you might want to take a moment to read this lot.'

'What is it?'

'Dad's accountant has come up with a reporting system he wants to implement. In his words, you need to bolt it to the back of the accounting package we use. This explains what he wants. Oh, and he says don't pad the estimate, or he'll have your danglies for ear-rings.'

'Always a very reasonable man, your father. When does he want it by?'

'He says no rush. This time next week is fine.' The folder must have been an inch thick.

'Rupert, we're gonna need a bigger whiteboard.'

We spent the rest of the morning turning the requirements into Post-it notes on the wall. The back wall was the only space big enough. It would have to do until we got some boards fitted.

'A week? Is he serious?'

Rupert grinned.

'Deadly serious. My dear papa tends to expect a lot.'

'We'd better get on with it then, I suppose. Can't see us getting much done on TWITYR this week.'

'Actually, it might not be as bad as you think. I happen to know that he had approached a certain company last month about something very similar. There's more to it now, but the basic design is the same.'

'Are you saying he got Brian to start this?'

'Oh yes. We put a good week into it before they had a big row. Storming out, throwing things, Brian went proper mental. That was after he'd put the phone down, of course. He wouldn't tell me what it had been about, but the upshot was that we stopped work immediately.'

'So, if only you had a copy of what you had produced so far…'

Rupert reached into his rucksack and pulled out a hard drive.

'If only!'

'You beauty. Shit. This is not technically legal, is it? That code belongs to Brian.'

'I wrote most of it.'

'Yes, but you were working for him at the time. He owns it.'

'What are you talking about. Brian shafted you and is shacked up with your ex.'

'True, the little shit can swivel. Just make sure you scan and replace any reference to him in the code. Right, you make a start on that. I'm going to set up the firewall and backups. Losing anything because we don't have a copy would be a disaster.'

'Here, you'll need this. It's the sign-on details for the Dexter network. We'll need full access to implement this lot.'

By the early afternoon, Rupert had removed any reference to Brian from the original code. The Post-its now reflected our progress. The music was pumping via a Bluetooth speaker that Rupert had retrieved from home at lunchtime. My phone was set to play at random.

'This accountant seems to know his way around.'

'He's a devious git, been a mate of Dad since they were at school.'

'But this stuff is clever. He's going to be able to take a set of accounts and re-format them to add and remove companies at the push of a button. It means you could have multiple sets of books, all controlled by one person. You could give the taxman a right runaround.'

'Rule number one with Dad: you never talk about the taxman. He's very protective of his books, that's all I'm saying.'

Was he as dodgy as Joe had hinted? I shrugged.

'We're just writing software. Bloody good software at that.'

I picked a Post-it and walked back to my desk, smirking as the music changed to the Beatles. Taxman.

14

Over the next week, life settled into a nice routine. We'd implemented the changes to the Dexter's system. With TWITYR in big letters at the top, the newly installed whiteboard was seeing a gradual move of Post-its from left to right. Jen was delivering an instalment every other day, which kept me busy coming up with twists and new storylines. Joe was dreaming up ever more complex clues. Robbie was a whirlwind of activity and had added colourful throws to the tatty sofa and implemented a complete accounting system (apparently). We'd even been paid, making my bank manager very happy.

We had done two more photoshoots to build a library of images to use on the website, all featuring the famous yellow raincoat. The animation was looking smooth and professional. I installed the beta version of the software on Robbie's PC, so she could do some additional user testing from her office. She loved it and gave me helpful feedback.

At home, things were going well, too. Robbie had become a regular overnight guest. We even had matching electric toothbrushes sitting side by side on the bathroom shelf. We completed the domestic picture at our first grown-up dinner party when I cooked. Ambrose and Stella were enthusiastic about the spicy beef, less so about the souffle. In short, I was happy. Little did I know that the Shitehawk Of Adversity would soon start to circle.

Rupert started the morning playlist with Hunky Dory. Like a dad taking the stabilisers off a kid's bike for the first time, I was so proud. He noticed me staring at him.

'What?'

'Nothing. Just thinking about how you wouldn't have chosen this six months ago.'

'I've been brainwashed. My dad warned me about joining cults, then I end up here enjoying fifty-year-old music. Anyway, big day today.' It was my turn to look puzzled. 'Last three Post-its on the board.' He pointed. Sure enough, only three left. We walked across and took one each.

It felt strange knowing that all our hard work was about to be put to the test. I'd already pulled together a plan for launch day. We'd had a countdown banner on the website for a week. Teasers had been placed on all social media platforms, and the buzz was growing. We still needed approval to get the app on the major markets, but I was confident that would come at any minute. We could always launch the app from our own website if it came to it.

'Tell you what, let's have a party to celebrate the launch.'

'Don't you need loads of mates for a party?'

'Cheeky sod.' Having said that, Rupert had a point. My social circle was quite limited these days. 'It doesn't have to be massive. We need everybody who helped make it happen. Robbie, Jen, Joe, Stella, Ambrose, even your dad. I wonder if Jen would use her contacts to get the press involved?'

Just then, a notification showed on my phone. When I looked, two emails had arrived within a minute of each other. We'd been accepted and could promote our app through the two big markets. We had no excuses now, and we could set a launch date. I phoned Jen immediately. It rang six times. I was about to hang up when she answered.

'Sorry about that. Took me a while to get the phone off Charley. How are you?'

'I'm great, thanks. We've just had the news that we are ready to launch. Just a few loose ends to finish here, but I wanted to talk about the plan. Are you free for coffee?'

'Okay. It looks like spring is here. Why don't we meet in the park? Charley can use the play area, and we can chat.'

'Great. Half an hour? I'll pick up some drinks and muffins and see you there. What does Charley drink?'

'She'll have a triple espresso.'

'Fine, I'll see you soon.'

'Hang on, you idiot. I'm joking. I'll bring her a drink, don't worry. The thought of a three-year-old with a triple espresso inside her is truly terrifying.'

I hung up and turned to Rupert, who'd been listening.

'I gather you're going out for a nice sit in the park.'

'Business meeting.'

'It's okay for some.'

When I arrived in the park, Charley had already found a friend, and Jen watched from a bench. I handed over a coffee and a muffin.

'Hi. Hope I haven't dragged you away from something important.'

'No. Just writing for some website. This is nice, sitting in the sun, watching Charley play. It's been a long winter,' she said.

'It sure has. But that website is all set to launch. By tonight, we'll have the coding finished. The apps can go live from tomorrow. We just need to crank up the publicity so that we get millions of downloads. Then we can start selling the advertising.'

'You've put a lot of work into this. You must be very proud.'

'You've put just as much into it. Yes, I suppose I do feel proud, a bit. It's more excitement than pride. This could really take off.'

'Do you really think millions of downloads?'

'Maybe not millions, but thousands, with a bit of luck. We're not charging, so being curious costs nothing. Hopefully, we can grab people's attention and keep them hooked. Actually, I need your help when it comes to grabbing their attention. Could you write a press release? You'd do it so much better than me.'

'Flattery will get you everywhere.' She took a drink. 'I can do better than that. I thought you might ask, so it's already done. Some of the editors I've worked for are prepped as well. You said that you'd be having a launch party. If that's still on, they'll be happy to cover it. Interview you, that sort of thing.'

'Interview you too, don't forget. You're just as much the story as I am. That would be fantastic. One more thing; actually, it's two more things. Robbie needs your bank details for when the millions start rolling in. Also, how are you fixed for making the party next Monday?'

'I'll have a chat with my mum about babysitting. It should be fine. That gives me time to get the word around the editors. Where are we having this soiree?'

'Interesting question. I hadn't thought that far ahead. Hang on a minute, we'll use our new office, it's huge. Thanks for this.'

'Thanks for the coffee and muffins.' There was a shriek from the play area. 'Looks like I'm needed.'

I headed back for the office, wondering how many people could fit in. This could be good.

15

The launch party was due to start at 6pm. I was back in the office by early afternoon, scrubbed, presentable, and very nervous. The press release had gone out, and our Twitter following had climbed steadily during the day. We'd chosen ten of the early followers to get advance access to the app, and we were confident that it downloaded okay. We could see that at least four of them had read the first instalment, but the vault (as we were calling it) would not open until an hour into the party. Rupert had rigged up a screen that updated in real-time to show the number of downloads and the number of correct clue answers.

Robbie had arranged catering with the cafe, and by 5.30, Ildiko and her husband, Imre, stood poised to swoop with trays of nibbles. We had plenty of booze, now all we needed were people. Ambrose was the first to arrive.

'This place has scrubbed up nicely.'

'You played a big part in that, mate. Come in, and have a beer. Stella, not with you?'

'She's coming later. She's on a train back from London. Wow! That looks fantastic.' He nodded to the larger-than-life poster with Robbie in the yellow coat and bright lettering against a black and white background: The Woman In The Yellow Raincoat. We'd also framed some photos we were using on the site and displayed them around the room.

'How do I get the app, by the way?'

I pointed to the bottom of the poster, where the instructions were printed. Ambrose took out his phone and tapped away. The counter clicked to eleven, and Rupert cheered from the other end of the room.

'Wish I always got a cheer when I walked into a room.' It was Joe. I introduced him to Ambrose and pointed out that Joe had set most of the clues.

'Joe runs the best record shop you could ever hope to visit.' Within seconds, they were chatting happily about Steel Pulse and Black Uhuru. I spotted Robbie arrive with Dex, and I left them to it.

'Look what Dad's brought you.' I kissed Robbie and accepted the bottle of champagne before shaking Dex's outstretched hand. Robbie slipped away to speak to Rupert.

'Congratulations, son. You've done a good job for me so far, and this looks like it's going to be a gigantic success too.'

'Thanks, that means a lot. I thought, at first, you thought I was a bit of an idiot and not good enough for Robbie.'

'I still think you're an idiot, and nobody's good enough for Roberta, but I'm willing to keep you busy.'

'Cheers. I think. Let me get you a drink.'

'Don't worry about that. I'm not shy when it comes to tracking down drink.' He laughed loudly, then the newcomer at the door caught his eye. 'I don't believe it. Is that young Jennifer? It is. Come here, you. It must be close on ten years.' Jen looked awkward as he enveloped her in a massive bear hug.

'Hello, Mr Dexter. It's good to see you.'

'Please, I think it's time you called me Dex. I can't believe it's you.'

'Jen is the genius writer that's made all this possible.'

'I thought you'd moved down south somewhere. Jennifer and Roberta were thick as thieves. Lots of sleepovers. She was like another daughter to me. Roberta said, you lost touch. Does she know you're here?'

'I've not seen her yet. Will you excuse me?' With that, Jen turned, heading straight for Ambrose and Joe. Dex seemed oblivious to Jen's discomfort and was soon in possession of a drink. I detached myself and followed Jen across the room.

'Sorry about that', she said when I reached her.

'At the risk of seeming indelicate, what happened with you and Robbie?'

'It was all a long time ago. Can we just leave it?'

'We can, but she is here, you know. I'm not sure you can avoid each other all night.'

'We've done it for the best part of ten years. Why change now?'

'But we do work together.'

'We do; you and me. Not me and Robbie. Don't worry, I'm pretty grown-up. There'll be no scratching and biting. Just don't expect us to be big chums.' So saying, she turned subtly and joined the conversation with Joe and Ambrose.

I headed for my desk and pretended to be doing something urgent. I'd never been good at conflict. Things had been going so well recently. Why couldn't they go back to being friends? What was so bad that the woman I'd used the 'L' word with and my new business partner hated each other so much? I didn't get long to mull things over as Rupert cheered again. It would be interesting to see how he kept this up if we ended up with a million downloads. I looked at the counter. Seventeen. A bit to go yet, then. Still, you had to start somewhere. We'd loaded up a series of tweets to go out every ten minutes or so, and I could see retweets and comments beginning to come in. We would release a new instalment each hour until midnight, then pause for a few days. I casually checked the number of followers — just short of seven hundred. That was promising. I felt Robbie's arms around my shoulders and leaned back slightly to rest my head against hers.

'Stop hiding, and talk to your guests.'

'I'm not hiding, just checking our numbers. We seem to be generating some noise on Twitter, but the number of downloads hasn't taken off yet.'

'Give it time. Come on, there's somebody I want you to meet. He's interested in advertising.'

The next couple of hours were a constant whirl of hands shaken, questions answered, and congratulations accepted. We signed up another three potential advertisers. Keeping them depended on the number of users increasing from the current 27, still frustratingly low. Jen introduced me to the reporter from the local newspaper and two freelance feature writers. I'd never been interviewed before, apart from the call-centre job. I felt like I'd spoken at a hundred miles an hour and made little sense, but they assured me they had what they needed. The room was bustling. I probably knew about a dozen of the people. Robbie and Jen seem to have done a great job of getting people here without speaking to each other at all.

Stella had arrived, and I made my way over to the group.

'Congratulations. Look at all these people,' she said, as I kissed her cheek.

'I don't know who they all are, but they're drinking the national debt of a small country. I'm hoping Robbie got a good deal on the booze.'

'From what I know of her, she will have. Don't worry. You just missed Jen, by the way. She had to get back to look after Charley, and you were tied up. She says well done and will call you tomorrow. Oh, and you might want to check in with Rupert. He's getting a bit tired and emotional.'

I looked across, and, sure enough, he was pissed. Not just lovely and pissed, but really, really pissed.

'Hey Rupert, how's it going?'

'Heeeeyyy. Happy St David's day, mate.'

'I didn't know you were Welsh.'

'I'm not.'

'Then why so pissed?'

'S'free.'

'Fair enough. Anyway, tomorrow is St David's day. First of March.'

"Today is the first of March, idiot.' Rupert swayed dangerously on his swivel chair.

'No. Today is the twenty-ninth of February. It's a leap year.'

'Bollocks.'

'It is, I promise, look.' I clicked the mouse and showed him the date in the corner of the screen.

'Oh. Bollocks.'

'What do you mean, oh bollocks?'

'I may have fucked up a bit.'

'What the hell have you done?' Then it hit me.

'You scheduled all the advertising on Facebook and Instagram for the first of March, didn't you? As in tomorrow.'

'No. Well, yes. Sorry. Twitter as well, actually. Fucking leap years. Who decided that?'

This would go some way towards explaining the slow take-up. I felt like murdering Rupert, but then I looked at him and grinned.

'Don't worry, mate. Leap years are fucking stupid. All it means is we get a big jump in numbers tomorrow.'

'Exactly.' We clinked glasses, and everybody wondered what we were finding so funny.

'You should make a speech.' It was Robbie again.

'I couldn't. I'd make a mess of it.'

'No, you won't. Just thank everybody for coming. They'll expect it.' With that, she tapped her pen against her glass and called for quiet. Every face was looking at me.

'Okay. I…'

'Speak up!' I impressed myself by using the swivel chair as a step and climbed onto the desk.

'Is that better? Right, I didn't prepare anything for this. I honestly didn't think so many of you would come, but I'm very pleased. I need to thank Robbie for everything she has done to knock me into shape and organise tonight.' There was a round of applause, and Robbie blushed. I was getting warmed up now. 'I also need to thank Jen for the great writing that has made all this possible.' The applause started again. 'Unfortunately, she had to leave to look after her daughter. I'd also like to thank Joe, our first sponsor — cheers, mate. Ambrose, without your intervention, I'd still be sitting in the corner of the pub muttering to myself. Dex, thanks for showing faith in me and Rupert. Sorry, Dom. I can't get used to him being a Dom. Can't we change it to Rupert by deed poll or something? Last, thanks Rupert, for all the hard work over the last few weeks. In particular, for the idea of making tonight what we in the trade call a soft launch. We kept the numbers of downloads low so that people here can be in the first wave and say to their kids that I got that download when fewer than a hundred readers had signed up. The publicity starts tomorrow. Please raise your glass to our millionth download — whenever it comes.'

I somehow made it down from the desk in one piece and started another lap of the room, shaking hands and generally being Billy-big-balls. All this with thirty-eight downloads!

People seemed to take the speech as the signal that the evening was drawing to a close, and they began to drift away. We were soon down to just me, Robbie, Rupert, Ambrose,

Stella and Joe.

Ambrose had produced a bottle of rum, and we congregated around the sofa on office chairs or on the floor. Stella looked at me.

'Great idea to start with the soft launch. I'm certainly pleased that I was in the first hundred,' she said.

'All carefully planned.' Rupert tipped his glass towards me and nodded. I looked around at this group of people. A month ago, I knew Ambrose and Stella from the pub and Rupert as a colleague. I hadn't even met the rest of them. Now I had the warm glow that these were my friends. I also needed a pee. I struggled to my feet and headed to the gents. When I got back, Ambrose and Stella were standing and making leaving noises.

'Sorry, guys. Stella's had a long day. In fact, it's ten minutes into the next day, so time for us to make a move. It also gets you off the hook for day five of the challenge again. I won't forget.'

'I know, just a lot going on at the moment. Hang on a minute. If it's after midnight, the ads have started running.' Just then, the monitor woke up. The number count had increased to 93. Then 104. We were all on our feet now as the monitor flashed again: 163. Word was spreading fast. I checked Twitter and saw we had nearly eight hundred followers. I pulled up the dashboard that we had created earlier. Fifteen people had already solved the first clue, and the sixth instalment had just gone live. We were up and running.

Robbie hugged me. 'Come on. Take me home. The genuine work starts tomorrow.'

I was still buzzing when we set off to walk back to my place. It was cold, and Robbie huddled in next to me, linking her arm through mine. She'd convinced me that the downloads would still be there in the morning and that I didn't need to watch the counter all night.

'That was a great night. Thanks for organising everything.'

'You deserved it. You've worked really hard and even got my idiot brother to concentrate.'

'Do you think he'll be OK?'

'What in life, or not throwing up in the taxi home?'

'Both, I suppose.'

'He'll be fine. He's certainly had plenty of practice as far as taxis go. Life probably not so much.' We rounded the corner by The Crown. The lights were still on in the bar, but Robbie just tugged at my arm, and we headed home.

'It must've been nice to see Jen again, after all this time?'

'Why do you say that? It's been nearly ten years since she spoke to me. Why would it all suddenly be lovely over a few vol-au-vents and cheap fizz?'

'You mean you didn't speak to her?'

'No, course not. Look, I don't mind you working with her, but she made it clear she wanted nothing to do with me. Why would I invite lots of grief by even trying?'

We walked on in silence. In the flat, the heating was still on. I made a mental note to sort out the timer. By the time I had got two glasses of water from the kitchen, Robbie was in bed. I quickly slipped in beside her, and she snuggled under my arm. I risked another question.

'Am I allowed to ask what happened between you two?'

'I suppose so.' There was another silence. I realised I had to actually ask.

'So, what happened between you two?'

'It's a long time ago, alright. We were only fifteen, so no judging. It was at a school disco. I copped off with Jen's boyfriend, Darrell. We'd had a few ciders, and I snogged him on the mound.' I sat up and looked down at her.

'The mound? What the f…'

'There was a small hill in the school grounds. We called it the mound, okay?'

'I thought for a minute that was a…'

'No, you didn't, you just saw the chance of a cheap gag, and no, that's not innuendo either — anyway, the day after, she totally blanked me. I tried to apologise, but she wasn't having any of it. She ran off and didn't come back to school for a week. It really upset me. I spoke to one teacher who knew us both. She told me to leave it for a bit, that Jen would calm down and get back to me when she was ready. She didn't. Term ended. I went to work for my dad; she started in the sixth form. I tried again later in the summer, but it was a bit awkward by then.'

'Why was that?'

'Well, she wouldn't talk to Darrell either, so we ended up seeing each other for a bit. '

'How long?'

'Two years. Look, don't judge, I was a teenager. I was going to go round to her house. I wanted to tell her I'd chuck him if she'd forgive me, but my dad talked me out of it. He said she wasn't worth putting myself through the upset and that I should stick with Darrell.'

'Have you really not spoken to each other in all that time? This is a small place, after all.'

'Obviously, we're both at the community centre a lot. We've been to the same pubs or parties, but just ignored each other. My mum suggested inviting her to their silver wedding, but Dad was against it. He said he didn't want to risk us fighting on the big day. Anyway, it's done now. You can carry on working with her. I'll carry on doing what I'm doing. I don't need to go back to all that grief.' With that, she kissed me on the cheek, turned over and went to sleep.

16

My phone woke me. It was Robbie. I actually looked to her side of the bed to confirm she wasn't there.

'Morning. What happened to you?'

'I couldn't convince you to wake up, so I thought you could have a lie in.'

'What time is it?'

'Ten o'clock. I've just phoned through an order for bacon butties. I thought you could pick them up on your way in.'

'My head hurts.'

'So it should. Drink some water, have a shower, and get yourself in here. I'll ring Dom next and try to get him moving. You've got a business to run now.'

'OK. Be there in a bit. Bye.'

I sat up and decided to have two minutes checking the dashboard. I logged in and stared at the downloads figure—almost nine hundred and just over a thousand Twitter followers. A text message flashed onto the screen.

'Stop looking at your phone and get in the shower! Xxx'

How the hell did she do that?

The bacon butty and coffee combination worked, and by

11.30, I had checked all the stats for the umpteenth time. This time, it was Joe on the phone.

'Whatever you did last night, do it again.'

'I beg your pardon?'

'I've taken more online orders this morning than I did in all of last month. I want to place more advertising.'

'I'm sure we can come to some arrangement. Why don't I come in later in the week, and we can sort it out?'

'So long as you don't bounce me out of the way when the big boys come knocking.'

'Wouldn't dream of it. Besides, you're my best puzzle setter.'

'Actually, I've had an idea about that, too. I'll flesh it out a bit before you come to the shop. Listen, got to go. There are three customers in the shop. This is like Christmas!'

One happy sponsor. Could it really be this easy?

I chose Madness to start the soundtrack of our day, just as Rupert arrived. He looked like death.

'You don't look well, mate.'

'Must be a bug. There's a lot of it going around.'

'Or it could be the hangover from hell. You really went for it last night.'

'My dad was chewing my ear for the first hour. I suppose that put me in a mood for a few.'

'Was he giving you a hard time?'

'When isn't he?'

'Do you need to talk about it?'

'Christ, no!' Phew. It's all very well offering to listen to other people's problems, but it's a real pain in the arse if they accept. 'What's the agenda for the day?'

'Social media hat on! We're swamped with messages and emails. We need to reply and stoke the fires a bit. You do Instagram. I'll make a start on Twitter. Remember the comms plan we worked out, and try not to piss anybody off.'

'Yes, boss. Shit, have you seen how many downloads? It's gone mad.'

I grinned at him before turning to the task of wading through hundreds of messages. After almost an hour, I sat back and stretched. The download counter had moved on again. We had passed two thousand. My mind wandered to thoughts of food. It must be nearly lunchtime. I set myself a target of clearing the rest of the replies, and then I would be allowed fish and chips. Stifling a yawn, a message that was halfway down the list caught my eye. It was the name of the account that did it. Ruckoats. Where had I seen that before? I clicked on the message.

'Congratulations on The Woman In The Yellow Raincoat. She shows great taste. We need to talk. Call me.' There was a phone number. It was bugging me where I'd seen the name before. Rupert was busy wrapping a scarf around the neck of his sister's cardboard cutout that was still in the corner from last night. It was then I saw it. The logo on the coat. Ruckoats. My heart pounded. I reread the message. It seemed upbeat. If they were going to be upset about us using the image, surely they would be a bit more formal? Only one way to find out. I paused the music and tapped the number into my phone. It was answered on the second ring.

'Ruckoats, Caroline speaking. How can I help?'

'Hello Caroline. This is Frankie from The Woman In The Yellow Raincoat. I just picked up your message.'

'Frankie, thanks for calling. I read the first instalment and loved it. I can see that your Twitter following is exploding. You must be very excited.'

'That, and hungover from the launch party, to be honest.'

'Well, I may have something to interest you. Would you be open to a sponsorship deal? I would love to work with you and leverage your following. This could drive big sales for us and make us both lots of money. Is that something you'd like to talk about?'

'That sounds fantastic. Sure. I'd be very interested.'

'I see from your website that you're based in West Yorkshire. My parents live in Ilkley. Why don't I get brownie points by visiting them and take you out to dinner while I'm up there? I don't suppose you're free tomorrow.'

'Let me just check.' I tried to stay calm, but whatever I was meant to be doing tomorrow could bugger off now. 'Tomorrow looks good.'

'Excellent. I assume I can get you on this number? I'll confirm the venue and time later. Oh, one more thing. Who's the model in the pictures?'

'It's actually my girlfriend, Robbie.'

'Great. I'd love to meet Robbie as well. Hopefully, I'll see you both tomorrow.' I put the phone down and just stared at Rupert.

'What's up with you?'

'Absolutely nowt. This is actually going to work. Come on. Chippy. On me.'

We were helpless with laughter by the time we got downstairs. We were trying to do the Madness walk while singing Baggy Trousers at the top of our voices. As we got to Robbie's office door, I thought it would be nice to see if she wanted to join us. We marched through the door. I stopped immediately, but Rupert carried on. The impact caused a tangle of legs, and we both crashed to the floor. Rupert was still singing, but I could see the look on Robbie's face. It wasn't good. The flash of anger must have lasted barely a second, but it stung.

'I apologise, Sir Alan. These two are the local village idiots. Actually, the lead idiot is my boyfriend Frankie, and I think you've met his backing singer.'

'I certainly have. It was the weekend that your father had

the suite at York races. Hello Dominic. Frankie, I'm pleased to meet you.'

I got to my feet and shook Sir Alan's hand. Robbie dragged a folder across the desk as she continued.

'Sir Alan is the chair of the planning committee. We were just discussing the plan to extend the main warehouse.'

I apologised for interrupting and grovelled as much as was workable in the circumstances. I was about to offer to include them in our chippy run, but Robbie's expression suggested that wouldn't be a good idea. We made our excuses and left. We were halfway to the chippy before either dare look at the other. Then the laughter started again. Life was good. It would be a lot better if Robbie didn't kill me before I'd explained about our night out tomorrow. That look she'd given me was scary. Also, I couldn't be sure, but I'm pretty convinced she'd moved the folder to stop me from seeing the thick envelope on the desk in front of her. Maybe I'd just been making up too many stories?

17

It was a challenge to take in what was happening. Last night had gone well. Correction, last night had been unbelievable. Our new friend treated us to a slap-up meal in Ilkley. After dinner, we shook hands on no less than three deals. We would integrate their online shop into our website, giving us a percentage of all sales through the site. They also wanted to have their logo on every page of the story and pay generously for the privilege. Third, and best of all, they wanted Robbie to become the "face of the company", as Caroline put it. A modelling contract! I was going out with a model.

They invited us to London to meet their technical team and sort out how the integration would work. We needed to agree on how the logo would be positioned. Robbie would do her first professional photoshoot. I was only slightly put out that they wouldn't just use my shots, but I could live with that. The figures they talked about were eye-watering, but it all depended on attracting the numbers to our site.

Caroline had arranged a car to drive us home. I say car; it was bigger than my flat. My heart was racing as I sank into the soft leather of the back seat. I reached out for Robbie's hand in the semi-darkness.

'This, I could get used to,' I said.

'It is rather nice, isn't it? Having said that, without wanting to be the voice of doom, it all goes away if the numbers don't stack up. You need to keep expanding the reader base, which means making sure the writing quality is kept up. You're very reliant on Jen at the moment, and, given how she feels about me…' She let the comment hang in the air.

'Surely it would help in that department if you two patched things up?'

'I honestly think it's too late. Too much water under the bridge and all that. Best not to rock the boat. We can't risk upsetting her. Let's just leave it.'

I started to say something, but Robbie was staring out of the window. I took that as a sign the subject was closed.

It was after midnight when we got to bed. By 6.30, I was aware of Robbie getting up.

'Is there a fire?'

'No fire. I just wanted to go for a run before I go to work.'

'I could come with you.' I understood why I laughed but was a bit hurt that she did.

'We both know that's not going to happen, don't we?'

'Fair enough.'

'Besides, my taxi's here. I'll be home, changed, out running, and showered before you've hauled yourself out of your pit. See you at the office.' A quick peck on the cheek, and she was gone. I turned over, intent on another couple of hours' sleep, but then thought about last night. Robbie was right. Everything still depended on the quality of the writing and growing the numbers. Kip was not coming back anytime soon, so I surprised myself by heading to work early.

I let myself into the office and said, 'lamps'. Pleasingly, the two lamps came to life and created pools of light by the desks. The new toys were making me very happy indeed. I flopped into my seat. I'd promised myself that I'd wade through my email inbox for half an hour, then go out to get takeaway coffee. Shit. Just over three hundred unread messages. What the hell was going on? I quickly scanned the list and spotted some alerts from the download sites with the latest figures. We were up to around three thousand, but the rate was slowing. I sorted the list into order by the sender and deleted the alerts.

The following frequent sender was Joe. There were over thirty messages, like a stream of consciousness, as he thought up new ideas for clues. I scanned them quickly. There were some really great ideas in there, including a virtual reality treasure hunt. I would set aside time later to work through them. I created a new folder just for Joe and moved on.

In the end, it took more than an hour, but I had tamed the inbox! There were some exciting sponsorship possibilities, but most of them were spam or good luck messages. There was one towards the end that caught my eye. The local radio station wanted to interview me on their afternoon show. Normally, I would run a mile rather than get involved in this sort of thing, but we had to get as much publicity as possible. I replied and included my phone number, suggesting they call me.

As I sat back in my chair, I noticed the '1' next to the text message icon. It was from Jen.

'First article online now. Will be in the paper this afternoon.' Clicking on the link took me to the online newspaper. I saw my face grinning back at me in front of the cardboard cut-out. I scrolled down to read the text, but it was quickly replaced by an advert. Before the pop up about cookies, I managed to read the headline. I knew from experience that clicking the 'Don't accept' button would just dump me out of the site. I clicked 'Accept' and scrolled down to the headline again. After reading the first line of text, another advert moved everything down the screen. I shouted at the screen.

'Will you stop doing that, and let me read the fucking article, you damned machine?' It was certainly worth making sure we never went down this route. Eventually, the screen seemed to have settled down, and I went back to reading. It was a really positive piece. I didn't think I came over as a dick at all. The article ended with a link to our website and the apps. I quickly tweeted the link to the report, as well as posting it on Facebook and Instagram.

Feeling pleased with myself, I ordered a reasonably extravagant bouquet for Jen to thank her for setting up the interview. I then ordered a second one for Robbie, just to be safe. I hadn't noticed Rupert coming in and leaning over my shoulder.

'Guilty conscience?'

'Not at all. Don't judge me by your lurid example. I just thought it would be a nice gesture. And stop sneaking up on me like that. You nearly gave me a heart attack.'

'Just bumped into my sister downstairs. She asked me to give you this.'

It was a manilla folder with, maybe, a dozen sheets of paper inside. I flicked through quickly and handed it back to Rupert.

'It's just a few changes to what we did last week for Dexter's. Could you handle it? I need to go out later.'

'Another picnic?'

'No. Meeting with potential sponsors, which will ultimately pay your meagre, yet somehow extravagant wages.'

'That's okay, then. You have my blessing. By the way, I've had an idea. Don't look at me like that, it happens occasionally. If people are struggling with clues, why don't we sell them the answers?'

'Actually, that's genius. Three answers for a quid! We'd need a module for taking bank details and stuff.'

'I'll add it to the list.'

He took the folder and wandered off to his desk. Thirty seconds later, The Arctic Monkeys filled the room, and we were off and running for another day.

I went back to the folder of ideas from Joe. So far, we had done cryptic crossword-type clues and general knowledge questions. Now his thoughts were moving to the next level. I still particularly liked the old spy movie cypher. Two people needed the same book to look up words given by references to the page and line. The book he suggested was actually my favourite, Nick Hornby's High Fidelity. I wondered how many copies Joe had in stock that he wanted to shift, but was happy with his choice. I would need pictures of Robbie reading the book. Setting that one up was simple. The next one on his list was far from simple.

Joe had an idea to set a treasure hunt, with actual clues hidden around the countryside. Five minutes later, in his following email, he'd realised that most of our readers weren't in easy reach of West Yorkshire. So, his ingenious plan was to make it a virtual reality treasure hunt. He'd gone into great detail about how it would look. I loved the idea, but could see one tiny snag. I didn't have the first idea of how to set about making it happen. Maybe I needed inspiration, not to mention the coffee I'd promised myself hours ago. I popped my laptop in my shoulder bag and made for the door. Rupert waved without looking up from his screen.

My plan was to go to the cafe, but as I stepped outside, a bus pulled up just ahead of me so I jumped on, and ten minutes later, I was sitting in See You Latte, with a massive Americano and a piece of shortbread. I was trying out the millionaire lifestyle for size. I opened my laptop and flicked through articles about virtual reality. Just ten minutes convinced me of what I had suspected from the start. We would need a big budget and a partner to handle the technology. It would also require our customers to have headsets. I resigned myself to this long-term plan and wondered about a lower-tech option. Surely we could do something based on good old-fashioned maps? We could have pictures of Robbie outside well-known landmarks to show a start point, then some clues about the map leading to a specific place, like a hospital or church? I made a few more notes before packing up and setting off to see the man himself.

Walking down the stairs into the vast record shop, I spotted a familiar face. It was Ambrose.

'I didn't expect to see you here,' I said.

'It's that element of surprise that keeps em coming back for more. Joe said he could do with an extra pair of hands, so I'm helping out a few days a week.'

'That's great. Is business that good?' I looked around at the two customers mooching through the racks.

'Joes says it's a bit busier in the shop, but it's the website that's taken off. We spend half our time packaging up orders and sending them out. Then there are the tee-shirts. I'm getting to be a dab hand at printing them. How're things with you?'

'Unbelievably busy, to be honest.' I told him about the latest with the coat company, then had to repeat the story as Joe arrived from the back room.

One customer had made his way over to the cash desk and was waiting nervously, praying that somebody would notice. It was Ambrose that did, and he made his way over. Joe ushered me through to the back room. I explained about virtual reality being a bit technically advanced for me at the moment. Joe looked a bit disappointed, but soon bought into the map idea and said he would get back to me.

'The other thing that I wanted to discuss was the tee-shirts. I've picked out half a dozen shots that I would like to go with and start selling them on the website. Could you supply them?'

'I could, but why don't I sell them? My shop already sells tee-shirts. It would just be a matter of you feeding the site traffic to my pages. I've no doubt you could do something clever to make it seamless to the customer. I could manufacture, process the sale, and dispatch. All for a huge fee, obviously.'

'It sounds like I don't have to do much.'

'You don't. A bit of website magic, maybe. Oh, and supply the customers in the first place. I thought you would want to get this moving at some point, so I took the liberty of putting some figures together.' He pushed a piece of paper across the desk. 'I've listed all my costs together with a suggested retail price. The number at the bottom is what we both make per shirt.'

'Wow. Very efficient.'

'I try to while away the hours down here by being useful. I've got the same breakdown for hoodies, baseball caps, beanies, mugs and tea towels when you want them.'

'Let's go with tee-shirts for now and add the rest in when we see how they go. What do we do next?'

'Have you got the photos?'

'I can email them from my phone.'

'Do that and give me a couple of hours. I'll see what I can do. Actually, before you go. As a thank you for choosing me as your supplier, I've got something for you. Hang on a minute.' He fiddled with the lock on the desk drawer before pulling out a copy of Ziggy Stardust. 'This is what I said you couldn't afford. Now I'm giving it as a gift. It's a first UK pressing, with the lyrics and a sheet advertising the tour.' He handed the album over. 'Nearly forgot. It's signed as well. By Bowie, not me, you'll be pleased to know.'

'Joe, I can't accept this. It's way too generous.'

'Nonsense. I can't think of a better home for it, and besides, you're making me a lot of money at the moment, with more to come. Now, bugger off and let me get on with creating our new range of tee-shirts.'

'OK, but email the figures to me. Robbie's insisting on proper contracts for everything we do. I'll get her to send you something, and thanks again. I'll treasure this.'

Ambrose was deep in conversation about the merits of Prince Far I and recommending various albums. He waved as I made my way to the stairs. I left the shop clutching the precious cargo in one of Joe's bags. Bags! That's something else we could put the images on.

A month ago, the bus would've shot past and sprayed standing water over me for good measure. Today it appeared, as if by magic, and I jumped on. A few minutes later, I was walking into Robbie's office.

'The very man.' She stood, threw her arms around my neck, and kissed me.

'What have I done to deserve that?'

'Probably not enough, but I'm feeling very affectionate towards you at the moment. I have news,' said Robbie.

'So have I, but you first.'

'Not one, but two potential sponsors. Both local companies but weren't frightened off by the rates I quoted. The contracts are here, waiting for you to read through.'

'Read a contract? Are you mad? Do they make me money and keep me out of jail?'

'They certainly do.'

'Good enough for me. Where do I sign?' She pointed, and I signed. 'My turn now. Joe has proposed a deal for supplying and selling tee-shirts using our images. I thought you might give the numbers a once over and generally do your stuff.'

'Does it make money and keep you out of prison?'

'I sincerely hope so.'

'Then I shall do my stuff.'

'You really should be getting paid for this, you know. You're doing so much more than I ever dreamed.'

'Oh aye?'

'Not like that. Well, yes, now that you come to mention it, but I'm definitely not paying you for that. But all the stuff you're doing, with the bank, the books, contracts. You're basically running the business while I dick around with Rupert.'

'They say to stick to what you do best. Look, I'm more than happy. Tell you what, I'll print the first set of accounts out and bring them over tonight. We can discuss it over a bottle of something nice.'

'Can we have pizza?'

'Yes, you can have pizza.'

'Stuffed crust?'

'Don't push it. Now, go do some work so you can keep me in stuffed crust pizza and fine wine.'

I went upstairs to be greeted by Paul Weller at full belt. Rupert lowered the volume slightly.

'What are you looking so miserable about?'

'Nothing. Just had a bit of a row with my dad.'

'Why?'

'Cos he's an arsehole.'

'Well, there is that but, he's the arsehole that has financed this little enterprise, so try not to piss him off too much,' I said.

'Don't worry. He went away happy enough. I finished the changes he wanted, and he has some ideas for more work for us.'

'That's all good, surely. We'll soon have the loan paid off at this rate.'

'I'll be on a bonus then, once it's paid off.'

'You never know, mate. The way things are going, we might all be on a bonus. Now, get some work done. I'll never be a millionaire if you just sit there gabbing. Give me half an hour to catch up on emails and stuff, then we need to start looking at what we need to do to integrate with Joe's website. We're going into the tee-shirt business.'

Weller was cranked up again. I was just about to start on the latest email when a text came through from Joe.

'Can you meet Ambrose in The Crown at 5.30? He'll have the tee-shirts with him.'

'Not like me to go to the pub, but it's business. Tell him I'll be there.'

I looked across at Rupert and grinned.

'Team building exercise at 5.30.'

'Pub?'

'Spot on. Got to cheer up your mardy arse.'

'Put a contract out on my dad; that'd cheer me up.'

'Sounds expensive. A couple of pints will have to do it.'

I settled at my desk and checked the dashboard. We seemed to be doing an excellent job on social media. There was a lovely gentle buzz from the newspaper interview without it quite exploding. The number of downloads had more or less stalled at around 3500. We needed to up our game a bit. But how? A call came through from an unrecognised number, so I lowered the music volume and answered. It was the producer at the local radio station. Could I do tomorrow afternoon at 2 o'clock? I certainly could. Maybe that would give us the boost we needed. I took down the details and hung up.

We spent the rest of the afternoon planning how to

integrate our apps and website with Joe's site for the tee-shirt sales. We soon had a re-assuring list of Post-its down the left of the whiteboard. That lot should keep Rupert entertained tomorrow while I was becoming a radio star.

We walked into The Crown at precisely half-past five. Punctuality was important, after all. Ambrose had already pulled two pints, admitting Rupert's was a gamble, but he seemed confident that we'd both turn up.

'They're on me. A sort of thank you for the introduction to Joe. He's just upped my hours, again thanks to you. Cheers.'

'Cheers. We're here to help!'

'Speaking of Joe, he sent you this.' He handed over a carrier bag, which appeared to be full of tee-shirts. We took our drinks to a table in the corner, and Ambrose joined us. I pulled out the first tee-shirt. It was black, with a monochrome image covering the front with the raincoat picked out in brilliant yellow. The others were in grey and burgundy, with the website name across the back. Each of the shirts was replicated in ladies' sizes.

'These are brilliant. One slight change. Can we have #TWITYR on the back as well as the address?'

Ambrose nodded. 'Will do.' I handed the extra-large grey one to Ambrose, along with one of the smaller ones. 'For you and Stella. Wear it with pride. One for you too, Rupert.' I handed him a woman's size.

'Hilarious. Can I have the black one?' I made a fuss of swapping but was quietly pleased I had the burgundy one. That left one each for Robbie and Jen. Rupert quickly whipped off his Blossoms tee-shirt and replaced it with the new one.

'Steady on, we don't have a licence for strippers.' As soon as he'd said it, Ambrose looked round the empty pub and did the same. In for a penny, making sure to keep my back out of sight, I was just pulling mine over my head when I felt it snag. Ambrose had grabbed the top to close the hole.

'The things you see when you don't have a gun.' It was Brenda, emerging from the cellar. Ambrose released me, and I resumed what passed for a dignified pose. 'You look like the world's crappest boy band,' laughed Brenda.

'These are this spring's must-haves, I'll have you know.' I held up the shirt I'd earmarked for Robbie.

'Bugger wouldn't even go over my head, you daft sod.' She was still laughing as she emptied the dishwasher. The conversation turned to Ambrose's new job and his skills as a tee-shirt printer before Bill and Jean shuffled in. Ambrose went off to serve them as Rupert finished his pint.

'Same again?'

'Go on then, if you're twisting my arm. Best make this the last one. I promised your sister we'd have a quiet night in with pizza and wine. I'm gonna be a good boy.'

'It's not like she's exactly a good girl.'

'What do you mean?'

'Ignore me. Robbie's just a bit too much like my dad when it comes to it, but cleverer.' He picked up the glasses and headed for the bar. My phone was on the table, so I saw the text as it came through. It was from Robbie.

'Just left the office. A quick shower and be at yours by 7. Don't forget the wine.'

Bugger. I'd forgotten about the wine. I wondered whether the stuff from the pub would be acceptable. Very doubtful, and she'd know that I'd forgotten and bought it here. Then I remembered the tweet about deliveries. I searched and found what I was looking for. One minute later, two bottles of the second most expensive Chianti they had were on their way to my flat. You've got to love the internet.

18

I was sitting in reception at the radio station, looking at the framed photos on the wall. Obviously, I know I was meant to recognise them all, but I had one out of five so far. I gave up, sat back in the seat, and exhaled noisily. Somebody would be along any minute to take me for my fifteen minutes of fame. More like ten, when they factored in the ad break, but I would get the chance to spread the word. My mind wandered back to what Rupert had said last night about Robbie being like her dad. Several people had warned me that Dex was dodgy. Was Rupert saying that Robbie was the same? She couldn't be that bad. She seemed to like me a lot. I certainly liked her. More than liked, if I was honest. Then there was all the work she was doing for the business, all without being paid.

No, she was a star. Plain and simple. But what about the woman in the yellow raincoat? Was she too good to be true? What if she had a dark side? What if she was a villain, head of a criminal gang? The world loves a bad girl, right? What would Jen call it, adding depth to the character?

The idea was great. I was just about to make some notes on

my phone when a teenager with a clipboard appeared. She whisked me through to the studio and introduced me to 'our afternoon show host, Dave.' We shook hands, and I put on the pair of headphones offered. It was weird when Dave spoke. I'd never seen his face before, but the voice seemed like that of an old friend. He explained he would introduce me, and I should outline the idea behind TWITYR. He'd ask me a few questions, then play a record. We'd then do a few more questions, and I get to finish by telling listeners how to download the app. He told me to relax and enjoy it, but this felt like the dentist's chair. I had a couple of cards with notes on them, so I didn't forget anything, and I placed them in front of me on the desk.

The god-awful power ballad faded, the 'On-Air' light glowed red, and Dave started to talk. My stomach took that as its cue to churn and let out an audible rumble. Before I knew it, the introduction was done, and I was speaking. Quietly, at first. Then I got into it. This was my baby. I knew my subject, and I soon forgot the cards as I went through everything: the story, the website, the app, the clues, and Jen. There was even time to get in a plug for Joe. I looked up, and Dave was leaning back in his seat, grinning at me. As I paused for breath, he held up a hand.

'This is Dave in the afternoon, and I'll be talking more with Frankie Dale about The Woman In The Yellow Raincoat after this classic from The Nolans.' The red light went off, and he took off his headphones. I followed his lead. 'That was great, Frankie. You realise you did ten minutes without me saying a word!'

'Sorry, I never thought.'

'Don't apologise, squire. It came over as enthusiasm. We'll need to keep the next bit fairly short, I'm afraid. We have the head of the council's planning committee coming in to talk about the extension of the industrial estate — gripping stuff.'

The teenager was back and huddled over the desk, pointing at the clipboard. I gathered that the committee leader was ready and agitating to get on the air as soon as possible. As The Nolans' mood for dancing wore off, Dave replaced his headphones and gave me the thumbs up. I followed suit. I could do this, an absolute doddle.

'Welcome back to Frankie Dale, co-author of The Woman In The Yellow Raincoat. Frankie, dare I say that your main character sounds like a bit of a goody-two-shoes, solving crime and generally going round being nice to people?'

'It's funny you should say that, Dave. Jen would say that the character has depth. In the coming instalments, we'll be introduced to her dark side. Believe me, she's tough and capable of anything. She's not averse to breaking the law if she needs to.'

'Everybody loves a bad girl.'

'Exactly.'

'What about your sponsors? How do they feel about her suddenly crossing to the dark side as it were?'

Shit, shit, shit. I hadn't thought of that. What if Caroline hated the idea and pulled the plug? Dave was looking at me. I smiled. 'They are really excited about it. Like you say, everybody loves a bad girl.'

'How can people join the TWITYR community?'

I reeled off the ways to download the app and the link to the website, and Dave moved on to Tony Christie, with the promise of the weather coming up. The red light went off. Dave came across and shook my hand.

'That was great, thank you. Good luck with it. I'll download the app as soon as I get off air.'

'Thanks, I really enjoyed it, once I got over the nerves. Thanks for the idea as well.'

'What idea?'

'You mentioned it being a community. I think you're right,

and we can make something of that. Cheers.'

'We'll have you back when you pass a million downloads.'

With that, I was back at reception. My old friend Sir Alan was busy giving the clipboard owner some aggravation, so I slipped out into the street. I felt good, but quickly needed a conversation with Jen and the potentially difficult one with Caroline.

I was almost running back to the office when I bumped into Jen just outside the Community Centre.

'Blimey, you're keen.'

'I'm still buzzing from this afternoon, to be honest.'

'I heard it. You were excellent.'

'It occurred to me that you should've been with me. You do the writing after all.'

'No thanks. Honestly, I'm quite content being behind the scenes these days. Besides, it wouldn't be half as surprising! A bit of a change in direction, isn't it?'

'You mean the bad girl thing? It was just something that came to me. We can shelve it if you don't like it.'

'Shelve it? No way. I love the idea. So much more freedom to write about villains. We just think of the worst thing she could do in a given situation and make it even darker. Obviously, the trick is keeping her likeable. What does the coat company think of it, really?'

'I am sure they will love it when they find out.' The look she gave me said everything. 'I'll phone Caroline next. I just wanted to discuss it with you first.'

'Thanks, I appreciate that. So, how do you want to develop things?'

'Well, we've already established the good side of her character. Now we can shake things up a bit, hint at the dark side. The fact that she handles all this money must be something bad: drug dealing, money laundering, bank robber. Maybe all three?'

'Protection. She could run a gang of thugs that lean on people who don't pay up,' said Jen, warming to the task.

'Like it. She could also use the thugs to beat the other bad guys when she's being the heroine.'

'We could alternate the instalments between good and bad. That way, you'll get feedback, so we know which side of the character is most popular. Look, I know you need to go. I think we could do with a longer, regular session to talk things through.'

'You're right. Could you do Thursday mornings? I drop Charley at her playgroup at nine. Meet at mine at, say, half nine? I'll supply the coffee and biscuits,' said Jen.

'Chocolate?'

'Chocolate and stem ginger. They'll blow your mind.'

'Done. I'll block the time out in my diary.'

'Great. Need to dash, I'm picking Charley up from Mum's.'

I realised I was smiling as I watched Jen head off up the hill.

In the office, I explained the idea of the community to Rupert.

'You mean like a members-only area?'

'That sort of thing. Chat room, extra content. We could charge a membership fee.'

'Sounds great. I'll start knocking something together.'

Back at home, I spent the rest of the evening playing with storylines, each one darker than the one before. If the public liked bad girls, they were going to love this one.

19

I'd fretted long and hard before making the call to Caroline. If she hated the idea of making the character darker, we could lose our sponsorship. Robbie was always confident that we had a contract that guaranteed that we keep control of the stories, but I was still worried. After I'd made the call, I realised how stupid I'd been. She loved the idea and the sample instalment I'd sent. She even suggested a couple of storylines I hadn't thought of. With the call out of the way, I could relax and enjoy the weekend with Robbie. We were both looking forward to our trip to the big city and, soon enough, it was Monday morning.

The sunny spring air matched my mood as we left the train at Kings Cross. Ahead of us were two days in the capital. I would spend most of the trip in a meeting room with the Ruckoats project team while Robbie got to be a model in the most exotic locations the city could offer. Secretly, I thought I had the better deal, but put on the expected act of making out I was missing out.

Twenty minutes later, we were leaving the lift on the seventh floor of a nondescript office block, just off Oxford

Street. Caroline was already waiting for us in reception, and we were greeted like long-lost friends. After coffee and danish pastries, they whisked Robbie off to meet the photographer. A nice lady called Tara arranged for our bags to be taken to the hotel. I was introduced to their project manager, Todd.

'I'm afraid we couldn't get the boardroom today, so we're stuck in room two. '

He opened the door, and I felt like I was up to my knees in carpet. The place was vast, with a glass-topped table that could seat twenty comfortably. As it was, three people clustered around one end. I was introduced to the team, but turned down the offer of more coffee. Todd picked up a remote control, and within seconds the lights had dimmed, and a vast screen had lowered from above the ceiling. It made my voice-activated lights seem tame. However, it soon became apparent that they had all the toys, but looked at me to do the clever stuff with the website. Once the standard presentation about their company vision was out of the way, we got down to business. They were initially put out when I pulled three packs of Post-its from my pocket, rather than using the high-tech whiteboard, but the session went well. In the end, we had the familiar column down the left and a clear picture of what needed to happen. Todd agreed to document everything we'd done. By 4.30, we were wrapping up, and after a final chat with Caroline, I would be in my cab on the way to the hotel.

We were in Caroline's office.

'Todd tells me things went well today.'

'Yes. Very constructive. Given a bit of luck, we should be ready to test inside a week.'

'How much of that luck depends on you?'

'How do you mean?'

'Are we relying on you personally to do most of the work?'

'No, not really. There's work on both sides. I'll do some of ours, but my colleague Rupert will do most of it.'

'That's good.' She smiled at me. What the hell was coming next? 'I think you're going to be busy with some promotion work, for both of us, if you're up for it.'

'What did you have in mind?'

'Well, my team has lined up a spot on breakfast TV tomorrow. They want to interview both you and Robbie.'

I laughed. 'Good one. Really, what are we doing?'

'You're sitting on a sofa discussing The Woman In The Yellow Raincoat and how that raincoat is exceptionally stylish, well made and available at a very reasonable price.'

'Telly? Me. Shit. Oh, sorry. Wow.' It was Caroline's turn to laugh while I got the familiar churning stomach.

'I hear you went down very well on your local radio debut. This is exactly the same, just with brighter lights and Robbie sitting next to you. Look, this is just the start. There is a chance we can get The One Show interested next week, as well as a couple of the Sunday supplements. So, what do you say? Are you ready to hit the big time?'

'Alright, Mr DeMille, I'm ready for my closeup now.'

'That's the spirit. I'll meet you there. The car will pick you up at your hotel at six.' I looked at my watch.

'That doesn't give me much time. Oh, you mean six in the morning?'

'Is that news to you that there are two six o'clocks in a day?'

'It'll be a shock to the system, but let's do it.'

I could get used to this kind of life. One of Caroline's team had already checked us into the hotel. My mouth dropped open as I took in the floodlit view of the Tower Of London from our suite and the champagne chilling nicely. My first reaction was to open the bottle and settle in with the Pringles and the giant TV, but Robbie was still hard at work. Even I could see it would be better to wait. I rechecked my phone just as a text came from Robbie.

'ETA 8.30ish. Knackered. Need bath and room service - sorry! xxx'

'Not a problem. Bubbles ready for drinking and soaking. I want to hear all about your day xxx'

Right, that settled it. A quick shower and an hour in the bar.

The bar turned out to be a very stylish roof terrace and was packed. I spotted a solitary stool in the corner and ordered a gin and tonic. When in Rome, and all that. I couldn't help smiling as I reflected on how far things had come since that night sitting in the corner of The Crown. I sneaked a selfie and texted it to Ambrose and Rupert to rub it in. Plenty of abuse came my way in return. I sent a more tactful text to Jen to make sure all was well. I sipped another four pounds-worth of gin and realised I was missing working on the storylines. London nightlife was all very nice, but I had a woman in a yellow raincoat waiting for me. I swigged another eight quid and went back to the suite.

I tapped away at the laptop happily until just before 9 o'clock. I was just about to check for messages when I heard the card in the lock, and Robbie bounced into the room.

'I want chips, and I want them now!'

'Your wish, madam, is my command. How was your day?'

'It was fantastic, but exhausting, ooh, bubbles. Want some, now!' I hugged her, happy as I'd ever been. 'Don't come too close. It's been a very long and hot day.'

'Why don't I run you a bath, order you some chips, and bring a drink through?'

'You're pretty close to perfect.'

'Pretty close? What else could I do?'

'I'll leave that to your imagination, but I'm knackered and

smelly at the moment, and we have an early start tomorrow. I can't believe we're going to be on telly.'

'I'm terrified, if I'm honest.'

'All in day's work for a top model like me.'

'Go on. Shift your big head through there, and I'll bring you a drink in a minute.'

Robbie headed to the bedroom, striking several poses on the way. I picked up the phone to call room service, but noticed a text alert. It was Rupert asking for reasons not to kill his dad. I texted back that he was providing work, and we needed to keep him sweet for a while longer, with a promise to get back to him tomorrow. I called through to the bedroom.

'Are you sure you just want chips?' There was no reply. I walked across the room and poked my head around the bedroom door. Robbie was curled up on the bed, fast asleep. She looked wonderful. I quickly set the alarm on my phone. I curled up next to her, pulling the decorative bedspread over us, and instantly fell fast asleep.

We were still in the same position when the alarm went off at five o'clock. Before I could move, I heard a quiet voice.

'Where's my chips?' I explained it was morning. Robbie considered this for a moment. 'Okay, but you still owe me chips and champagne.'

'I promise you can have chips and champagne later, but now you need to fling yourself in the shower. We gonna make you a star!'

20

Robbie was in her element at the TV studio. She seemed to breeze through the interview. I was just glad I didn't make an idiot of myself. Actually, no, I did okay. Lorraine told me afterwards that I came across as very enthusiastic. I think she meant I jabbered on a bit. There was one awkward moment towards the end when she referred to Robbie as my fiancee. I was about to correct her, but Robbie was already talking about her favourite coat.

By ten o'clock, we were in Covent Garden, sipping coffee. Robbie brushed crumbs from the front of my shirt.

'Look at the state of you. You're a TV star now. Appearance is everything.'

'I think you're the star. You're so natural,' I said.

'You're right. I'm a star! What's your plan for the rest of the day?'

'No idea. I'm in your hands.'

'I want to go shopping. Don't worry. You're excused. The last thing I need is you moping around outside changing rooms.'

'Why don't you do that, and I can catch up with Rupert?

He's tried to call three times in the last hour, but I couldn't answer.'

'There's probably a spider in the office or something else that he's scared of. Call him. I'll do my thing and meet back at the hotel this afternoon. You still owe me chips and champagne, don't forget.'

As she disappeared into the crowds, I picked up my phone. 'Rupert, what's up?'

'Thought you'd gone all big time on me after you'd been on the telly.'

'I have. I'm charging a fee for you to speak to me.'

'Bollocks. I won't tell you the news if you're not careful.'

'What news?'

'I take it you haven't seen the download numbers today?'

'No. I haven't had a chance since last night. How are we doing?'

'Just short of three hundred thousand!'

'Fuck me!' I held my hand up in apology to the waitress as she collected Robbie's empty cup.

'It's gone mad. TWITYR is trending on Twitter. Traffic on the website has gone mental. Sponsorship enquiries are coming in all the time.'

'Unbelievable. Let me get back to the hotel and get signed on. We can start working through the emails. How many instalments are live?'

'We've uploaded eight so far, but some people have already got through the clues for all of them.'

'Upload another two, and I'll be online in half an hour.'

Things were getting a bit crazy. I paid the bill and set off to find a cab. I started answering emails before he was in third gear and spent the rest of the day hunched over my laptop. Joe had been busy with clues for the treasure hunt, which was now ready. Rupert had finished the coding, and I set aside an hour to have a trial run. I was very impressed with the integration of the online maps and knew that this would take off. It was more than two hours before I took a break, having successfully solved two clues. Hopefully, this would keep our audience busy and engaged for ages.

I started working through the new batch of emails. Some just needed me to send a standard reply with rates for ads. Others were a bit more ambitious, and I arranged meetings for the following week with three of them. Then came the big one. It was from a media production company. They were interested in speaking to me about the possibility of working together. I was getting used to calling people back and decided not to put it off. They put me through to one of the partners, Jason, something or other. After a fair bit of flattery and waffle about their company, he said something that stopped me in my tracks.

'We'd be interested in working with you to produce a TV show based on The Woman In The Yellow Raincoat. I've already had informal talks with a certain American streaming service who are quietly optimistic. We also see possibilities for a video game. We're talking big production money here. Would that sort of thing be of interest?'

I was about to make a crack about what the pope does in the woods, but thought better of it.

'Err, yes. It all sounds exciting.'

'Great. We have an office in Leeds. Why don't I set something up for early next week, and we can chat?'

'Sounds great. I'll see you next week.'

Holy shit! Was this really happening? I was dancing around the room when Robbie came through the door. She was almost hidden behind several large and expensive-looking bags. I told her about the call; the bags were dropped, and she joined in the dance.

I said, 'Let's go find that champagne.'

'Chips as well. You owe me chips.'

'You can have a wheelbarrow full of chips, if that's what you want.'

We headed for the rooftop bar in the hotel. It was quiet at this time, and we soon had a table with a prime view across the London skyline. The champagne arrived quickly, and, ten minutes later, two bowls of chips. Triple cooked with tomato sauce. I knew how to show a woman a good time. We chatted excitedly about how things were going and what the future looked like. As the bar filled up, the second bottle arrived.

'Do you want me to get the concierge to recommend a restaurant for later?' I asked.

'I don't know about you, but I'm delighted sitting here, as long as there are more chips.'

A tequila bottle, a plate of lime pieces, and a bowl of salt also accompanied the second round of chips. Things got blurry after that. I know that there was a lot of laughter, and a feeling of euphoria, induced in equal parts by success, champagne and tequila. I looked at Robbie, trying hard to keep her in focus.

'How do you feel, Ms Dexter?'

'I feel lovely and a bit pissed, if I'm honest.'

'I always want to feel as happy as this. Let's get married.'

It was Robbie's turn to try to focus on me. 'What did you say?'

'I said, will you marry me?'

'Ask me again when you're sober.' I must have looked totally crushed. 'Scrub that. You're rarely sober. Do it properly, then. One knee and all that.'

I did my best to stand up, but the low sofa defeated me. 'Not sure I'd be able to get up again if I got on one knee.'

'Fair enough. Yes, you idiot. Course I'll marry you.'

'Really?'

'Yes, really. You provided chips and bubbles. You can be a

bit scruffy, but you'll do for me. Make it happen.'

'Think I might need to sleep first.'

'Me too. Come on, Bertie Big Bollocks, take me to bed.'

21

'A TV deal? Wait a minute. You want me to write for TV?' We were in Jen's kitchen for the first of our Thursday morning story sessions.

'Not just you and me. There'd be an entire team, which we would lead. We get to set storylines just like now. The team would do most of the heavy lifting, to put those into a script that the producers are happy with.'

'What about Charley?'

'I think she's a bit young for the team, but I can always ask.'

'Idiot. You know what I mean. Do we have to be in London?'

'No. The company has a base in Leeds, we can work from there. We don't even have to be in the office. You can work from here and use video conferencing to join meetings. Look, this thing is exploding, and most of that is down to you. This could be the one chance we get to set ourselves up for life.' Jen refilled my coffee cup from the pot. I could see she was close to tears. I put the cup down. 'What is it? You look really upset.'

'I don't know how to tell you.' She sat back at the table and put her head in her hands. 'I've been offered a job.'

'A job?'

'Yes, my old editor at the paper. He wants me to do a weekly column.'

'That's great. Surely it's not full time. We can still work together. Jen, this is really taking off.'

'I'm scared the work will take over, and Charley has to come first.'

'I totally understand that. Any deals we do, I promise that your time with Charley won't be affected. She's a great kid. Speaking as somebody with zero experience with kids, apart from Rupert, I actually enjoy spending time with her. So, I agree, she has to come first. Don't forget, we are talking about a lot of money potentially. Surely that would make life easier.'

'It would, but, like you say, it's potential.'

'But it's about to be real. Robbie is going to produce our first set of accounts this week. You should get your first payout. It's happening.' Jen was in tears now. 'Jen. Talk to me. What is it?'

'I'm just silly. I'll be fine.'

'You're obviously not fine. Come on, tell me what's wrong. Please. Whatever it is, we can fix it.'

Jen produced a tissue from her sleeve and blew her nose. After a moment, she seemed to compose herself.

'I'm finding it awkward. No, that's not the right word. It's upsetting me, knowing that you and Robbie are so close. Congratulations, by the way. I bumped into Ambrose yesterday and he tells me you got engaged.' I nodded and mumbled my thanks. 'It's just that I don't trust her, and I certainly don't trust her dad. Look, you're a lovely bloke, and I don't want to see you get hurt, but they're poison.'

'I can't believe you still feel that way over some stupid kid when you were fifteen. So she stole your boyfriend, and you got the hump. So what? It happens. Don't let it ruin your life. Holding a grudge like that is just crazy.'

'Is that what she told you, that it was over her stealing my boyfriend?'

'Is that not true?'

'Well, she hooked up with Darrell all right, but after I'd broken things off. I can't believe that's what she told you. Unless that's really what she believes.'

'If you're saying there's more to it than that, I think you need to tell me the truth, don't you?'

Jen blew her nose again before getting up to throw the tissue in the bin. She took a square of kitchen roll and screwed it up in her right hand. She leaned back against the sink and took a deep breath.

'OK. It was the night of the disco. Robbie's dad had arranged to pick us up at ten o'clock. She'd disappeared with Darrell, or so I assumed. One of the other kids shouted across that Robbie had set off with Darrell. Dex told me to jump in the car, and he would take me home. When I was in the car, I realised he'd been drinking. I could smell it on his breath. I said I would walk, but he wouldn't hear of it and set off. Only, instead of going straight home, he took a detour down the lane that runs along the back of the cricket club. He stopped the car and tried to kiss me. He said he'd always fancied me; crap like that. His hands were everywhere. I tried to push him away, but he's powerful. He leaned in close, and I head-butted him, right on the bridge of the nose. I know it hurt him cos it certainly hurt me. There was a loud crack and lots of blood. He was swearing and shouting, grabbing at my clothes. I hit him, a proper punch, right on the nose again. He howled, and somehow I opened the door and ran off. I climbed the gate and headed across the cricket field. I was terrified, but kept running. '

'Jesus Jen, that's awful. What did you do?'

'I made my way home. I went straight to bed. My mum came up, but I wouldn't let her in the bedroom. I just made out I was upset about Darrell, and she left me alone. I've never told a soul about what really happened.'

'What I don't understand is why the big fallout with Robbie? Surely it's Dex that you hate?'

'The thing is, she covered for him. She put the story around at school that she'd been with her dad when he got mugged. Supposedly, two big guys jumped him, broke his nose, and stole his wallet and phone. I suspect he needed a way of explaining the nose to his wife. Robbie provided him with an alibi, but she must've had some idea about what happened. People had seen me get in the car with him. It's true what they say. Blood is thicker than water, and she is so under daddy's spell. She'd do anything for him. That's why I worry about her being so closely involved with the business. I don't trust her.'

I was horrified. Jen just looked so small and vulnerable. I fought the urge to throw my arms around her.

'Jen, I don't know what to say.'

'Don't say anything. Like you say. The business is exploding. Making it a success can be my revenge on Dex. In fact, our lead character needs a dad. Let's make him a complete bastard, and string him up.'

'We're going to need more Post-its.' Jen actually smiled.

'Thank you for listening, and thanks for being a good friend. Now, let's destroy Dexter.'

We set about re-shaping the stories still to be written, but I was already worried. Was I engaged to somebody that I couldn't trust? More to the point, what would I do about it?

I went into Robbie's office to make coffee.

'I've got something for my fiancé. Is he interested?'

'Depends what it is. I suspect you could use your wily

ways to distract me from coffee making duties if you must.'

'Dream on, you can make me one as well. It's your accounts up to yesterday. Shall I walk you through them?'

'Will I understand at the end of it?'

'Probably not.'

'In that case, let's save both of us a lot of heartaches, and you just tell me how much I can spend on frivolous purchases.'

'Fair enough, as long as those purchases include things for the love of your life.'

'Bowie can buy his own stuff. I've got you to buy for now.' I ducked and then picked up the stapler she'd thrown at me. 'So, can I buy the yacht yet?'

'Not quite, but things are looking good. Obviously, the TV and game production deals haven't paid out yet, but revenue is good from all the other streams. I think you could justify taking twenty grand as a payout this month.'

'What the f…'

'Yep. It's not bad, is it?'

'That's five thousand for Jen, don't forget.' I wondered whether to talk to Robbie about what Jen had told me, but I bottled it. 'A few more paydays like this, and we could buy a really nice place to live when we get married. Any more thoughts on a date yet?'

'Funnily enough, I was speaking to my dad about it last night. How does Christmas Eve sound?'

'Sounds fantastic. I certainly should be able to remember anniversaries. Won't it be impossible to book somewhere? Surely all the decent venues will be booked up ages in advance?'

'Don't forget, Dad's got contacts. He's sure he could sort it.'

'In that case, Christmas Eve it is. We are getting married at Christmas! Now come here. I want to seal the deal.'

'You romantic old bugger.'

22

The last couple of weeks have been hard work but enjoyable, apart from the 'One Show'. Caroline was good to her word, and we got a slot a week ago. I still get the sweats when I think about it. I was so nervous I spent the entire show throwing up in the loo. Robbie did the interview alone and was very good. They sort of glossed over why I wasn't there; not my finest moment. We'd reached the last week of March, and spring was in the air. For once, the sun was shining when Robbie stuck her head around our office door.

'Come on, I'm taking you for a walk.'

'What if I'm busy doing important things?'

'Are you?'

'I'm picking a playlist for tomorrow. I suppose I could finish it in the morning,' I said.

'You're on dodgy ground, mate.' I laughed and asked Rupert to lock up.

Once we were outside, I set off confidently.

'Not that way. Follow me.'

'I just assumed you were taking me to the pub.'

'Maybe later.'

'So going for a walk actually means, you know, going for a walk? Not just walking to the pub?'

'That's right. A novel concept for you, but I'm sure you'll cope.'

'Not sure I like setting a precedent, but where are we going?'

'I thought we'd go through the park, and drop down to the river, make a bit of a loop, across the bridge, and back towards your place.'

'But that's miles.'

'What if we stop off at the pub on the way back? That must knock at least a hundred metres off.'

'Sounds more manageable.'

'Come on, idiot. Can't you just enjoy a walk in the sunshine with your beautiful fiancee?'

'Now you put it like that. What's not to like?'

If I'm honest, it was nice to feel the warm sunshine on my face. We talked and laughed in equal parts. The conversation always seemed to come back to the wedding, but I'd taken the decision early on that, when it came to planning nuptials, I was way out of my depth. It was better, not to mention safer, just to agree with everything.

'What was the last thing I suggested?' Panic swept over me. I'd been rumbled.

'Peacocks.'

'What about them?'

'You want them at the reception?'

'Gotcha. I suggested roasting them and having them as a starter, and you agreed. You weren't listening, were you?' She dug me hard in the ribs with her elbow.

'I just want you to have the perfect day. Whatever you want is fine by me. Probably taste like chicken anyway.'

'Of course, I don't want roasted peacocks for starters. I was testing you, and you failed miserably.'

'But you're so much better at this sort of thing. I'd be so happy and proud just to have you turn up on the day. If I'm honest, I'd be just as happy at the registry office, then back to the pub to watch the football results.'

'You say the most romantic things.' Elbow again.

'I wish you'd stop doing that. It really hurts.'

'Good. Look, I think what you just said was lovely. I really do. If it was up to me, that's exactly what we'd do. But my mum and dad would never forgive us. They want the big day, with all of their friends, to see what a great time we have.'

'I thought it was meant to be our day?'

'Dream on. Have you met my dad?' I assumed Robbie was joking, but couldn't be sure. We'd come to the point where the path veered away from the river to skirt around an old barn. Robbie pulled herself up to sit on the wall. I was slightly less elegant as I joined her. I dislodged the loose top stone, and I over-balanced, dropping into the field below. Robbie almost cried with laughter.

'Stop showing off and get up here.'

I picked up the offending stone and wedged it back into position. The wall was a lot higher on this side. I was going to look stupid if I couldn't climb back up. Instead, I held out my arms.

'Jump down. Let's walk on this side.'

'Okay.' That was lucky. 'Actually, I wanted to have a closer look at the barn, anyway.'

'Why's that?'

'It's the reason I brought you here. It's for sale, or at least it will be in the next couple of days. I was wondering what you thought of us buying it? Our first home? I just happen to have a key.' She unlocked the padlock on the door and slid it open.

'There's a big hole in the roof. We'd get wet.'

'Granted, it needs converting, but just think about what we

could do with it.'

'Surely we couldn't afford to buy this and convert it.'

'I think we could. Do you remember Sir Alan from the council planning committee?' I nodded, remembering the embarrassing first meeting. 'Well, he let Dad know that they've refused the planning permission.'

'So why would we buy it then?'

'It's been refused, which means the current owner is desperate to sell and would accept a lot less money than you'd think.'

'But we'd still need planning permission.'

'We would, and Sir Alan has indicated that, with a few minor alterations, it would then be granted. Bargain.'

'Isn't that a bit dodgy, like insider trading, or something?'

'Don't worry. It happens all the time. He owes Dad a favour. This is his way of paying off the debt.'

'Can we really afford it?'

'Yes. Dad's already said he'll give me a chunk of my inheritance, and the business is very profitable. Getting a mortgage would be no problem. Just think about what we could do with the place. You could have your own music room.'

'Can I have a jukebox?'

'You can have two.'

'In that case, let's do it.'

It was my dad that had answered the phone.

'Hang on, I'll get your mum.'

Was that it? No, hello son, not heard from you for a while? How's it going? None of that. How had we got to where we couldn't communicate? Of course, I knew what it was. He blamed me for the fire. Chatting to Mum was easier. She told me every detail of her entire week. I just added approving noises at various points. It was ten minutes out of my day and made her very happy. I really ought to do it more often. Finally, under any other business, I casually dropped in my news that I had met Robbie and would like to bring her over for tea on Sunday. That had thrown Mum into full organisational meltdown mode. I could tell she wanted to start dusting immediately, so I said my goodbyes.

Now it was Sunday, and we were in Robbie's car heading east towards the coast. It was the first time I'd actually been driven by my fiancee, and I was ever so slightly terrified. The world seemed to whizz past the window at an alarming rate. I realised I was gripping the sides of my seat so hard my hands hurt. Eventually, I convinced myself that she couldn't be driving as fast as I'd thought and reasoned that she'd never actually killed herself so far, so it must be safe. I pushed back into the leather seat and took several deep breaths to relax.

'You seem tense. What's up? Am I driving too fast?'

'No. I feel very safe,' I lied. 'I suppose I'm a bit on edge. It's not every day I take my future wife to meet my parents.'

'From what you've told me, they sound very nice.'

'They are, I suppose. My dad's just been a bit weird in recent years, since the fire.'

'Surely you can't believe that he blames you? Especially after all these years.'

'I've tried to convince myself, honest I have. It just seems to have taken all the life from him.'

'How about I turn on the charm? He couldn't possibly resist.'

'Mmm. Actually, we're almost there. Take the next left. It's the cottage at the end.'

My mum was standing in the drive, almost bouncing on the spot with excitement. After quick introductions and hugs, she whisked us inside to be force-fed tea and sandwiches.

'Frankie, give your dad a shout. He's in the backroom.'

I left the women chatting as if they'd known each other for years and made my way to the back room, expecting to find my dad engrossed in some new project. I was shocked at how much he seemed to have shrunk in the last few months. He was sitting in his armchair, seemingly just staring into space.

'Hi, Dad. I thought you'd have the music on full blast.' I scanned the room and realised there was no music system. 'Come through to the kitchen and meet Robbie.'

He sighed as he stood up and followed me down the hall. I thought it might be incredibly awkward, but a couple of minutes of Robbie flirting with him seemed to bring out a bit of the dad I remembered. We were soon getting tales of the new neighbours, old friends, cousins, the lot. When we announced the wedding, the last of the Christmas sherry was produced, and all was good.

Before we headed for home, I took my mum to one side to ask what had happened to the hi-fi. That was the only time she'd looked less than ecstatic all day. Everything was still in packing cases in the garage. He just hadn't bothered to unpack, and it had been two years. I just couldn't picture two years without music, and it gave me the seed of an idea.

23

When somebody makes a film of my story, this is the bit where newspapers spin and headlines jump out. Honestly, the next few months were just like that. Everything was happening so fast. While the rest of the country was obsessed with the referendum, I had my eyes firmly on my future. Besides, I was against the idea of a referendum in the first place. I read a quote once that, to be successful, you should observe the masses and do the opposite. If this was true, a referendum is pretty much guaranteed to come up with the wrong answer. Anyway, life was crazy: the wedding plans, the business, even more fame on telly, and all the time, the money kept coming.

Jen enjoyed taking the character based on Robbie even darker. In fact, the Woman In The Yellow Raincoat had turned pretty evil. I think Jen found it therapeutic somehow. I tried to tackle Robbie several times about what really happened on the night of the school disco, but each time I lost my nerve. They seemed to be existing quite successfully without ever meeting. A Venn diagram would show each of them in their own big circle, with the tiny overlap being me. Based on 'if it's not broken, don't fix it', I bumbled onwards.

The online stories went from strength to strength. By the end of the summer, we measured users and followers in hundreds of thousands. A million was passed, and the numbers kept growing. The stories got darker and more involved, as did the clues and challenges to progress. We started a vast community that swapped hints or simply bragged about how far they'd got. Rupert had become a minor celebrity in his own right by creating a podcast regularly featuring on national charts. He was actually quite good at it, but that didn't stop me from taking the piss.

Joe was excited that a virtual reality company that could produce the global treasure hunt had approached us. He was still enthusiastically creating problems to be solved (in a good way) and still refused payment. I managed to get him to accept some free advertising, and his business was booming. Ambrose now had a small team working for him and seemed thrilled. A nice little bonus of him being so busy was that he seemed to have forgotten day five of the challenge. I had no intention of reminding him. The thought of what it might throw up still made me uneasy. Best to let sleeping Ambroses lie.

As I spent more time working alongside Jen on storylines and popping up on radio and TV anywhere and everywhere, we were in danger of spreading too thinly. So, our small team in the office had now grown, with the addition of two mini Ruperts. I'd love to say they were called Rupert 2 and Rupert 3, but that's not true. There was Spud (real name) and Clive (not real name). Actually, maybe it was the other way round, and Spud was the nickname. That makes more sense now I think of it. Rupert had daily battles about the music to be played, and I was regularly called on to impose sanity. I saw myself as a kind and benign dictator who liked a lot of Bowie while working.

I had learned to drive and could now be seen posing in my ten-year-old Eos — cool! Technically, I could afford a brand new car. Still, the Yorkshireman in me wanted to have any new-driver scrapes in an older car that was a bit battered already. In fact, it got two new scratches, but we don't need to dwell on that.

The wedding plans were extravagant, to say the least. Dex had been true to his word and arranged a small castle for Christmas Eve. Nothing was too much for his princess, apparently. The invitations had gone out, and four hundred guests were expected. I think I know about ten of them, including my mum and dad. Joe wants to DJ at the reception. Ambrose has agreed to be the best man, and Rupert will be the chief usher (assuming he hasn't killed his dad by then). Things are obviously strained between them. He tries to brush it off, but there's clearly a big problem.

Robbie's dress has been chosen, and I'm not allowed to know anything about it. Even the bridesmaid outfits for her three cousins are top secret. I did try to tell her that we had ordered Ziggy costumes for Ambrose and me, but she pointed out how expensive a Christmas day divorce would be.

Ruckoats had brought out a new range of clothes to go with the yellow raincoat, and Robbie was now the brand's face. I don't know how she has the energy. However, she still runs Dexter's and TWITYR, on top of her modelling career, and all the time, the wedding plans grew, as did the sales figures for yellow raincoats.

My seed of an idea for Dad was growing. Several trips to Joe's had yielded an embryonic new record collection. Original copies of the albums I'd grown up with. The Four Tops Greatest Hits (the one with the green lettering), Highway 61 Revisited, Blue, The Idiot and, of course, the entire Bowie back catalogue. The plan was to present them to my dad and help him unpack the hi-fi and get everything set up.

We'd also had an offer accepted on the barn conversion near the river. We had submitted our bid before it went on the market and now employed an architect and a builder. The builder was even called Bob. Honest. Work would be finished in February, and we could move in when we got back from our honeymoon in New Orleans. We were doing the whole music tour, visiting Nashville and Memphis, before heading to the Big Easy for Mardi Gras.

Before all that, we had the small matter of a TV series to produce. The writing team was lined up, and our first workshop with them took place in early October. To allow us to spend more time on that, we had recruited two new writers of our own. Ollie and Polly, I kid you not. Both worked remotely, but seemed to get on well with each other. Jen was working with them to ensure the style and quality stayed consistent. Jen was still Jen. She was so organised, always there for Charley and still running the writer's workshops. Jen was delighted with the cheques that had regularly hit her bank account and never referred to the incident with Dex. I'd tried to get her to come to the wedding, but she said that was too much. Besides, it was Christmas for a very excited three-year-old.

On October 31st we hit two million downloads. On November 10th, we passed the half-million-pound profit mark, less than a year after I had that idea. I was on top of the world and a big success. I had an OEIC, for god's sake (whatever that is). I was about to marry a beautiful model and move into my dream home. I even had a signed copy of Ziggy Stardust and a new electric toothbrush. With extra plaque-removing action.

On November 11th I was just getting ready to meet Robbie in the pub when I answered the intercom at my front door. It was the police.

24

'Mr Frankie Dale? I'm Detective Inspector Cagney, and this is Sergeant Casey. May we come in?'

I pushed the entry button and told them to come up. I opened the door. My heart was pounding as my mind raced through what I could possibly have done wrong. I decided humour was the best policy. I was wrong.

'I thought for a minute you were going to say, Sergeant…'

'Lacy. Don't worry, sir. We've heard them all over the years.' The two policemen sat on the sofa, and I perched nervously on my armchair. I immediately stood up again.

'Can I get you something to drink? Tea? Coffee?'

'No, thank you, sir. We're fine.' I sat down again. 'You seem a little nervous, sir. No need to worry.'

'It's just the last time there was a policeman in my house I was eight years old. I'd punched the kid next door, and my mum thought it would be a good idea to get the local patrol officer round, to give me a shock.'

'Did it work, sir?'

'Frightened the shit out of me, to be fair.'

'Quite. It never happened again, I take it?'

'No. Total pacifist since then.'

'We will rest safely in our beds with that knowledge, sir. Thank you.'

He's taking the piss, I thought, as I sat back, fingers tapping on the chair arm.

'I'd just like to ask a few questions, if I may?' I nodded. I was going to say something about hope it's not geography but thought better of it. 'Do you know Thomas Dexter? Also known as Dex?'

'Yes. He's going to be my father-in-law. Is everything okay?'

'Aside from your engagement to his daughter, do you have any other relationship with Mr Dexter?'

'My company does some work for him. He loaned me some start-up capital, but that's all paid back now. His son, Rupert, works for me.' Cagney looked at his notebook. 'Sorry, Dominic, his name's Dominic. Rupert is a sort of nickname.'

'What about his daughter, Roberta? Does she work for your company as well?'

'Not officially. She helped out by doing the books and admin when we first started. She's continued with that, but she's happy with her full-time job, working for her dad.'

'And you're due to be married later this year, I understand?'

'Yes, Christmas Eve. Can I ask what this is about?'

'Nothing to worry about, sir. Just a few questions. We're almost done. What's the nature of the work you do for Mr Dexter?'

'We are a software company. We maintain and develop the IT systems.'

'How many people do you employ?'

'Three, including Rupert.'

'From an office at the local community centre?'

'Yes.'

'Thank you, sir. That's all for this evening. We may need to speak to you again, but for now, we'll leave you in peace.' Cagney and Casey stood up, shook my hand, and made for the door. 'Oh, one last thing, sir. Are you the sole signatory on your company bank account?'

'No. Robbie, Roberta has full access too. She does the admin, as I said.'

'Thanks again, sir. Enjoy the rest of your evening.'

I closed the door behind them and went back to the chair. My hands were shaking. What the fuck was all that about? I called Robbie, but it went to voicemail.

'Hello, love. It's only me. Sorry, I'm a bit late. I'll be there in five. Bye.'

Ambrose put a pint in front of me, and I downed it in one.

'Steady on, mate. What's got into you?' He started to pull another pint.

'I've just had the police round at my place.'

'You been a bad lad?'

'No.' I leaned closer and dropped my voice. 'They were asking questions about Robbie's dad. I'm meeting her here, but her phone's going straight to voicemail. I don't suppose she's here yet?'

'Not unless she's hiding behind the dartboard.' I actually looked towards the dartboard. 'I'm sure there's nothing to worry about. Just calm down. You don't wanna be pissed when she gets here, do you?'

'True. It just shook me up, that's all. I wonder what's going on.'

'Look, I'm due a break in a minute when Brenda gets back. Have a seat, and I'll keep you company.'

I sat in the corner just as my phone rang. It was Jen.

'Hi, Jen. How're things?'

'I'm great, thanks. Are you OK to talk?'

'Yes. I'm in the pub waiting for Robbie. What is it?'

'I just had a call from Bob, the editor at the local paper. He reckons that Dex is being interviewed by the police. Did you know?'

'I knew something was up. I had the police at my place, half an hour ago. They were asking questions about him but wouldn't say what it was about.'

'There's more. Bob thinks the accountant is being questioned as well.'

'Shit. You don't think he could've been laundering money through the company, do you?'

'You mean the sort of thing we've been attributing to our fictional character, who just happens to be the father of our fictional heroine, who looks incredibly like Robbie?'

'Fuck me. What if it's true?'

'More to the point, what if they think we knew about it?' I was really panicking now.

'What if they think we were in on it? All that money we've made.'

'Look. Keep calm. We're doing a lot of guessing here. I'm sure Robbie'll be able to tell you more.'

'She's late, and her phone is switched off. What if…'

'Try not to worry. I'm sure Robbie's fine. Sorry, I have to go. Charley's calling. Speak soon.'

I quickly looked at the local paper online. There was nothing about Dexter's. It was either too soon, or there really was nothing to worry about. Ambrose was now beside me. I told him what Jen had said.

'Look. You've done nothing wrong, have you?'

' No.'

'And Robbie's not daft. She won't have done anything either.'

'But you think Dex might?'

'Well, there are rumours. You must know that.'

'Everything's been going so well.'

'Why not wait and see what Robbie says before you get into a spin about this? It could be summat and nowt, as Brenda would say.'

'You're right.'

25

I waited at home until after two in the morning. Still, I heard nothing from Robbie despite trying her mobile every five minutes. I'd called her dad's mobile and the landline but no answer — the same with Rupert. By four o'clock, I gave up trying to sleep. By six, I was on my way to the office, frantic with worry. I fumbled for my keys to the main door and let myself in. I'd never been first in the building, and it felt strange. Somehow, I found the light switch and made my way down the corridor to Robbie's office. It was locked and in darkness.

When I got upstairs, I went straight to my desk. In the middle of my screen was a Post-it. It read, 'Sorry. Rupert.' What the fuck had he done? I tried his phone, but it went straight to voicemail. I was really panicking now. Moving my mouse brought my monitor to life. I typed my password and quickly scanned the email inbox. Nothing stood out. My stomach was churning, and I couldn't settle. Maybe caffeine would calm me down. I grabbed my jacket and locked the door again as I headed to the cafe. I was the first customer and soon headed back to my office with a bacon butty and a coffee.

Spud arrived just after eight o'clock.

'Morning, boss. You're early.'

'Morning Spud. I couldn't sleep, so I came in to get an early start. I take it you've not heard from Rupert this morning?'

'No. A bit early for him as well, to be honest. He was still here last night when I left. He was in a really arsey mood, if you ask me.'

'Why? What do you mean?'

'I think he had a row with his dad. Then he got a right hump on. Turned the music off.'

'That's not like him.'

'No. He had a real pop at Clive, too. Started off about his taste in music, but he turned nasty, had a go about the work he'd been doing, threatened to sack him if he didn't pull his finger out.'

'Nobody's getting sacked. I'm sure he'll have calmed down when he gets in. I'll have a word with Clive too; just settle things down a bit.'

'Thanks. I'd offer to get you a coffee, but Robbie's office is locked up. She not in today?'

'Erm, I'm sure she'll be here soon. Wait until the others get in, then I'll stand a round from the cafe.'

By nine o'clock, I'd smoothed things over with Clive, but there was still no sign of Rupert. Spud went off with my twenty-pound note to do the coffee run. Again, no answer from Robbie. I was just putting the phone down when it rang. I looked at the screen, but it was Bob, the builder (not that one, the one that was doing the barn conversion).

'Bob, how are things going?'

'Morning, Frankie. I think it's going well. If anything, we are a couple of days ahead of schedule. The trouble is we were due a payment yesterday, and nothing arrived. I wouldn't normally bother you, but the steel company is chasing me for their money. I've tried Robbie, but no answer. Sorry to bother you with it.'

'Don't apologise, mate. Give me this morning, and I'll get the money over to you. How much is due?'

'Eight grand.'

'Fair enough, leave it with me.'

In theory, I could sign in to the bank account online and send the payment. In practice, I needed Robbie. The phone rang again. This had to be her, although I didn't recognise the number.

'Hello. Mr Dale?'

'Speaking.'

'Morning, Mr Dale. My name is Dawn Riley. I'm a reporter for the Mail On Sunday. I'd like to speak to you about your involvement with Thomas Dexter. Would you agree to an interview?'

'No, leave me alone.' I hung up. What the hell is happening? The reporter rang back, but I cancelled the call. I sat back in my swivel chair and sighed heavily. It looked very much like the entire Dexter family had gone to ground, and the papers seemed to scent a story. And what the fuck was Rupert sorry for?

Spud returned with the coffee. I pocketed my change and half-heartedly held a progress meeting with the two-thirds of my team that had turned up. At ten o'clock, I checked downstairs again, but still no sign of Robbie. It was time to be brave and get out the little black book. This was Robbie's high-tech method to make sure I knew how to sign in to the bank account. As a security measure, I'd insisted that the username was on a page at the front of the book, and the password was at the back. We had a similar system for both the business accounts, my personal account and the investments account. The plan had worked smoothly so far, mainly because I had never used it. It turned out the instructions were perfect and, after a false start, thanks to getting the password wrong, I was in.

I didn't understand what I was looking at. This was the joint account we'd set up for the house purchase. There was a long list of transactions. I could see Bob's payment in the 'Money out' column, but then it had the same amount under 'Money In'. According to the screen, the balance was zero. That couldn't be right. I was in a definite panic now. Surely I was just reading it wrong? I went down the list again. I could see payments for thousands in 'Money In' but just one more amount under 'Money Out'. It was for over three hundred thousand pounds. The money had gone. The balance really was zero. Oh, fuck! I felt sick and tapped Robbie's number again. Nothing. I did have a text. It was from Jen.

'You coming for our session? Kettle's on, and I'm eating all the biscuits! x'

Of course, it was Thursday. I grabbed my jacket and waved to Spud and Clive. Ten minutes later, Jen answered my knock at the door. She was dressed in a very sharp burgundy suit and crisp white shirt.

'You look smart. What happened?'

'I'll take that as a compliment, you smooth-talking bugger. I'm interviewing somebody for a magazine piece later, and need to look my best. You, on the other hand, look like shit. Come in before you scare the neighbours.' We went through to the cosy kitchen at the back of the house. It felt nice.

Jen looked at me and asked, 'What's happened?'

'I'm worried sick, to be honest. Robbie never showed last night. Both Rupert and her have dropped off the face of the earth, and I'm worried she's taken a lot of money with her. Somebody has cleaned out the joint account. I'm hoping she's just moving money around, and she'll turn up later today, having invested it and made us millions.'

'You don't look as if you believe that if you don't mind me saying. Have you checked the hospitals?'

'No. Christ, you don't think Robbie's had an accident, do you?'

'It's a possibility, isn't it? It would explain why she's not answering your calls. Do you want me to ring around?'

'Yes, please.'

'You get a cup of tea down you. There's more biscuits in the cupboard above the sink. You look like you need some sugar.' I felt numb as I raided the biscuit cupboard and sipped the hot tea. Five minutes later, Jen put down her phone. 'Right, I think we can rule out the hospital theory. Have you been to her flat?'

'No. I tried ringing the house as well as all the mobile numbers.'

'Why don't we go round there? If nothing else, it will give you something to do. I suspect we aren't doing much writing today. Come on. We can take my new car.'

I hadn't noticed the new Yaris parked outside when I arrived. We jumped in, and soon, we were at the gates of the Dexter house. I jumped out and pressed the intercom for Robbie's flat. No answer. I tried the main house with the same result. I gave up and trudged back to the car.

'Have you more accounts, other than the joint one?'

'Yes. There's my personal one, and one each for the software business and the yellow raincoat. Then there are a couple of savings accounts.'

'Can you check them on your phone?'

'In theory, but I need my little black book for the passwords. It's at the office.'

'Okay. Let's go.'

As we walked into the office, Spud came across to ask something. Jen obviously gave him a look. He swerved away and ended up back at his desk. Both he and Clive stayed silent.

'Right. Come on. Check these accounts.'

Deep down, I knew what I would find. All the accounts had been emptied. Even the OEIC, whatever that was. Not only that, the credit card was up to the limit. By the time I'd checked the last one, I was shaking and close to tears. Jen had a quiet word with Spud and Clive, who kept their heads down and trooped out of the office. Jen put a consoling arm around my shoulders. I turned towards her and sobbed helplessly.

'I'm all for letting it out, but you're going to get snot on my suit.'

'Sorry.' At this point, I laughed, and my nose seemed to explode.

'Told you.'

'Sorry. I'll pay to get it cleaned.'

'Don't make promises you can't keep.' We hugged each other tight, then she took control. 'Right, I think it's time we called the police, don't you?'

'I'll just try Robbie's phone again.'

'Frankie, she's legged it. She's taken your money and scarpered. The police obviously suspect something's going on. They need to know about this.'

'You're right.' I couldn't resist ringing Robbie one more time, but, again, it went straight to voicemail. Next, I phoned the police. I explained that Robbie appeared to be missing, along with close to half a million pounds of my money. The woman on the phone promised to send somebody round. Jen patted my hand.

'Well done. I know that was difficult. The police'll soon get to the bottom of this.'

Two minutes later, Cagney and Casey were at the office door.

'Blimey, that was quick.'

'Mr Dale, may we come in?'

'Of course. I just wasn't expecting you yet.'

'So you were expecting us?'

'Yes. Of course, I assumed you'd be here sometime today.'

'Quite. Well, here is a warrant that allows me to take away all of your computer equipment for full analysis. These officers will bag everything up, and we'll give you a receipt.' Four big blokes in uniform came through the door, and each moved to a different desk.

'Wait. No, hang on. You can't take that lot. I need them to keep my business going. What about the money? You need to find Robbie.'

'All in good time. Right now, we need the equipment to continue our inquiries into your business dealings with Mr Dexter.' It was Jen who spoke next.

'Hang on. Frankie just reported a missing person and the likely theft of half a million pounds, and you're treating him like a suspect. What's going on?' Just then, Cagney's phone rang. He held up a finger and listened intently.

'I see. Thanks.' He put the phone back in his overcoat pocket. 'It appears there is some confusion. I've just been informed of your call to the station. However, we were already on the way here to execute the warrant. I suggest that while my officers bag up the evidence, we sit and have a chat.'

Half an hour later, Cagney closed his notebook. He thanked me for my co-operation and promised to be in touch. I suddenly felt exhausted. Jen put her head on one side and looked at me.

'You look like shit.'

'Ta. I needed a lift.'

'Look, you need to get some sleep. Why don't I drop you off at home? That way, if Robbie turns up, you'll be there. Get some sleep, I'll go and do my interview, and I'll call in later when I've picked Charley up from the nursery.'

She took my hand and led me to the door. I fumbled with the keys before Jen took them, locked the door, and put the keys in her pocket. Five minutes later, she used them to let me into my flat. I flopped into the armchair. I felt numb.

'Is there anything I can get you before I go? Something to eat, a drink?'

'No, thanks. You've been brilliant today. Thank you. Like you say, I need to get some sleep.'

Jen handed me the keys and kissed me lightly on the cheek. Her perfume smelt good, and I smiled at her.

'You look after yourself this afternoon. Don't worry, we'll sort this out. Call me if you need anything.'

I remember the door closing behind her, but nothing else. I must've fallen asleep immediately. When I woke up, it was dark and cold. I really needed to sort out the timer for the heating. I rubbed my neck and fumbled for the reading lamp next to the chair. At last, the heating controller clicked into action. I felt grubby and needed a pee. After I'd had a shower and a change of clothes, I felt human again. I checked my phone, but still nothing. Could Robbie really have taken the money and run, or was she a victim in all this, too? What if she'd been kidnapped? I'd never considered that. A whole new set of worries descended. The phone ringing snapped me out of this. Robbie? It was Jen.

'How are you feeling? Did you manage to sleep?'

'Yes. I got a couple of hours. I feel a bit better.'

'No arguments. You're coming to my place for tea. Charley wants to see you, and she's got something for you.'

'Sounds lovely, but I don't think I'd be terrific company.'

'We don't care about that. I make a mean spag-bol, and Charley isn't used to taking no for an answer. Don't spend the evening moping on your own. Come and mope with us.

There's wine!'

'In that case, you're on. What time do you want me?'

'As soon as you can, so Charley gets to see you before she goes to bed.'

'I'm on my way. Do you want me to bring anything?'

'Not being rude, but have you got anything?'

'Funny. You should be writing for a living. I'm on my way.'

The cooking smells in Jen's kitchen reminded me of Sundays as a kid. It felt safe and warm. Charley had painted me a picture of a rainbow over a house. There was a scarecrow as big as the building.

'Thank you, Charley, that's lovely. Why is the scarecrow bigger than the house?'

'I's not a scarecrow. It's you.' I was about to ask why I was bigger than the house, but she got the giggles and went back to her juice.

'I'll put this on my wall at home.' I turned to Jen. 'See, things are looking up, and I'm accumulating stuff again.'

'It's good to see you smile. It's been a tough day.'

'It's been a shit-fest, to be honest.'

'What's a shit-fest?' asked the big-eared three-year-old.

'It's just uncle Frankie being silly.' The admonishment in the look she gave me reminded me to behave.

'You said uncle Frankie was a…'

'Never you mind what I said or didn't say. It's time you were in bed, young lady. Why don't you go and pick which story you want me to read for you?'

Charley sprang up and went off in search of a book.

'She's a great kid.'

'She is, but she hears everything!'

'Sorry about that. I'm not used to being around kids. They somehow sense my fear and exploit it.'

'You seem to be doing okay with that one.'

Charley bounced back in with a book almost as big as she was. Jen scooped her up. 'Say goodnight to uncle Frankie.'

'Not yet. I want uncle Frankie to read my story.' Jen saw the look of absolute terror on my face. She laughed.

'Alright. Uncle Frankie can read you a story. Let's get you washed and into bed.' Jen stuck her tongue out at me as she passed. 'I'll give you a shout when she's ready. Have another glass of wine.'

I was horrified at the thought of reading the story and certainly needed some liquid courage. Within a couple of minutes, they summoned me upstairs. I was made to sit on a tiny wooden stool and handed the book. Charley introduced me to Muriel, the stuffed cow that was beside Charley on the pillow. Jen switched off the overhead light, leaving just the soft pool of light from the tiny lamp. She tapped my shoulder and motioned that she would be downstairs. Hesitantly, I started to read.

'You have to do the voices.'

'Who says?'

'I do. It's not a story if you don't do the voices.'

'Bossy boots.' I screwed my face up, and she giggled. Before long, I was into my stride, trying to do a different voice for each character while keeping my voice as low as possible so that Jen couldn't hear. As I finished the last page, I became aware of Jen behind me. She whispered.

'That was lovely. By the way, she's been fast asleep for the last five minutes. Come on, let's have another drink.' I placed the book on the bedside table and followed Jen downstairs. 'You're a natural.'

'Rubbish. I felt very awkward.'

'She didn't think so. You're certainly honoured to be asked. Only me and my mum have ever had that privilege before. You'll stay for another drink? I've got another bottle in the cupboard.'

'Thanks. I've nothing else to do.'

'Charming.'

'No. I didn't mean it like that.'

'I know, just teasing. I'll get the bottle.'

We sat side by side on the sofa. Jen drew her feet up beneath her and cradled the wine glass.

'How did your interview go today?'

'I enjoyed it, to be honest. It was a local woman who's just landed a part in the West End. She was so excited and bubbly. It's the start of a big adventure for her.'

'I must admit, I've felt that way myself for the last few months. Until today.'

'How do you feel now?'

'Numb, I suppose. I was meant to be getting married in a few weeks, buying a new house. Now I suspect I'm skint and probably single again. Back to square one.'

Jen stretched out a leg and playfully pushed her foot against my knee. It felt nice, natural.

'Not quite. The Woman In The Yellow Raincoat is a big success. We're writing a TV script. People would kill to be in that position.'

'True. Look, whatever happens, I really appreciate everything you've done over the last year. Without you, the business would be nowhere.'

'You've been the driving force behind it. Don't forget that. You had the idea. You saw where it could go and did the coding to make it all happen. It's your ideas that give us the storylines. We seem to work well as a team. Besides, the bank deposits every month have come in very handy.'

'Without the computers, I'm not sure where we go now.'

'The police will release them soon, surely. We can carry on writing. I've got my laptop. Can you keep the website updated with new content?'

'That's why I need the kit. I use my phone for personal

emails, but all of the business stuff is accessed on the Mac. Hang on a minute.' I sat up, almost spilling the wine on the coffee table. 'I've got my old laptop at home. They only took the computers from the office. Why didn't I think of that before? Once I sign on to the laptop, I've got access to all the online passwords. At least we should be able to keep things going, and I can get at the business emails and messages.'

'What if the police come to the flat and take the laptop?'

'I'll make a backup disk so we can effectively use any laptop.' My heart was pounding now. I needed to make that back up quickly. Just in case. 'Now that I've thought about it…'

'I know. You need to get it done. Are you sure you'll be okay?'

'Yes. Look, I've got something positive I can be doing now. Sorry to dash off. It's been a lovely evening. The spag-bol was lovely. Thanks again.'

After a quick hug, I was out of the door and almost running home.

26

I wasn't sure what I expected to find when I powered up the laptop. The police had taken away the central server. Still, I could access all the social media platforms and email. Maybe Robbie would've been in touch that way. Quickly scanning the new emails, nothing stood out. There was a lot I needed to answer for TWITYR, but they would have to wait. The number of downloads was still rising. I checked Facebook and Twitter, but nothing from Robbie. My heart sank. It was like I'd had a flash of inspiration at Jen's that the laptop would hold the key to understanding what was going on. Now I could see that, as usual, I was wrong. The low battery indicator began to flash on the laptop. I was about to close the lid in frustration when I noticed the new file indicator on Dropbox. We used the service for moving files between the TV team and us or other partners. I reached into the zipped pocket of the rucksack and retrieved the power cable. I plugged it in and clicked to view the file. It was encrypted. Why would somebody be placing an encrypted file on the system used to share information? I was intrigued, but didn't have the password. I could see that the file had been created this afternoon. Was this Robbie's way of getting in touch?

I tried a couple of passwords. 'TWITYR' failed miserably, and 'Robbie' prompted me that I had only one chance left. I sat back and stared at the screen. What if it wasn't Robbie that had put the file there? Rupert was much more likely to use an encrypted file on Dropbox. I grinned to myself and typed in Z-I-G-G-Y. The screen changed and showed a page of text — I was in.

If you're reading this, you successfully cracked the password—well-done, boss.

First, I wanted to apologise for what I've done. You've been a perfect mate to me, and working with you for the last few months has been great. Ultimately, I suppose, blood is thicker than water. That's what they say, isn't it? So many times, I've been close to telling you, but I couldn't.

The rows with my dad were about the business, and, in the end, I did what he wanted me to do. You know what he's like. I stood no chance, really. For that, I am genuinely sorry, but it might not be too late. You need to check the app code carefully. It has quietly been harvesting passwords, bank details and any other personal data we thought would be handy. The code itself doesn't look suspicious, apart from the fact that it writes data to a file on our system. A suite of programs on the server checks the major shopping sites for a combination of email address and password being reused. When it finds one, it has the card details to buy whatever it feels like. In the hands of a well-organised gang, it would be worth millions. The plan was to sell the entire system, but the police came sniffing before I could. If you're quick, you might be able to delete the code and cover your tracks. Nobody needs to know. In fact, a better plan would be to get rid of the module to register and enter bank details altogether. Start again and don't reuse any of the code. It would also be a good idea to get rid of the version marked 'beta'. I was playing with a version that contained a virus to record keystrokes on infected machines. Couldn't get it past the virus police, so I abandoned it.

As you may have realised, the entire family has relocated. Don't try to work out where we are. Needless to say, we are a long way from the police investigation and extradition treaties. Robbie did an excellent job of moving cash around. I feel bad that you lost so much, but we need it for a fresh start. I'm hoping you could do me a favour and not show this to the police. Robbie wants you to know how sorry she is as well. The little idiot really loves you, but loves her dad even more.

At least I didn't kill the man, but I had to break up the band. Sorry again. R

I stared at the screen. The whole family had gone. The money was all gone. The wedding was off. The entire rose-tinted future I'd dreamt about for the last few months was all gone. I felt the overpowering urge to sit there and sob. Then the terror hit me. The police had all the software on the server. What if they found the code, or the harvested data? They'd come after me then. Shit. Did Cagney and Casey already suspect? Is that what all the questions had been about? Hang on! Deep breath. Calm down. I'd done nothing wrong. Why would they come after me? Then again, the real culprit had done a runner to who knows where. Of course, they'll try to pin it on me. It was almost midnight. Too late to call Jen for advice now. Who would still be up? Ambrose. I tried his number, but it went straight to voicemail. Joe never slept. I tried him.

'Frankie, my boy, how are things?'

'It's all gone a bit shit. I need to talk.'

'You need what? You'll have to speak up. The band's just come on.'

The background noise shot through the roof, and three seconds later, the call was ended. Typical. He was at a bloody club. At least somebody is having a good night. I sat back. A text arrived almost immediately, promising to ring me in the morning. The room was silent until I heard a car pull up outside. Had Jen come to check on me? I strode across to the window and looked down at the street. The car was bigger than Jen's, and two figures emerged into the streetlights. It was Cagney and Casey. They introduced themselves on the intercom, and I pushed the button to let them in. There was no other way out. I was trapped. Then again, where was I going to run to? May as well put the kettle on, I suppose.

I was about to offer them a drink, but the look on Cagney's face said it all. Then his voice confirmed it.

'Mr Dale, we'd like you to come to the station and answer a few more questions.' Two minutes later, I was sitting in the back of their car. The ten-year-old me would've been very disappointed that it wasn't a proper police car, but the grown-up me was too busy trying not to wet himself to care. When we got to the station, they parked in the underground car park and walked with me to the security door. We took the lift and emerged into a brightly lit corridor. Casey pushed open a door with a large '3' on it. I stepped inside. At least it wasn't a cell. It was the kind of interview room I'd seen on TV a million times. It was so familiar it felt weird. Cagney took a seat opposite the door and waved his hand at a chair for me. Casey sort of hovered by the door.

'Mr Dale. Can I call you Frankie?' So long as he didn't call me the prisoner, I didn't care. I nodded. 'Frankie, thank you for agreeing to come in for a chat.' Agreeing? Nobody thought to point out I had a choice in the matter. 'Now, as we discussed at our last meeting, we are interested in your business dealings with Mr Thomas Dexter.' He looked at the notes in front of him. 'You told us last time your company carried out the development and maintenance of Dexter's computer systems. Is that correct?' I nodded again. It occurred to me that on the telly, at this point, he would have said something about me nodding for the benefit of the tape. I realised there was no tape. Was that good or bad? 'Were you involved in any other business dealings with Mr Dexter?'

'No, apart from the loan he made, to give me the startup capital.'

'Did Mr Dexter ask you, at any time, to deposit any money into a bank account? To look after it, as it were?'

'No. Never.'

'Are you aware of any money being paid into your account that you were not entitled to receive? Money that you subsequently paid back.'

'No.'

'Did you ever purchase any insurance or life assurance policies through the business accounts?'

'No.'

'Did anybody else purchase such products on your behalf?'

'Not to my knowledge.'

'Not to your knowledge?'

'No. My fiancee, Robbie, managed the accounts, but she never mentioned life assurance to me.'

'You say that Mr Dexter loaned money to you.'

'Yes. I needed some startup capital, and Dex offered the loan so that I could do some maintenance work for him.'

'Was this a commercial arrangement?'

'Sorry. What do you mean?'

'What interest rate did he charge you?'

'He didn't. I paid the money back fairly quickly once I started to do the work for him.'

'Did Mr Dexter make loans to other people or businesses?'

'I've no idea.'

'As part of the work you did, you had access to the company's software systems?'

'Yes.'

'Did anything you saw give you any concerns?'

'No.'

'Nothing that suggested malware, stealing data, that sort of thing?' Oh, double shit. He knew.

'I saw nothing that would suggest that.' Not a lie.

Cagney pushed back his seat and stared at me for what seemed like ages before he spoke again.

'The Woman In The Yellow Raincoat. This is a work of online fiction that you produce. Is that correct?'

'Yes.'

'Is it true that the woman featured in the images on the website is Roberta Dexter, Mr Dexter's daughter and your fiancee?'

'Yes.'

'It's just that I've been reading a few of the pieces. The characters would appear to have a lot in common with the Dexters. In the story, the lead character is involved with money laundering, money lending and drug dealing. Is that right?'

'Yes, the fictional character.'

'Yes. The fictional character. However, would it surprise you to learn that we have been investigating the business dealings of the real Mr Dexter? Would it also surprise you to learn that we believe his real-life business dealings are varied? They include, but are not limited to, drug distribution, illegal money lending and money laundering?' Holy shit. We thought we'd made that lot up. 'You see, I believe that you knew all about Mr Dexter's little empire and had a ready-made storyline for your work of fiction. I believe that you were part of the empire yourself and gained financially from that connection.' Now I really did need the toilet. 'Well? What have you got to say for yourself?'

'Can I go to the toilet?'

'No. Answer the question first.'

'Look. I knew nothing about this. It's fiction. Part of my

role was to make things up. Okay, I based the characters on Robbie and Dex, but only the physical side. I made everything else up.'

'You really expect me to believe that?'

'Yes. Because it is true.'

'Very well. We'll leave it there for now, but we will need to speak again. Sergeant Casey will show you to the facilities. Have a good evening.'

27

I decided to walk home. It was almost three in the morning and cold. As I walked, I thought about the events of the last couple of days. I'd basically started the week from hell, a near millionaire, about to get married to the woman I loved, with a successful business. Now I was penniless, single, and being investigated by the police. Could things get any worse? It started to rain. Typical. I pulled the zip of my jacket up and increased my pace. At least I hadn't been arrested, which meant they had no proof. What was I talking about? There was no proof because I hadn't done anything.

My only crime seemed to be having an over-active imagination. Oh, and trusting people. I trusted Robbie with everything. That hurt the most. Had she abused that trust and used the bank account to launder money from Dex's other businesses? How could she betray me at the same time as making plans to marry me? Strangely, I was walking past the end of the lane where our new house was being converted. I pulled myself up onto the wall and sat looking at the silhouette of the barn. In a few weeks, I should've been moving in there to start my married life. Now, if Cagney got his way, I would be in a prison cell. I had to prove I was innocent — but how?

I wasn't sure why, but a picture of Jen's cosy house flashed across my mind. I wished I was there now, enjoying a glass of wine and a chat. The wind whipped more rain into my face, so I clambered down and started to walk again. Now, on top of everything else, I had a wet bum from the wall. It also occurred to me that, assuming I could no longer afford the house, I would be homeless. I'd given notice to leave the flat. Shit. I needed a backup, and fast. Hang on a minute. Backup! That's it. I'd set up a backup for our systems and included Dexter's as well. I had a remote copy of everything done in the business since I set it up. It would take time, but I could trace every change that Rupert had made to insert the malicious code in theory. I could also log every financial transaction that Robbie had made. I needed to speak to Ambrose quickly.

I finally made it home and peeled off my wet clothes. A hot shower left me feeling better. I went into the bedroom to get dressed, but the bed looked too inviting. I crawled in and fell into an exhausted sleep until I was woken just before nine o'clock by the ringing phone. It was Ambrose.

'Morning, mate. I saw you tried to call last night. Thought I'd better ring back. What's up?'

'You're not going to believe the night I've had. I need your help. What are you doing this morning?'

'I'm due at Joe's for twelve. I'm free until then.'

'Can we meet at the cafe? I need caffeine and bacon. Ten minutes?'

'You're on. I'll see you there.'

Ildiko waved from behind the counter as I pulled out the seat opposite Ambrose.

'I've ordered. What's up? You sounded worried.'

'More than worried.' I told him about the events of the last couple of days.

'What are you going to do?'

'I'm not entirely sure. I was hoping you could offer some advice, given your legal background.'

'I'd love to, but I was strictly corporate, nothing like this.'

'If I could get the gear released by the police, I might stand a chance. I set up a backup on a remote server. Every time anything changed on any computer, it wrote away a copy. I'm hoping I can piece together what happened and prove my innocence. The trouble is, I would need some pretty hefty kit to collate everything.'

'Sounds like you also need Stella. That's exactly the sort of thing she does for a living.' I grinned at him. 'But then again, you knew that, didn't you?'

'I was hoping she could do something.'

'Look, I've got a mate that may be able to help on the legal side. We were at university together. I chased the big bucks and went to corporate and hated it. He went into criminal law and was damned good at it. Made a mint as well, which is a lesson to me.'

'Trouble is, I'm skint. All the money has gone.'

'Don't worry about that. Leave it to me.' Ambrose took out his phone and started to scroll through his contacts. The food and drinks arrived, and I tucked in. Ildiko patted me on the back as she left. The rumour mill was obviously in full flow. I was carefully wiping egg yolk from my chin when Ambrose finished his call. 'Right. Gavin is confident he can help. I pulled in a favour, so he says not to worry about the fee. He's happy to work on it, and you can pay him when all this is sorted. I've just sent you his number. He says to call at one o'clock this afternoon. He'll take the details and go after the computers.'

'Thanks for this, mate. I owe you big time.'

'It's not me you need to worry about. We were looking for last-minute flights to Spain, for Stella's week off next week. It sounds like you could do with her being at home instead. I'll go back via the wine merchant. She might need a bit of persuasion.'

'Whatever you do, don't cause any hassle between you two. Then again, if we can get this sorted and get the money back, I'll buy you a house in Spain!' I finished my sandwich and fiddled with the tomato sauce bottle. 'There is one other thing I need your advice on.' Ambrose picked up his coffee and nodded. I leaned closer and dropped my voice to a near whisper. 'It seems that Rupert was being forced by his dad to add some dodgy code to the apps.'

'He's been in touch?'

'He sent an encrypted file with a message in it.'

'Very James Bond. Where is he?'

'He didn't say. Just that the whole family has gone abroad. His dad was spooked by the police attention and had a plan B. That involved cashing in everything they could lay their hands on, including my accounts. Presumably, they plan to live very comfortably on all the money they've spirited away.'

'What does this code do?'

'It sounds like it is stealing bank details and as much personal info as he could get. I think the plan was to sell it. The thing is, it's not been used. He hasn't sold anything. Now that I know it's there, I should be able to strip it out and delete the data. If word got out, that would be the end of the business. Nobody would trust us again.'

'What if the police find it? If this is as big as you think, they'll be diving deep into everything. Even if you strip it, they have copies of the software as it stands now.'

'So, the options are, amend the software, and hope they don't notice, or confess everything, and try to prove it was nothing to do with me.'

'Either way, you run a real risk of losing everything. If they don't believe you, you'd be looking at prison. If they do believe you, then chances are the business is finished anyway.'

'I still think I prefer the option without prison.'

The call to Gavin went well. I told him everything I knew. He advised that it was probably best to come clean with the police about the data harvesting, but to wait a day or two. He wanted to try to get the computers back and see which way the police were going to move. Did they see me as a victim of the Dexters or an accomplice? We arranged to meet in a couple of days. In the meantime, he advised me to stay calm. Stay calm? How could I stay calm with all this going on? Our sponsors were getting twitchy for a start. I had a voicemail from Caroline. She was just 'checking in' but couldn't help noticing that there hadn't been a new instalment this week. The old me resurfaced, and I pretended that I hadn't seen the message.

Even though it was Saturday morning, I called both Spud and Clive. I explained the situation, leaving out the bit about the dodgy code. Spud took it very well and said he would carry on working from home as he had his laptop. Clive, on the other hand, suggested I do something which I'm pretty sure is impossible. I certainly wouldn't be able to walk afterwards. My workforce had effectively gone from three to one in a couple of days. Fuck it. Clive was the least of my problems. I was wondering what to do with the rest of the afternoon when the phone rang. I crossed my fingers that it wasn't Caroline. It was Jen.

'Thought I'd better check that you were OK.'

'I'm a bit twitchy, but other than that, I'm fine. How about you?'

'Funny you should ask. I've just been offered work, writing

an in-depth profile of a well-known star of stage and screen.'

'That's great. Who is this well-known star of stage and screen? Brad Pitt?'

'He's called Zac.'

'Zac Efron? Wow, that's great.'

'No, Zac Arundel.'

'Zac fucking Arundel? Who the fuck is Zac fucking Arundel? Never heard of him.'

'Peasant. He was in that thing on a Sunday night on ITV. The one with that woman from Downton Abbey. He has a bit of a limp.'

'Are you speaking a foreign language here? I have no idea who you're talking about, but I'm very pleased for you.'

'How pleased?'

'Pretty pleased. Maybe not as much as if it was Zac Efron but pleased.'

'Pleased enough to do me a favour?'

'Course I will. Name it.'

'Would you babysit? My mum is busy, and the meeting with Zac is tonight or never.'

'You mean be responsible for a small child? Me? Have we met before?'

'You'll be fine. You made a big impression on Charley the other night. I'll feed you and make sure there's beer in the fridge. It'll be three, four hours tops. Even you can keep a three-year-old alive for four hours. Just make sure there's no playing with matches or knives.'

'Where's she going to get matches from?'

'I didn't mean her. I meant you. Does that mean you'll do it then? Thanks. See you at 6.30.'

I was about to speak when I realised the phone was dead. It looked like I was babysitting tonight. The phone rang again. Had Jen seen sense and changed her mind? It wasn't her.

'Gavin. I didn't expect to hear from you today. What's wrong?'

'Nothing's wrong. Well, nothing new anyway. Can you be at your office at four o'clock today?' I looked at my watch.

'Yes, if I set off now.'

'Good. The police are delivering your computers.'

'Seriously. That's fantastic.'

'I told you I was good. The police have taken copies of everything, but at least you can keep working while we sort the rest of it out. You need to identify the dodgy code and prove that it was Rupert that did the work. Then we can tell them what we know. One bit of bad news, I'm afraid. They've got a court order to freeze the bank accounts, so you won't be able to access them.'

'They're all empty anyway, so it makes no difference to me.'

'Sorry, got another call coming in. Let me know if there's a problem. Cheers.'

I grabbed my jacket and headed for work. I went via Robbie's office. It was all locked up and in darkness, but I could see through the window that the computer and filing cabinets had gone. The front door was covered in the tape that said it was a crime scene and not to enter. I wished we had our own kettle.

The delivery turned up at ten past four. I signed the receipt and started to put everything back together. An hour and a half later, we had a functioning office again. I let Spud know that he could come back on Monday and I was about to start looking for the criminal code when I realised what time it was. I grabbed my jacket, locked the doors, and headed for Jen's.

'Wow.'

Probably not what Jen expected as she opened the door.

'Wow to you, too. Am I to take that as a compliment?'

'Yes, sorry. I just haven't seen you with your hair down before. Zac what's-his-face won't know what's hit him.'

'That's the plan.' I stepped inside, and Jen closed the door. She looked fantastic. Her hair was almost waist length, a mass of soft red curls. She was wearing a knee-length cocktail dress. The black material made her pale skin and red hair glow. 'And, for once, I don't have sick down my front.'

'Probably best for Zac what's-his-face.'

'Arundel.'

'Is he? That doesn't surprise me.'

'Come on, say hello to Charley.' She turned left into the small living room. Charley was on the rug in front of the TV, watching something pink.

'Hi, Charley.'

'Shh.'

I quickly apologised to the three-year-old. 'Sorry.'

'Charley, don't be rude.' Jen turned to me. 'Sorry, nothing comes between her and Peppa Pig. She will turn back into a delightful child as soon as it finishes. Can I get you a beer?'

'Lovely.' I followed Jen through to the kitchen. She handed over the beer and pointed at the pizza menu on the table. There was a twenty-pound note beside it.

'I know I said I would feed you, but didn't think you'd fancy alphabetti spaghetti, which is what madam had. So, I'm paying, no arguments, and save me a slice for when I get back.' I started to protest.

'There's really no need to pay.'

'I insist. You're doing me a big favour. This way, I can ask you again!'

'Any time. My social life seems to have taken a bit of a dive this week. Glad to make myself useful.'

'It must be tough for you. I can't imagine how you're feeling. We'll chat when I get back if that's okay. Peppa should be finishing now. Time to get Charley to bed. My taxi will be here in a minute.' I sat at the kitchen table and swigged the beer. Jen disappeared upstairs with Charley. Two minutes later, she was back.

'Her majesty is requesting a story from uncle Frankie. Any chance?'

'How can I say no?' Jen's phone flashed into life.

'That's my taxi.'

'You get off. I'll sort out Charley. Don't worry about anything.'

'Thanks. See you later.'

With that, she was gone. I was actually responsible for another human being for the first time in my life. I climbed the stairs and found Charley tucked up in bed, clutching another jumbo storybook. She demanded a big hug before sliding down beneath the duvet. I read the story, complete with voices. This time I remembered to keep an eye out for my audience nodding off. She was fast asleep well before the end of the story, but I wanted to know how it ended. I stopped reading out loud, but stayed until I got to the end. Very quietly, I moved to the door and turned out the light. I positioned the door partly open, as Jen had done. I was just about to go downstairs when I heard a tiny, very sleepy voice.

'Night night, uncle Frankie.'

'Night night Charley. Sleep well.' I felt very pleased with myself as I went back downstairs. I ordered a table-sized pizza and settled in front of the TV to await its arrival. Flicking through the channels, I found The Blues Brothers had started an hour ago. Missing the start was hardly a problem as I knew the dialogue, almost by heart. When the pizza arrived, the driver joked that he wanted to come and watch it with me. I think it's just one of those movies. Usually, I would be enthralled, but not tonight. I ate a couple of slices of pizza but couldn't concentrate on the film. The events of the last couple of weeks started flying around my head. I switched off the TV and picked up another beer from the fridge. Before I opened it, I went upstairs to check on Charley. She was fast asleep, not a care in the world.

Back downstairs, I flicked through Jen's CD collection. I was delighted and surprised that they were in alphabetical order. Less surprising and less impressive, the first two albums were by ABBA and Air Supply. No Bowie! When I saw Cherry Ghost, I'd been about to give up. I put the CD in the player and checked that the volume was low to make sure I didn't disturb Charley. I sat on the sofa and spotted a text. It was from Jen. She was obviously slightly nervous about leaving her daughter with me. I replied to say that everything was fine. I asked how it was going and received a one-word reply—'DULL'. Old Zac Whats-his-face obviously wasn't up to much.

I finally gave in and took my laptop from my shoulder bag. At least I could answer a few emails rather than dwelling on problems. There were a couple of enquiries about advertising. That was really frustrating. Outwardly, we were still very successful. Behind the facade of success, the business was probably doomed. I could end up in prison. So much for emails distracting me from my problems. I was about to give up when I spotted a message from the TV producer we worked with. He'd sent me a copy of the draft script for episode one. I was to review it ahead of the next meeting in a couple of days. I opened the document and felt a real buzz at seeing myself and Jen as part of the writing team. It seemed crazy as I was about to read the script for the first time. I suppose the characters and the storylines were mine and Jen's creations. Reading the first scene felt very strange. I knew the characters and what was going to happen, but the dialogue was so unfamiliar. There was something about the way the two main characters spoke to each other. It wasn't quite right.

I started to make small changes, substituting the odd word, inserting phrases here and there, discarding others. Before I knew it, I had basically rewritten the first two scenes. Not drastically. It just felt more natural. I was quietly pleased with myself.

Cherry Ghost was still playing on repeat when Jen let herself back in.

'Hi. I wasn't expecting you so soon.' She looked at her watch.

'It's gone ten o'clock. Believe me, that's long enough for this evening.'

'Not good?'

'Let's just say he's as thick as two short planks, with an ego the size of China. Hope there's pizza left in that box.'

'There is. Would you like me to warm it up for you?'

'No need. Cold pizza is one of the biggest treats going.' Jen kicked off her shoes and seemed to drop six inches. 'I don't suppose you fancy opening the bottle of white that's in the fridge while I go up and change?'

'Will do. Charley has been fast asleep for hours, good as the proverbial gold.'

'That's great. You're a natural. Back in a minute.'

I took the wine from the fridge and located the glasses in only the second cupboard. I poured us both a generous measure and grabbed an extra plate for Jen, just as she re-appeared in black jogging bottoms and a white fleece top.

'Thanks for this, cheers', she said, then raised her glass. She took a long drink and almost dived headfirst into the pizza box.' I helped myself to another slice too.

'So old Zac wasn't up to much.'

'Bit of a creep. Couldn't understand why I didn't want to go back to his room. Trying to bore the pants off me for two hours was an unusual tactic, granted. I'm not even sure I want to write the piece now. I suppose I should, don't want to piss off the editor.'

'You may not have to worry about that. They've sent us copies of the script for the first TV episode.'

'Brilliant. Is it any good?'

'I think it's better, now that I've had a go at it. We need to book some time tomorrow to get your expert touch on the job, but I think it will work. Obviously, my experience in producing a prime time show for a major network is limited.'

'You mean zero?'

'Fair enough.'

'You seem more upbeat than you have been for the last couple of days.'

'You wouldn't have thought that a couple of hours ago. I suppose it was getting my hands on the script and getting some work done that helped. That and reading a story to Charley. That felt good. Like somebody needed me.'

'How was she?'

'She was perfect. I read the story. She fell asleep, and that was it.'

'What about you?'

'I played with matches for a while, but she took them off me and put them back with the knives.'

'Idiot. You know what I mean?' She topped up the wineglasses and took more pizza. 'You still haven't heard from Robbie?'

'No. Nada. Not a word. I think I could cope better if she'd had an affair, or we'd had a big row. It hurt when Cheryl left me, but at least we talked about it, and I accepted things. This feels more like she's been in an accident. Gone. Like a bereavement, I suppose. Actually, no, not a bereavement. If anything, it's worse. At least if she'd been hit by a bus, I'd understand not being able to talk to her. This way, she's choosing not to contact me. She's taken everything we'd worked for, everything we'd planned, and just binned it like an empty wine bottle.'

'It's only been a couple of days. I suppose a lot depends on how bad the trouble with the police is. If she turned up tomorrow and said it had all been a dreadful mistake, you'd take her back in a shot, wouldn't you?'

I sat and thought for a moment.

'You know, I'm not sure I would. This has flattened me so much. I should maybe have listened to you in the first place.'

'How do you mean?'

'You never trusted her. You, more or less, warned me against her. How she would put her dad first, before anything else. You were right. If the police are to be believed, it looks like she was up to her neck in whatever scams and illegal businesses he had on the go.'

'Have the police said what happens next?'

'They're still making their enquiries. On the plus side, Gavin, my solicitor, has managed to get the computers back. I was setting everything up again before I came here tonight.'

'That's promising, surely? They wouldn't let you get back to work if they thought you were guilty of anything.'

'There's still a massive problem.' I took a deep breath before explaining what Rupert had been up to.

'Do the police know about this?'

'We don't think so. I'm starting work tomorrow to try to understand exactly what he's done. That's why I was so desperate to get the kit back. Gavin thinks we should get a clear picture, then confess to the police. At least I should be able to prove I had nothing to do with it. The trouble is if the word gets out, the app is finished. Nobody will use it. We'd have data protection regulators crawling all over us. Big fines, maybe prison. Don't worry, Gavin assures me that you're not at risk.'

'I'm not thinking about me. You must feel awful. Everything you've worked for.'

'There's all your work, too.'

'For which I have been paid, thank you very much.'

'True. At least Robbie couldn't get her hands on that.' Jen thought for a few seconds, swirling the wine in her glass.

'What about the TV deal?'

'I'm not sure. I suppose there is no reason for them to pull out yet. It may be an entirely different story if this all goes public.'

'I suppose it is all a bit shite at the moment.'

'Eloquently put. At least we have pizza and wine.'

'Shall I get the other bottle?'

'Go on then. After all, tomorrow is another day.'

28

I groaned as the alarm went off at seven. It must have been almost one o'clock when I'd left Jen's last night. It had done me a lot of good to talk things through. Jen was proving to be a good friend, as well as an excellent writing partner. Maybe the second bottle wasn't good preparation for today, but I think I needed it. I dragged myself into the bathroom. The flat was freezing. I really must sort out the timer on the heating.

Today was a big day. I needed to trawl through the code for Rupert's little time bombs. I was annoyed at myself. Usually, we would review each other's code as a way of spotting errors. In truth, we were working so quickly; we skimped on that bit, idiot.

The rain stopped somewhere between leaving the shower and heading out of the front door. Maybe my luck was changing. I grabbed some breakfast from the cafe to take away and was soon at my desk. I opened the code for the module that requests bank details and went through line by line but could see nothing out of the ordinary. A second pass had the same result. It was only on the third review that I spotted the extra file being populated with passwords, bank details and answers to the typical security questions asked. In the end, I did what Rupert had suggested and set about writing the module again from scratch. I printed the originals and used a marker to highlight the anomalies, and encrypted the dodgy file.

Spud arrived at just before ten, followed shortly after by Stella.

'Morning, Frankie. I gather you could do with some help,' she said.

'First of all, thank you for coming in on a Sunday, and sorry for screwing up your holiday plans.'

'Don't worry about that. I'm not one for sunbathing. Give me a good book and a roaring fire, and I'm happy. We're planning that for next weekend, so you've got me now. This sort of challenge will be like a nice brief diversion from the stuff I'm into at work at the moment.'

'So, what do you need?' I called Spud across and explained what we were trying to do. We took notes and created the regular Post-it column as Stella talked us through how she needed the data presenting. After half an hour, Spud had a project and was coding immediately. I made sure Stella had access to everything on the system and was happily ensconced at Rupert's desk.

I concentrated on the dodgy module. The office seemed silent, but I figured Stella wouldn't be used to working with the music volume up high. There was no way I was going to disturb her. I've never seen anybody work as hard. She was totally absorbed in what she was doing. I delivered coffee at regular intervals and a salad at lunchtime. She never even looked up when the police arrived and asked me to go with them to the station. It seemed I was being arrested.

At the station, I was allowed to phone Gavin. He told me to

say nothing until he could get there, but warned me it would be a couple of hours. My heart was pounding. Cagney seemed to be busy elsewhere. Casey explained I was being arrested on suspicion of being involved in money laundering and fraudulent accounting. There was no mention of the data that was being stolen. As I declined to be interviewed without my solicitor, they put me in a cell. The place smelt vaguely like grandads and I was terrified. My imagination went into overdrive. What the hell did they think they knew? It made things worse because they'd taken my phone. I couldn't even read. I just sat there, stared at the wall, and felt the panic rising.

Gavin eventually arrived.

'Frankie, sorry it took so long. I was just taking the kids to see my parents when you called, and I couldn't really cancel it. You have my full and undivided attention now. I'm sure we can get you out fairly quickly.'

'Why do you think they've arrested me?'

'I suspect they're just trying to scare you. See if you crack and tell them something.'

'The first bit is certainly working. I've never been so scared in my life. The only thing I can tell them is that I think I've found the dodgy code that Rupert had installed.'

'That's certainly a start.'

'Trouble is, I don't understand how it works. Most of it is straightforward enough, but then there is some really complex stuff. Rupert certainly had some outside help, some Serbian contact.'

'Do you know a name?'

'No, but I'm pretty sure Rupert couldn't have thought of it alone, let alone build it. I'm also pretty sure that he did nothing with the data he stole. I found the file. There are over six thousand bank accounts involved, but he reckons they never had time to sell them. I've moved the files to make sure he can't access them.'

'Right, I think now is the time to talk to the police. You should just answer their questions. Don't volunteer anything just yet. Remember, you're a victim in all this. I think we can convince them. Are you ready?'

'I suppose so. The sooner we do this, the sooner I can go home.'

Gavin banged on the door. A uniformed officer collected us and took us to an interview room. I think it was the same room as last time. Gavin sat beside me as Cagney entered and placed a file on the desk. This time, I was warned that the conversation was being recorded. The rest was a bit of an anti-climax. Not that I'm complaining. Maybe I've watched too many episodes of Line Of Duty, but I expected to be grilled, hauled across the coals. Interrogated until I confessed, not that I'd done anything. None of that happened. Casey simply repeated the questions about the company and the work I did for Dex. I was told not to take a holiday without contacting them first, and we were shown the door.

'What was all that about?' I looked at Gavin for answers.

'It's just part of the dance. I'd say they don't have anything incriminating on you. Still, given that the entire Dexter family's evaporated, they're looking for somebody to blame.'

'So, what happens now?'

'You go home. You work with Stella and hope she comes up with something that can help the police without dropping yourself in it.'

I was absolutely exhausted, so Gavin gave me a lift home. When I switched my phone on, there was a message from Stella.

'Interesting day! Gavin phoned to explain. Hope all is okay with you. Spud has locked up. Plenty to talk about in the morning. Will be in for nine. Get some sleep. Xx'

Typically, after a day like this, I would head straight for the pub. Instead, it was a shower, tomato soup and bed.

29

I must've fallen into a deep sleep, but woke at four o'clock, after dreaming that I was using the wardrobe as a toilet. The brain does remarkable things when you have a full bladder. I hauled myself out of bed and padded to the bathroom. The radiators were banging out the heat. Very useful at this time in the morning. I needed to sort out the timer. The electricity bill had arrived yesterday as well. I added that to my mental to-do list and climbed back into bed. I looked at the clock and realised I hadn't set the alarm. To be ready for Stella, I needed to be in the office before nine. I tried to get back to sleep after fixing the alarm, but was soon replaying yesterday's events. Could I really end up in prison? I tried to push that image from my mind, but it was no good. Any chance of sleep had gone as I was wide awake. I gave in and got up. Five minutes after raiding the freezer for the emergency bread, I was seated with coffee and strawberry jam-covered toast.

The day ahead seemed to all revolve around what, if anything, Stella had found. I needed to get my head into a place where I could concentrate on the upcoming script review, but there was no chance of that with the police thing hovering. Let's hope Stella is as good as Ambrose says she is. At six-thirty, the heating made a click, and the radiators started to cool. I took that as a sign to go into the office.

The office door closing woke me up. I was at my desk, sitting back, and must've fallen asleep. It was Stella.

'Have you been here all night?'

'No. I woke up at stupid o'clock, and couldn't get back to sleep. I came in, rested my eyes for a minute, and I must've nodded off. It's good to see you. I'm really grateful for your help. Thank you.'

'Don't thank me just yet.' She dragged a seat across to sit beside me. 'I haven't exactly found the smoking gun yet, but I have made a start. Basically, as we thought, Robbie was moving money in and out of your accounts. Medium sums. A few hundred quid here and there. The kind of transactions you §probably wouldn't notice or question.'

'To be honest, I never looked at the accounts. I left everything to Robbie. What an idiot.'

'Don't beat yourself up. You trusted her. You were planning to get married. Why would you worry she was up to anything? Anyway, as the weeks went on, the sums got bigger. I need your help to cross-check a list that I've created. It shows all the companies that have paid money into your business. Advertising, sponsorship, that sort of thing. There's a similar list of companies buying IT services from the other business.'

'But we only did work for Dexter's.'

'Precisely. A lot of these payments were in cash. We have to assume the cash was dodgy and needed to be cleaned. The money goes into your account. You buy goods and services from one of Dexter's many companies. The money goes out of your account and into Dexter's and is now clean. They got it from a legitimate source, namely you, and they have the purchase orders to prove it.'

'What sort of stuff have I been buying?'

'Easier to say what you haven't, to be honest. Would you be surprised to know that you've rented storage units in seventeen different locations? How about removal vans with a full crew on eleven occasions in the last four months?'

'I didn't.'

'We know that, but nobody has been questioning the transactions, and the money has gone through the system.'

'Shit.'

'Precisely. At the moment, all I can show is the movement into other accounts. What I can't do is prove where the money has ended up. My guess is that the accounts were off shore. These banks are incredibly secretive and protect their clients.'

'At least we can show the police what's been going on.'

'What good does that do? The police could just say that you knew about the scam. How could it operate without your knowledge and cooperation?'

'You think I'm a dick?'

'No. I think you're guilty of trusting someone you loved. You weren't to know she was pulling off a very sophisticated and successful fraud. What we really need to do is follow the money. Prove that you haven't benefitted from it in any way.' I pulled a crumpled ten-pound note and two twenty pence coins from my pocket.

'That pretty much sums up my net worth at the moment. Hardly points to huge benefits from a scam, does it?'

'Quite, but how do we trace the money? It's not as if we can beat a confession out of a computer system.'

'More's the pity. So, what's the plan?' Stella reached into her briefcase and produced a file of papers.

'We go through the list, and you confirm which firms are genuine and which are part of the scam. At least then we can confirm the scale of what's been happening.'

'OK. I would offer to buy you breakfast, but I appear to be in reduced circumstances!'

'Don't worry about that. Just concentrate on the list.' Stella placed the list between us and made notes as we reviewed the names. Then I sat bolt upright.

'Hang on. You said we can't beat a confession out of a computer system. Maybe I can.' I was pretty animated now.

'What do you mean?'

'I'm an idiot for not thinking of this before. Part of Rupert's treacherous role in all this was to build dodgy code into the app.' Stella nodded and chewed the end of her pen. 'One bit he abandoned was a program that scraped keystrokes from any computer we installed it on. It wrote that information out to a file, to be harvested later. He couldn't disguise the program, and the anti-malware kept picking it up. That's why he abandoned it.'

'How does that help us?'

'Well, he'd been testing it under a version he called "beta". That's the version I installed on Robbie's PC. If it worked, it would've been recording everything she typed: account numbers, sort codes, passwords, the lot. If we can get that file, we could piece everything together. It only occurred to me when you said "beat a confession"'

'Wouldn't the anti-virus software have deleted it?'

'I'm hoping not. Robbie had the check being run as part of her month-end procedures. She said it slowed everything down too much to be doing it every day. Even if we only got a few days' worth of data, there's a chance we could retrieve what we need. Surely it's worth a shot?'

'It sounds incredible. How do you access the file?'

'I don't know yet. I need to trace the software, find out where it was being written to, and hope that we have a backed-up copy of it that Rupert didn't remove.'

'How long will that take?'

'A couple of hours, tops.'

'You get started, I'll go on the coffee and bacon butty run.' Stella hugged me, then headed for the door. 'Brown sauce or tomato?'

'Surprise me. I think my luck is changing!'

'Found it!' Stella had arrived with breakfast, and Spud was beside her.

'Well done. Your reward is a bacon butty with brown sauce,' she said.

'Excellent. Morning Spud. Food first!' We all sat at the table next to my desk and tucked in. This was breakfast number two for me, but I was ready for it. As I pushed the last piece into my mouth, I motioned for everybody to shuffle across. We gathered around my monitor, and I opened the file. I wasn't sure whether or not it was good news. There were records in the file, lots of them. The trouble was, it just looked like random characters.

'Bugger.' Stella put down her coffee and picked up her USB drive.

'Don't be downhearted. It would never say in big letters, "this is what you wanted to know," was it? Here, open the file marked URLs.' I plugged in the drive and quickly found the file. 'This is a list of over a thousand banks from all over the world. Each record contains the URL of its website. Which one of you two fine gentlemen is going to write the program that scans the first file for any matches on the URL?'

Spud reacted first.

'I'll do it.' He started to move towards his desk, but Stella stopped him.

'Hang on a minute. Think about keying in a URL. If you've used it before, the system will guess the rest of it. That way, you only key three or four characters. So, the program needs to be clever, scanning small strings of characters. Then, if it gets a hit, display that bit of the file.'

'Got it. Give me half an hour.' He scurried across the room. I looked at Stella.

'Is this going to work?'

'I hope so. I think it's the best chance we've got. How much data is there?'

'It looks like there are about four weeks, which is lucky. I installed the software on the 24th of the month. The file was last updated on the 22nd of the following month. That was probably when she ran the month-end, and the anti-virus deleted our little worm.'

'While we wait for Spud, I'll get set up. I've got all the bank transactions in and out of your account. With luck, we should be able to spot them on the file.' I appeared to have nothing to do for now. I took the opportunity to call Jen and explain what was happening.

'You sound like you've got your hands full.'

'Just a bit, but we're making progress. I can feel it.'

'Look, you obviously don't have time to work on the script today.'

'The script! I'd totally forgotten that. We've got the meeting with the team tomorrow.'

'Don't worry. I loved the changes you'd made. It really tightened things up. I'll work through the rest today and give it the same treatment where I can. If it's not too much in one week, do you fancy coming over for dinner tonight? We can review what I've done and make sure we're ready for the meeting.'

'The neighbour's curtains'll be twitching. Entertaining again.'

'I think my reputation will cope. Besides, when else can we work together?'

'You're right. What can I bring?'

'Just yourself. Do you eat chicken?'

'I do, and don't call me chicken.'

'Idiot. Six-thirty. Call me if anything goes wrong.'

'I will. See you tonight.' I ended the call just as Spud cheered and raised both hands in the air. I took that as a sign he was ready for us. We all gathered, this time around Stella's desk. Spud pointed to an icon that had appeared. Stella clicked it, and the screen displayed two columns of data. On the left was the list of banks. On the right were the seemingly random characters from my file.

'Just click start.' Spud was looking very pleased with himself. A blue bar gradually made its way down the list of banks. It stopped after about ten seconds. I leaned closer.

'That's ours,' I said, pointing at the highlighted name. Stella used the cursor as a pointer on the right-hand portion of the screen.

'Were you brought up on Smith Lane, by any chance?'

'Yes, I was.'

'First part of the login. Looks like the bank sends a six-digit code to a mobile phone.'

'That's right.'

'Look, there, six digits being entered.' Stella flicked across to the list of bank transactions and positioned the list at the 17th of the month. 'Right, on that day, there was a transfer out of £8600.' She went back to the log and pointed at the screen. 'There "8-6-0-0-0-0" - she'd keyed in the amount. It works.' I was excited, but a bit confused.

'OK. I can see that we can prove that Robbie moved money out of the account, but how do we know where to?'

'This is where we need to get lucky. I use the same bank as you, so I know how this bit works. Making a payment to an account you've used before is done by selecting it from a list —nothing we can do about that. But setting up a new payee means entering all the details. The number of accounts she used, there is every chance that she set up a new one in the weeks that we've got. It's just a matter of finding it. Spud, we need another version of this program. We need to be able to scan for an amount.' Spud went back to his desk and started coding.

'I still don't get it.'

'Just hang on a minute. All will become clear.' Spud was back quickly, apologising as he sat down.

'It's a bit rough and ready, but I figured speed was what you're looking for.' Stella agreed and clicked on the new icon. She arranged the tabs on the screen, so she saw both programs side by side.

'Right. The next transfer out was £12000.' She scanned for the amount. Sure enough, the number was highlighted on the screen. 'OK, if our luck is in, this would be a new account, and we will see it just before the amount in the list.' We scanned the screen but could see nothing that looked like a payee. 'Next on the list. £27,000.' She keyed the digits.

'How could I not know that these amounts were going out of the account?'

'As I said before, you trusted her. There you go, £27000, and the words Baronia Banking Corporation. That's an offshore bank, if I'm not mistaken. Look at the account she's moving the money to.'

'The devious sod.' I couldn't believe it. The account was in the name of Stardust Raincoats.

'Right, I need time to work. I'll make my way through the rest of the file and see if we drop lucky with any more names.'

I went back to my desk and stared across the office at the whiteboard at the far end. Brian used to take the piss, accusing me of just staring into space. I always told him I was thinking. I joked that he should do the running around, and I'd do the thinking. This was how I did it best, staring. I must have been there a while. I had slouched low in my seat, right on the front edge of the padding. My mind wandered. I could do with a holiday. Maybe, when this was all sorted, I could have a couple of weeks away on a beach somewhere. Then again, I was skint. Possibly Stella would be able to somehow retrieve some of the money I'd lost. Even a cheap flight would do, as long as it was warm.

Flight!

Hang on. I pushed myself upright, almost tipping the seat over. I regained a bit of dignity and hunched over my keyboard. I pulled up a copy of the source code for the program Spud had written. Changing the input parameters, I created an empty file and started to type. I trawled the internet, trying as many relevant searches as I could think of. Before long, I had a list with sixty entries on it.

I hit the button and ran the scan, using my new file as input. Bingo! I had a hit, and it was close to the top of the list. The list included every airline I could think of. Robbie had looked at flights with American Airlines. I stared at the keystroke file. The characters MAN jumped out. I'd flown from there many times. It was the code for Manchester airport. The following letters were TZA. Where the hell was that? Tanzania? I did a quick internet search. It was Belize. I copied a chunk of the file out to a document and began highlighting words on the screen. I used the American Airlines website to understand the keystrokes needed to book flights and looked at the highlights on the document. Four surnames but none of them Dexter. Could they have got hold of fake passports in other names? Given Dexter's contacts, the answer was obviously yes.

Stella was still working flat out. I didn't want to disturb her. Instead, I wrote another version of the program. This one was looking for words common in emails such as "regards" and "Thanks". If Robbie had used her work PC for booking flights, who knows what the emails would reveal? I ran the scan. Each time I got a hit, I copied the text into a document. I picked out common phrases and added them to the input file. A quick tweak meant the system ignored any records that had already been processed. In two hours, I'd recreated over a hundred emails that Robbie had written. They were illuminating, to say the least.

Finally, Stella stood up and stretched. I moved across, and we sat on the sofa. Spud wheeled his seat over and joined us.

'Any success?' I asked hopefully.

'You could say that. Robbie was using at least a dozen bank accounts in different names to bounce the money around.'

'Were any of them in Belize?'

Stella raised an eyebrow. 'Yes. What made you ask that?'

'I've been busy myself. I think she booked flights to Belize for her parents, Rupert and herself, but under false names.'

'Any of those names, Morgan by any chance?'

'Yes. What I assumed to be Robbie's parents. How did you know?'

'Several of the accounts are under Morgan.' Spud spoke next.

'Dexter Morgan. It's a character in that TV series.'

'Which TV series?'

'Dexter.'

'Never seen it.' Stella coughed loudly.

'Focus, guys. We can now guess that the money is offshore, probably in Belize, and that the Dexters are there too, or at least have been. What else do we know?' It was my turn.

'Well, I think that their mate, Sir Alan from the council, is up to his eyes in this. I found outgoing emails that thank him for providing several services, for which he was paid very well. I think he sourced the false passports. Never did like him, so it would be nice if we dragged him into it. Do we have enough to go to the police yet?'

'It's certainly a start. The police are better equipped to take this further.'

'Is there any more that we could do?'

'I'll put together a report to help with your statement to the police. It's what, four o'clock now? I'll have it done by lunchtime tomorrow.'

'I'll phone Gavin and see how he wants to tackle this. Stella, how can I thank you for what you've done? You've been brilliant. You too, Spud.'

Stella laughed.

'A trip to Belize to take them out would be nice if you can fix it.'

'Where is Belize exactly?' asked Spud. I was about to waffle a general answer, but Stella rescued me.

'It's just off the bottom of Mexico, in the Caribbean.'

'Sounds nice. Can I come too?' I stood up.

'If we get the money back, we can all go — staff jolly to Belize. Until then, I'm skint, so I suggest we bugger off home for the night. Thanks again.'

I got to Jen's just after six-thirty. When she opened the door, the sound of a screaming child flooded out.

'Somebody sounds very unhappy.'

'Come in. Charley's terrified of spiders, and we just found a monster. To be honest, I'm just as bad. It's probably where she gets it from. Can you rescue two ladies in distress?' The truth was, I was none too keen myself, but I couldn't lose face.

'Where is it?'

'In the kitchen.' I hoped I looked confident as I strode down the hall. Jen almost cowered behind me. Charley clung to her mum's hand. I picked up a glass from the draining board and a sheet of paper from Jen's notepad.

'Right. Where was it last seen?'

'Over there, by the back door.' I stepped across.

'Woah. We're gonna need a bigger glass.' It was, indeed, a monster. Jen quickly swapped the small glass for a pint. I approached carefully and reached out with the glass. The beast saw it coming and set off for the corner of the room. All three of us jumped back. At least two of us screamed. I'd like to say I was the odd one out but… 'Okay. Jen, can you open the back door for me?'

'What are you going to do, chase it out?'

'Very funny.' I lunged again, and this time trapped the monster behind the glass. I slid the paper down between the wall and the glass. 'Voila.' I stepped through the open door and into the back garden.'

'Not there. It'll just come back in. Put it over the fence into next door's garden.'

Bravely, I launched the spider over the fence, carefully checking that the glass was empty before going back to the house. Jen was carrying Charley, who had her arms wrapped tightly around her mum's neck. 'All gone. He won't be back.'

'Promise?' the sobs subsiding.

'I promise.' Charley threw her arms around me in one move, and I carried her back to the living room. Jen followed.

'You just cemented yourself as her hero. You're very brave.' Jen pecked me on the cheek. She smelt of vanilla.

'You didn't see how much I was shaking.'

'I hope you're hungry after all that.'

'Starving, as always.'

'There's steak pie in the oven. Hope it's okay. Technically, it should've come out of the oven five minutes ago, but I wasn't risking it. How about I put madam here to bed, and you open the bottle of red that's next to the fridge?'

'Sounds like a plan.'

'Frankie, will you read me a story?'

How could I refuse? Jen went ahead, and I followed, with

Charley still clinging around my neck. I sat on the tiny stool while Jen supervised teeth cleaning, then she tucked Charley in.

'Be good for uncle Frankie, and go to sleep quickly!' Jen kissed Charley and turned to go. We both pulled a face as Jen made her way back downstairs. Charley giggled and snuggled further down in bed.

'There's no need to be scared of spiders, you know.' Two eyes on the pillow got bigger and rounder. 'Honestly. Some of my best friends are spiders.'

'Really?'

'Really. Would you like me to tell you about them?' Charley nodded. 'Well, when I was not much bigger than you, I met a boy called Ziggy. He could play the guitar. I was very impressed. He came to my house one day with two other friends, called Weird and Gilly. Yes, they are silly names, but I haven't told you the best bit yet. They had friends that were spiders. They came all the way from Mars.' Charley was giggling almost uncontrollably by now. I wasn't too sure where the story was going, but at least she wasn't screaming now. Lowering my voice slightly had the desired effect, and within minutes, she was fast asleep. I slipped out of the bedroom, switching out the light as I went. Jen was in the kitchen.

'Did you just tell my daughter a story about Ziggy Stardust and the spiders from Mars?'

'You weren't meant to be listening.'

'I just hope you didn't mention his god-given ass.'

'Nah, I'll save that for another time.'

'You really are good with her, you know. She rarely takes to people easily.'

'To be honest, I usually avoid kids altogether, but she's great.'

'Here. I opened the bottle. Cheers.'

'Cheers. This smells good. I'd almost forgotten you could cook.'

'I try. I thought we could eat and you tell me what you've been up to, and then I'll let you read the script changes.'

'Fair enough.'

The food was lovely. We chatted easily and were soon at the bottom of the bottle. As Jen opened the second, I filled her in on the day with Stella.

'So, still no word from Robbie.'

'Nothing. I suppose the family is concentrating on staying out of the way of the police.'

'Have you told the police what you've found yet?'

'No. I'm meeting Gavin tomorrow afternoon. Stella should have her report by then. I'm assuming I'll make a statement and hand over the evidence so the police can run with it. Gavin seemed hopeful that they'll see me as a victim instead of a criminal, which would be nice.'

'Let's hope so. Listen, before you get too pissed, we need to go through the script changes. Make sure you're happy with them. I take it you won't be able to make the meeting tomorrow?'

'I must admit I'd forgotten about it.'

'Don't worry. Get the police sorted. I'll go to the meeting and present the changes.'

Jen had printed out two copies of the script. We sat at the kitchen table and read it through.

'This is good. You're much better than me, a proper writer,' I said.

'Don't put yourself down. You set the tone for this. All I did was imitate your style. I think we make a good team. We should maybe think about another project once the yellow raincoat woman has gone.'

'Do you think she's going?'

'I think she's gone, to be honest. Realistically, Robbie was the face of the stories on the website. Without her, we'd struggle to carry on in the same format.'

'I hadn't thought of that. Plus, there's the tie-up with Ruckoats. I wonder what they'll do when they find out what's happened.'

'Again, difficult to base a campaign around a model who's done a runner.'

'True.' I stared at the wine in my glass and saw my reflection looking back. 'Let's kill her.'

'What?'

'Seriously. Why don't we kill her off? The character, not the fraudster. We could go for one last storyline. Make it spectacular, but kill her at the end of it. Think of Shakespeare. The bad guy never wins. We made her an evil character. Let's kill her off and have a bit of fun with it. Maybe torture her a bit.'

'We are still talking about the character, aren't we? Not Robbie.'

'Yes, but I can dream, can't I?'

'What about the TV guys and the advertisers?'

'They'd get used to the idea. Besides, the TV series doesn't have to follow the arc of our stories. There are loads of examples of TV characters that veer away from what happens in the original books. Like you say, we'd then be free to work on other characters. What do you say? Can we kill her?'

'Why the hell not? She's fucking toast! Cheers.' Jen raised her glass.

'Cheers.'

'I've never signed anybody's death warrant before.'

'I should hope not. Remember, it's the character we're killing, not your ex.'

'I know.' I sat quietly for a moment, staring at the glass again. 'It's such a mess.'

'Yes, but you're taking steps forward. It'll be a big relief to speak to the police tomorrow. Let them do the heavy lifting then.'

'That one will be a doddle. Gavin will do most of the work. It's breaking the news to Caroline I'm not looking forward to.'

'Just come clean. Tell her everything. I'm sure she'll be fine.'

'Or she'll sue me for every penny I've got.'

'Look on the bright side. That's not exactly a lot.'

'Very true. More wine?'

'Go on then. I shouldn't but, then again, I've never sat and planned a murder before. How should we do it?'

'Now you're getting into it.'

30

'Hi Frankie, it's Caroline.'

'Hi, Caroline. I was just about to call you.' I was annoyed with myself that I'd picked up the phone without checking who was calling.

'Pleased to hear it. It's been a few days since I left a voicemail.'

'Yes, sorry, been hectic here.'

'So I gather. Look, I hear rumours. Are they true?'

'I suppose it depends what you've heard.'

'Why don't you tell me? Then we know it's the truth.'

'Okay. You've probably heard that Robbie has disappeared, along with the rest of her family. They are being investigated by the police for all sorts, money laundering, drugs, people trafficking. I couldn't believe half of what the police have been saying.'

'So you've been in touch with the police?'

'Yes. Actually, they thought I was involved but, so far, I've not been charged. My solicitor is pretty confident we can prove I'm a victim of all this.'

'Victim?'

'Before she left, Robbie emptied all of my bank accounts. I've lost everything. In fact, it's worse than that, as I have a builder screaming at me for unpaid bills and an eye-watering mortgage on a property I can't now afford.'

'So it wouldn't be a good time for me to tell you we are on the verge of pulling out? The marketing guys are very twitchy. They seem to be split down the middle and looking for me to make a call. On the one hand, we said we'd go for the bad girl image. On the other hand, there's bad and bad. I hate to kick you while you're down, but I'm leaning towards ending things. There's a certain actress that's been spotted wearing the yellow coat, and we may switch to her.'

I took a deep breath. 'How would you feel about one last dramatic story? After that, we shake hands and go our separate ways.'

'Go on, I'm listening.'

'What if we killed her off? Big dramatic finish but a definite ending. Bad girl gets her comeuppance sort of thing. We could have her bumped off by the bad guys.'

'I'm not sure that bullet holes and a blood-spattered yellow raincoat are quite the image we were looking for, to be quite honest.'

'Maybe you're right. Okay, what if she wasn't wearing the coat when it happens? What if the reason she gets killed is that she wasn't wearing her trusty coat?'

'I like that message more, I have to admit.'

'Just off the top of my head. What if she gave the coat to a well-known actress? What if that well-known actress was then cast in a new TV series called The Woman In The Yellow Raincoat? The series could pick up where our website ends.'

'If only we had a TV series.'

'Would you believe me if I said we have a script meeting with a production company this afternoon? The draft of the first episode is up for review. I suspect we could change it, especially if I could go to them with a major new sponsor lined up?'

'How much were you thinking?'

'I've got no idea. Why don't you talk to your marketing team, and I'll speak to the producer. We can arrange a meeting if everybody gives it the thumbs up.'

'Excellent. Give me twenty-four hours.'

'Great. I'll call you tomorrow.' I hung up. I couldn't believe how well that went. Had you told me ten minutes ago that I would be pitching this to our producer, I'd have laughed at you. Sometimes I think I could get the hang of this life lark.

Gavin met me in the reception area of the police station. I handed over the report from Stella and all the stuff that I had pulled together. He flicked through it.

'This is good.'

'Good enough to convince them I'm innocent?'

'Should be. The false name is an excellent find. Couple that with the flights to Belize. They should be able to track them down.'

'Isn't Belize one of these places without extradition to the UK?'

'Apparently not. The government has no formal treaty, but they've kicked people out if the evidence is strong enough. Maybe that's what Dexter was thinking, too. It could be his downfall.'

We were called through by Casey and taken to the now-familiar interview room. Cagney was already sitting at the table, and he told us to sit.

'I believe you have something for us?' I handed over the two files.

'The blue folder contains a report put together by a forensic accountant. The yellow one has dozens of emails taken from Robbie Dexter's PC.'

'How did you come across evidence from the PC when we have it in a storage room here at the station?'

'We have a remote system that automatically backs up everything on my systems and those at Dexter's. Also, I became aware that Dominic Dexter had installed malicious code as part of a version of our TWITYR app. This version was never released to the public but was installed on Robbie's PC. It was recording keystrokes made at the computer and sending the data to a file.'

'So you admit to installing illegal software?' Gavin leaned forward.

'My client played no part in either the creation or use of that software. It was done entirely without his knowledge.' I was nervous about contradicting my solicitor, but I wanted to be totally honest.

'Actually, I was the one who installed it on the PC, but inadvertently. Robbie wanted to use the app, and I installed what I believed to be the latest version.'

'So if you had nothing to do with the malware, how did you come to access the information?'

'I received a message from Rupert, Dominic, in which he confessed and explained what he'd done.'

'We found no such message on your equipment when we examined it.'

'The message was encrypted. You wouldn't' have been able to access it without a password.'

'And you knew the password?'

'I worked it out. It was Ziggy. We played Ziggy Stardust a lot at work.'

'Well, I commend your taste, but you didn't think to mention this last time we spoke to you?'

'I only received the file after I'd spoken to you.'

Gavin interjected again.

'Look, my client has been able to piece together very

incriminating emails. He has uncovered the false names used by the Dexter family to evade capture. Frankie has traced the accounts that the money was moved to. He has even typed it all up for you in an elegant report. Short of going out and arresting them for you, I suggest he has done enough to convince you he is a victim in all of this, not a perpetrator.' Cagney looked stunned. I almost wet myself. Nobody moved for what seemed like ages. Cagney broke the silence.

'For all we know, this is simply another of your works of fiction. How do we know that what you're saying is true?' I pointed to the file.

'Everything is documented in there. How we came to have the data, how we interpreted it, copies of the software and files are included on the thumb drive in the folder. It explains everything.'

'Very well. I will get my team to go over this with a fine-tooth comb. We'll follow up on any leads. If, and only if, we believe the evidence is real, then we may accept your innocence. For now, I suggest you leave the detective work to the professionals.'

For once, I bit my tongue. I'd just handed the idiot enough evidence to nail them, and he says all that. Twat.

Gavin dropped me off back at the office. There was no sign of Spud. Still, I wasn't paying him at the moment, so that was fair enough. It was too late to make it to Leeds in time for the script review. Instead, I called the producer.

'Jason? Hi, it's Frankie Dale?'

'Frankie, hi. Are you in the building?'

'No, I'm afraid I won't be able to make it. Jen will be there, and she's more than capable of representing us both.'

'I've no doubt.'

'Have you got a minute? I need to bring you up to date.'

'Sounds ominous. I'm all ears.'

Over the next twenty minutes, I told him everything about Robbie, the money, the police — everything. I finished with fingers actually crossed when I came to the bit about killing off the main character in his brand new series.

'Wow. You don't mess about, do you? But, not to put too fine a point on it. Where the fuck does that leave our production? A dead lead character before we even start?'

'This is where it gets interesting, I think. What if I were to say we could pivot the story to a new lead character who inherits the yellow raincoat? Even better, it comes with a ready-made sponsor and a big name, lead actress, thrown in.'

'You said the magic word with sponsor. Tell me more.'

I did. I stressed Caroline hadn't signed up to it yet, and we hadn't even spoken to the actress, but in principle, were they interested?

'You've got some balls, I'll give you that. Let's set up a meeting with Caroline to start with. We'll go ahead with the review as if we never spoke. I don't want to change direction until we know it is a goer.'

'Thanks, Jason. I'll set something up.'

I sat back and spun around in my seat. Anything else for me to sort out today? Peace in the Middle East? Put Oasis back together? Bigger Curly-Wurlys? I'd never actually had a Curly-Wurly, giant or otherwise, but my dad always brought it up every Christmas. Why are Curly-Wurlys shrinking? I always told him it was something to do with climate change, but if I could fix it for him, I may as well, now that I was on a hot streak.

I hit play on Ziggy and filled the room with music. I wanted to enjoy the next couple of hours as much as possible. After all, it's not every day you get to plot a murder. Unless you're a professional murderer. Is that a job? I suppose that applies to assassins, but I don't suppose you get to do it every day. I realised I was getting off track. It's often said that the most challenging bit of writing is actually making a start. Just staring at an empty page can be intimidating. The temptation to check social media, or tidy your sock drawer, suddenly proves critical to your very existence. This is particularly stupid when you're either writing for pure pleasure or probably more so when it's for financial gain. I made a start by typing 'How to murder the woman in the yellow raincoat.' Then I grabbed my jacket and headed for the cafe to get coffee and some cake before they closed.

As I walked down the street, I toyed with the idea of heading straight to the pub. I fancied settling into the corner of the bar and talking bollocks with Ambrose all night. Ildiko waved from the front window of the cafe. I made a snap decision in favour of the cake and went inside to order. I could always go to the pub once I'd planned my murder.

Back at the office, the combined rush of sugar and caffeine triggered a burst of energy. It turns out I had quite a grisly imagination when it came to murder. I made a surprisingly long list of possible options. Then it hit me. I was planning to get rid of the character based on the woman that, until a few days ago, I was planning to spend the rest of my life with. I stared at the computer screen as tears streamed down my face. How had it got to this? How could Robbie do this to me? To us? How could she go from picking out curtains to emptying bank accounts? What had I done to trigger it?

The phone ringing snapped me out of my thoughts. It was Jen.

'Hi Jen, how did it go?'

'It went well. They were more than happy with the edits we'd made. Jason was a bit mysterious, though. He came into the session just before the end and gave a strange speech about things developing and watching this space. Any idea what's going on?'

'It all happened very quickly. I spoke to Caroline about

killing off Daisy. She was okay with it. In fact, she was more than okay. Her marketing team was looking at getting some actress involved in a campaign. I managed to sell the idea that we could tie everything up by introducing a new character, who takes on the yellow raincoat, a bit like Dr Who regenerating. We could write that into both the online version and the TV series. If we can also get the actress cast in the role, Caroline may be interested in sponsoring the series.'

'Wow! That's a win all round! Is it likely to come off?'

'It's all down to Caroline and Jason to do a deal. I'm hoping to set up a meeting in the next couple of days.'

'Assuming that comes off, what would you want to do with the online stories?'

'To be honest, I think we are in the hands of the gods. If we can get the clean software out as an update to the app, and nobody finds out about the data, I think we could carry on. On the other hand, if word gets out about what Rupert did, we'd be up shit creek. In the meantime, I've been planning how to kill Daisy. Could you take a look and start to pull her final instalment together?'

'I'll get on to it first thing tomorrow. Right now, I need to get to the writer's workshop, although I would give anything for a soak in the bath and an early night.'

''The workshop. Are you okay if I give it a miss?'

'Of course. I'll speak to you tomorrow.'

'Bye Jen, speak tomorrow.'

31

Things seemed to happen quickly over the next couple of days. Caroline and Jason agreed on a deal for Ruckoats to sponsor the new show. Jen and I worked up the final instalment featuring Daisy. We got approval from the others that they were happy with the story. Joe came up with a highly complex task that involved ads placed in newspapers over four successive days. The only way to solve the clue was to have access to all the ads.

Spud and I pushed the boat out as far as social media was concerned. Rumours of the storyline spread like wildfire. We stoked the fires and spread lots of stories and counter rumours. We seeded misinformation far and wide. The newspapers got involved and started to run competitions to see if any readers could guess where the story was going next. Even our old friends at the 'One Show' did a piece on us. Excitement grew to a fever pitch. We'd launched the newly updated software, and around half of our three million readers had downloaded it. New readers were coming in every day, trying to catch up, and find out what all the fuss was about.

The first part of the clue appeared in The Times. Sales exploded, and their servers struggled to keep up with demand for the online version. We'd done deals with three other papers, which meant they were actually paying us to advertise with them. We could monitor numbers for who had solved the first part of the clue. Almost forty thousand by the end of the first day. By the time the second clue came out, we were over two hundred thousand and climbing all the time.

All the extra publicity pushed us to another two million downloads of the app. The New York Times described us as a publishing phenomenon. To say we were excited doesn't come close to the atmosphere in the office. Jen had joined us for the day. Charley was with her gran but had contributed a picture of a woman in a yellow raincoat, and it had pride of place on the wall. Joe and Ambrose joined us for a quick video conference to share the moment. They didn't stay long, as Joe's business had gone through the roof with the increased traffic. We were trending on Twitter, and there was a fevered discussion on the first of the clues.

Caroline had paid the latest instalment of our deal, so I had proper cash at long last. I blew some of it on bottles of champagne. The local press was there to record the opening of the bottles and sample the atmosphere. Never has hatching a murder been so much fun. Joe even decided later that he'd made enough money for the day, and he and Ambrose joined Stella in the office. Needless to say, Ziggy on repeat provided a soundtrack for the celebrations. We all joined in whenever Starman blasted out, the renditions getting more exuberant as the day continued.

At just after five o'clock somebody, it may have been me, started the chant of 'pub, pub, pub', and a huge cheer erupted. It was only when that died down that we noticed the latest visitor peering around the door. It was Cagney. Casey, as ever, hovered just behind him.

'Sorry to interrupt, you're obviously busy. Do you think we might have a word?'

I called out to the rest to set off for the pub, and I would join them soon. Somebody cut the music, and the office suddenly fell quiet. When everybody had left, Cagney moved closer.

'I didn't mean to break up the party, but I thought you would be interested to know that the Dexter family has been detained by customs officers in Spain. They were trying to enter the country on the false documents that you pointed us towards.'

'So what happens now?'

'The two of us are flying out to Spain this evening to interview them. The rest depends on what they have to say, but if what you've told us is true, they'll be arrested and flown back to face trial.'

'Do you need anything from me?'

'Not at the moment. It was just a courtesy call to let you know that we've got them.'

'I don't suppose they had a big suitcase full of my money?'

'If only. I'll leave you to join your friends. Have a good evening.'

They left. I felt a bit strange, sitting in the silent office amongst the debris of champagne bottles and plastic cups. I should be elated that the Dexters had been caught. In truth, the woman I'd fallen in love with was being held in a cell in Spain. Was that a cause for celebration or something to make me feel extremely sad? Should I go to the pub and celebrate or go home and feel miserable? I decided to compromise and go to the pub, but feel a bit sad on the way there. It's what she would've wanted.

I found the others in the snug at The Crown. Ambrose waved me across. He'd already got me a pint.

'What was all that about?' he asked.

'They've caught Robbie and family trying to get into Spain.'

'That's good news, surely? It's just that your face doesn't seem to think so.'

'It's just the thought of her, sitting in a cell in a foreign country. We were meant to be getting married soon.'

'Yes, but she then decided to rob you blind. Kind of trumps the marriage thing in my book.' Stella stuck her elbow in his ribs.

'Does that mean you'd ditch me if I robbed you?'

'No, my sweet. My love for you would conquer any loss.' Nice recovery. 'Besides, I'm skint, whereas Frankie had just made half a million.'

Own goal, and another dig in the ribs from Stella. Spud was fiddling with his phone. Then he spoke.

'It's on the BBC news site. Yorkshire family, suspected of massive fraud, detained in Spain. The family were attempting to enter the country using false passports. UK detectives are believed to be flying out to interview them.'

Joe asked the obvious question.

'Does this mean you'll get your money back?'

Stella answered.

'It's a complicated business. We'd have to prove that Frankie's money wasn't made through criminal activities. The trail was so complicated, it's difficult to tell what were real transactions and which were fake. It's possible but could take years in the courts and cost a fortune if you lost.'

'That's a sobering thought', I said. 'Who wants another drink?' Joe, Ambrose, Stella and Spud all nodded, but Jen put her hand over her orange juice.

'Not for me, thanks. I need to go after this and pick Charley up from Mum's.'

'Okay. We probably need to start work sketching out the

new story arc for the TV series. Are you free tomorrow morning?'

'Sure. My place, as usual, ten o'clock?'

'Great. I'll see you tomorrow.'

Jen drained her drink, said her goodbyes to everybody, and I watched as she headed for the door. Brenda took the order and told me to sit down. She said she'd bring the drinks over. When I got back, the conversation had moved on to favourite holiday destinations. I thought of the holiday with Cheryl in Spain. We'd rented an old farmhouse just outside Hondarribia and had a wonderful couple of weeks. Now Spain was where Robbie was sitting, alone in a cell. I found it difficult to settle back into the rhythm of the night out. The others were getting louder as the drink was consumed. I could feel myself getting quieter. It was Stella that noticed and came to sit beside me.

'Are you okay?'

'Take no notice of me. Just a few mixed feelings.'

'It must be difficult. You obviously still care about Robbie.'

'I do, probably more than I should. She used me and scarpered with all my money.'

'There is that. At least you got the chance to kill off her character. Not many get to do that.'

I laughed at the thought.

'But are we killing the goose that lays the golden eggs? I can't see anything in the future being as successful as TWITYR.'

'Don't forget that success was down to you and Jen. You make a great team. You can do it again. The TV work is exciting, isn't it?'

'True.'

'And they've unfrozen the bank accounts, so at least you can cash in properly on the final episode. Look, why don't you get an early night? I'm sure things will look a lot brighter in the morning.' I put my empty glass on the table and prepared to leave.

'You're right.' As it turned out, she was wrong. Very wrong.

32

Joe called very early the following morning. It was dark, and I fumbled on the bedside table for my phone.

'Morning Joe, do you never sleep?'

'Been out with Spud and his mates. Just got in. You need to put the BBC news on. There's a bit in the local reports you need to see.'

'Can't you just tell me, and I can go back to sleep?'

'No. I think you need to see this. Hurry up. It'll be on again in the next few minutes.'

I got out of bed and made my way to the kitchen. It was cold. Fucking heating timer. I flicked on the kettle and TV. I just had time to make coffee before the local report. They led with the story of the arrests in Spain, then cut to an interview with Casey on some ornate looking building's steps. He waffled on a bit, then the following sentence made my blood run cold.

'The arrests were made possible by the IT firm that wrote the software for the Woman In The Yellow Raincoat online fiction site. The fact that it recorded keystrokes from the user's computer led directly to us intercepting the false names in use by the family. Police officers in Yorkshire then tracked the family to Belize in Central America and finally to a flight to Spain.'

The monumental bell-end. Not only claiming credit for what I did, but dropping us right in the shit. Everybody now knew about the illegal software. The fallout was quick to start. Twenty minutes later, I got a call from a reporter. No comment. As it was still early, I texted Gavin. He rang back immediately.

'I've seen it.'

'What do we do?'

'You say nothing to anybody. I'll draft a statement for the press. I'll point out that the software was inserted without your knowledge by a member of the Dexter family. It was never deployed as part of the standard app, and only one PC was affected. As we talked about, the biggest risk is that you're seen as guilty by association. The public sees you as dodgy and deletes the app.'

'What's the legal position if that happens?'

'You're fucked.'

'Thought so.'

'Leave it with me for now. I'll get something out ASAP.'

I thought about going back to bed and ignoring today, but my stomach was churning so much, I knew I wouldn't be able to sleep. Maybe it wouldn't be that bad? Gavin would get the story out that nobody was affected, and people would continue to use the app. People would be supportive, see me as a victim in all of this. Support so far had been unbelievable. Why would it change now? I opened Twitter. Shit! TWITYR was trending again. This time not so positively. The politest had already deleted the app. The not polite ones ranged from foul-mouthed rants to suggestions that life in prison would be too good for me.

The phone flashed again — the same reporter. I declined

the call. A minute later, I had a new voicemail. It was the reporter, wanting me to put my side of the story. I was tempted to call him back, but decided to resist and wait for Gavin. The front door intercom rang, and I almost jumped out of my skin. It was the same reporter, only now he was actually on my doorstep. I looked down at the street. Sure enough, there was a small gaggle of reporters with microphones and coffee cups. I was attracting the paparazzi! I needed to get out, but didn't fancy going through that lot. Then I remembered, there was a fire escape at the back of the building. I grabbed my jacket and laptop bag and headed for the door.

The fire exit had a prominent notice saying only to be used in case of an emergency. I figured this was an emergency and pushed on the bar. The door swung open. I expected some sort of alarm, but there was nothing. I managed to close the door again and clambered down the steps into the yard. This was the first time I'd been here, but there was a gate in the far corner of the very high wall. I headed for it and emerged onto the street, almost opposite The Crown. All that time living there, and I never realised I had a shortcut to the pub. It's amazing what you learn in a crisis. I headed up the street without any clear plan of where to go.

The phone came to my rescue. It was Jen, inviting me for coffee. She'd seen the news and thought, I may need somewhere to hide — what a clever woman. Five minutes later, I was sitting in the comfortable, tiny kitchen with homemade chocolate brownies and strong black coffee. Jen joined me at the table and put her head on one side.

'How are you coping?'

'I'm angry more than anything. I did nothing wrong. It was bloody Rupert.'

'Any idea what we're going to do?'

'Not a clue, to be honest. Gavin is working on a statement

for the press, but I suspect the damage is done. The app is seen as something that is stealing passwords and bank details.'

'How do you feel about being in the public eye?' I looked at her as if she'd fallen out of a tree.

'It's a bit shit at the moment, to be honest.'

'Sorry, I don't mean now, this minute, with everything that's happening. I mean generally. When you were doing the TV and radio stuff. How did it make you feel?'

'It was exciting, at first. Something new.'

'What about when that wore off?'

'It was a pain in the arse, to be fair. I missed being at home, and it was exhausting, dashing from one place to another.'

'Is it fair to say that you'd be much happier sitting in the pub, with Ambrose and Joe, taking the piss and hitting your head on the beam?'

'Apart from the beam bit, yes, I suppose I would.'

'Then why don't we kill you off?' Now she was worrying me. 'I mean, we killed off Daisy. The app was coming to an end. Why can't you just tell everybody to fuck right off and walk away?'

'It sounds attractive apart from two points. Firstly, I may actually be prosecuted for this. There's so much work to do to convince the police that I'm the victim. Secondly, what would I do for an income?'

'Well, I can't do a lot about the police, but like you say, you did nothing wrong. The income bit, I may have a plan. You said yourself, now there's money in the account from the latest payment from Caroline. You could live on that for several months.'

'A chunk of that is yours, don't forget.'

'Fair enough, but I have learned a lot from the last few months. I love writing, and I think I'm quite good at it.'

'You're more than good.' Jen held up her hand to cut me

off.

'Second, I would hate the kind of profile that you've had in that time. I've had the best of both worlds. I get to embellish and polish the ideas you come up with, but stay completely anonymous. Nobody has a clue who I am. I get to close that door at night, and it's just Charley and me. I adore that I can do a job that I love, make a decent living, and put Charley first. What I'm saying is, I think you might just enjoy that anonymity as well.'

'But isn't it too late? My name will always be attached to "that bloke that stole passwords and bank details", assuming I avoid prison.'

'You're not going to prison. You did nothing wrong. As for the name, kill it off. Become anonymous again.'

I started to protest about it not being possible, but the hand came up again. My god, she was good at that.

'We write well together. What I'm suggesting is we write as a partnership under a completely new name. We invent a persona, a name, even a backstory for a writer. It's been done before. We wouldn't be the first. We've already got contacts like Jason for breaking into TV.'

'But the writing teams would know who we were.'

'Forget writing teams. The script that we came up with together was far better than anything they produced. Anyway, as you would say, that's detail. In principle, are you up for killing Frankie Dale and reinventing yourself?' I sat back and had a slurp of coffee. My heart was pounding. Eventually, I leaned forward again.

'In principle, I'm intrigued by what you're saying. I do have two conditions.' Jen nodded and looked at me inquisitively. 'First, I get to have the last brownie.' Jen broke off a corner for herself before pushing the plate to me. 'Thank you. Second, I get to pick a really cool name.'

'As long as it's not Mac De La Riviere, we have a deal.'

'What's wrong with Mac De La Riviere?'

'I'll take the brownie back if you're not careful.'

'Okay. Let me think about it for a bit.' It was a big step. Throughout all this, I'd assumed I was going to be famous. I got a real kick out of seeing my face on the telly. On the other hand, being Frankie Dale was a bit shit at the moment. I could simply walk away from all the hassle, let it go, just become anonymous. What was the most important to me, being famous or earning a living doing something I really enjoy? Creating something. That was the key, and working with Jen made all that relatively easy. 'Let me get this straight. We're talking writing under a nom-de-plume?'

'Get you with the French. Yes. Being anonymous.'

'Good, cos the other way sounds a bit murdery and painful, to be honest. In that case, I'm in. Frankie's gone. Mac lives.'

'Not Mac.'

'Spoilsport. Can I make a list of names?'

'You can make a list of names. You can even use Charley's crayons if you want.'

'Ta. I might just do that.' I finished the brownie and looked hopefully at the coffee pot for a refill.

I phoned Gavin to tell him the plan.

'Before you make any big decisions, let me tell you what's happened so far today, and it's only what? 1.30?'

'I take it you've been busy?'

'You could say that. The press release has gone out. I tried to get hold of you to approve it, but you weren't answering. I'll send you a copy now, so at least you know what you've said. The other thing that happened was that your former business partner has been in touch with the police.'

'Brian Docherty? Is he sticking the boot in?'

'On the contrary. Mr Docherty has made a statement to the

effect that Dexter tried to get him to put similar software onto the council's planning system. Apparently, he had the co-operation of the head of the planning committee in loading it up. Mr Docherty refused. They had a huge row about it, and he refused to work with Dexter in the future. All of which has convinced the police, you are indeed a victim in this and are no longer under investigation.'

'Good old Brian. Who would've thought that he would come to the rescue?'

'I don't think you're out of the woods just yet. Public opinion was pretty hostile. Why not see how the next couple of days pans out? The press may take a different stance when Mr Docherty's statement gets out. Keep your head down, but try to keep it business as usual. Sleep on it. Come to my office at 2 o'clock tomorrow. We can talk about it then.'

'I will. Thanks for your help, Gavin. Oh, before you go. You said Brian mentioned the head of planning, Sir Alan wotsit. What's happening to him?'

'I believe he is assisting the police with their enquiries.'

'Good. Never liked him. See you tomorrow.'

Jen had made more coffee, and I helped myself. I looked at the cupboard.

'Don't even think about asking for more brownies. You'll be hyper enough with the coffee, and you won't eat your tea!' She had a point.

'Could you hear the news from Gavin?'

'I got the gist, yes. I think its good advice. Keep your head down today, see how things shape up, then look again tomorrow.'

'What about the reporters outside the flat? I can't face going through that lot to get home.'

'Stay here. I'll make up the spare room. Charley would love to have a friend sleepover.'

'I don't know what to say.'

'Just say yes, and promise not to sneak into the brownie cupboard.'

'I promise. Thanks, Jen. I don't know how I would cope without you these days.'

'Don't mention it, just come up with a better name than Mac De La Riviere.'

'How about Vince Taylor?'

'That's an interesting choice. No doubt you'll have some very clever reason for choosing it, but, do you know what? I don't need to know. From now on, I'm Vince Taylor.'

'And I'm Vince Taylor or at least half of him. That's one thing we are changing, no arguments. The split is fifty-fifty, agreed?'

'Agreed. Who is Vince Taylor?'

'I am Vince Taylor.'

'So am I. Right, I'm off to make up the spare room, then I need to pick up Charley. Make yourself at home, apart from the brownies.'

I nodded and reached for my laptop. I had some research to do.

'You're in danger of becoming a bad influence on me,' said Jen later that evening.

'How do you mean?'

She glanced at the second glass of red that I'd just poured for her. I suppose we had been drinking more than usual. I went to pick both glasses up.

'I could just pour yours into mine, save you from yourself.'

'Don't you dare! Give it here.'

We chinked glasses and settled back on the sofa. Charley was safely in bed, story done, and very pleased that Uncle Frankie was staying over. To be honest, Uncle Frankie was quite pleased, too. After all the upheaval, Jen was a genuine friend. I felt better just spending time with her. She put her head on one side and looked at me.

'You didn't answer my question.'

'What was the question?'

'You know what it was. I was only gone five minutes to check on Charley.'

'It was a hard one. Can't we start with football as a specialist subject? Even geography, but not chemistry. I'm crap at chemistry. We had double chemistry straight after PE. The lab was on the third floor, and I was always so knackered when I got there I just sat at the back in a sweaty heap.'

'A lovely picture, but you, sir, are avoiding the question. What are you looking for out of life?'

I sighed and took a sip of Rioja.

'I suppose I thought I had it all sussed. Marry Robbie, make loads of money, become a big writer — sorted.'

Jen smiled and said, 'How's that working out?'

'Ouch.'

'What about kids? Are they on your list? You'd make a wonderful dad.'

'I suppose I'd always assumed kids would be part of it, but, as the years have gone on, that's looking less likely.'

'You seem to have ruled Robbie out of the picture.'

'Seems like a long way back, to be honest.'

I took another drink and watched the flames on the gas fire in silence. It didn't feel awkward. It felt comfortable.

'I want to put things right with my dad, too.'

I told Jen the complete story about the fire, the scars, how Dad blamed me and the gulf that had opened up between us. By the end of it, I was blinking back the tears.

'Sorry, need the loo.'

When I got back, I was over the top cheerful.

'So, enough about me. What about you? Goals and aspirations are your chosen subjects. Go.'

'I think you know most of it. Charley is the focus, has to be, but, I suppose, being creative is important. I'm determined to make a success of being Vince Taylor for a start,' said Jen.

'Money important?'

'I don't think money makes you happy. I think the absence of money can make you unhappy, but it's not something that drives me. If I can keep a roof over Charley's head and pay the leccy bill, a few essentials, I'll be happy.'

'What about things like good wine, holidays, shiny things?'

'Obviously, they come under the heading of essentials.'

'Obviously.' We raised our glasses. 'What about travel? Where would you really like to visit?'

Jen swirled the last of her wine before reaching for a refill.

'Empire State Building.'

'Sleepless In Seattle by any chance?' Jen looked at me and laughed.

'Am I that obvious?'

'Not at all. I'm just very clever. It's also on your DVD shelf.'

'It was our favourite film. We must've seen it a dozen times.'

'We?'

'Sean. Charley's dad. You'd have liked him. A similar sense of humour.'

She turned away. It was her turn to stare at the fire, suddenly quiet. I could see a single tear rolling slowly down her cheek.

'Jen. Are you OK?'

She nodded and reached out to the coffee table for a tissue.

'I'm sorry. Just ignore me.'

'No, don't be daft.'

'It just gets to me occasionally.'

We sat quietly for a few moments. Jen seemed lost in her thoughts, and I didn't have a clue what to say. Then she took a deep breath and spoke very quietly.

'Cancer. I was three months pregnant when he started getting headaches. He eventually went to the doctor, but it was too late for them to do much. He died two weeks after Charley was born.'

'Christ, Jen, I'm so sorry.' Another tear escaped, and I reached out and covered her hand with mine. She squeezed it tightly, and we just sat like that. It was as if she was clinging to her life. After a few minutes, I sensed Jen's breathing was slowing, and her hand relaxed. I gently started to pull my hand away, but she tightened her grip briefly. We sat like that for a while. Silently, she lifted her hand and gently kissed the back of mine before busying herself by opening another bottle of wine.

'Fancy a film?'

I shrugged. 'Yeah, sounds great.'

I smiled as Jen went to the DVD shelf. She turned before opening the case.

'Could we watch this?'

'Perfect.'

'No laughing when I cry.'

'I can't promise, but I'll try.'

Five minutes into Sleepless In Seattle, Jen shuffled along the sofa and moved my arm around her shoulders. She snuggled in close, and we watched the film in silence. There was a little bit of sobbing at one point, but I think I got away with it.

33

Gavin welcomed me to his office with a firm handshake.

'Come in, sit down. How are you feeling?'

'I was okay until I walked in here. Solicitor's offices always give me the willies,' I said.

'If I'm honest, same here.'

'That must make the job interesting.'

'I think it's because it feels like walking into the headmaster's office at school. I've never told anybody that before, so keep it as our little secret.'

'Right you are. So, what news from the police?'

'Actually, I've just got off the phone with Cagney. He confirmed that all four Dexters have been charged. They've thrown the book at the old man, a list of changes as long as your arm.'

'What about Robbie?'

'Almost as bad, I'm afraid. False accounting, money laundering, VAT fraud, the lot. Dominic and Mrs Dexter have lesser charges relating to aiding and abetting.'

'What about Sir Alan?'

'The investigation is ongoing but looks like all manner of

corruption going back years. However, the good news is that you, my friend, have been completely exonerated. No charges. You will remain a free man.'

I allowed myself a slight grin.

'That's fantastic.'

'I take it the press has backed off a little?'

'It looks like it. Jen, my business partner, put me up last night. I called at home a couple of hours ago for a change of clothes, and the reporters had all gone. I was so pleased when it rained last night. Hope they all got piss wet through.'

'What about the fallout from the bad publicity? How's that been?'

'Funny you should ask. That's what I wanted to talk to you about.' I told him about the plan to wind up the company and for us to become Vince Taylor. Gavin listened intently. I pulled some papers from my laptop bag.

'This is a bank statement as of this morning. As you can see, there is almost forty grand that has come in from contract payments that were due over the last few days. There is more to come. Jen and I stayed up half the night discussing this. We want you to take over as administrator for the company. We would like to be paid ten thousand pounds each to relinquish all rights as owners of the company. The last episode of the story is due to be published tomorrow. It could take a few weeks for any stragglers to work through the clues. At the end of that time, we'd like you to seek offers from newspapers and magazines, to publish the entire story without clues, more like a conventional book. After that, you should wind up the company. Any money left after deducting your fees should be given to two charities, the local hospice and cancer research. Any residual rights should be assigned to the hospice. If they can make more money from it in years to come, that would be great. Does that sound doable?'

'Obviously, I can make that happen. You do realise you'd

be giving up substantial financial rewards?'

'Yes, but the anonymity will be worth it. To be honest, the TV company will deal with us from now on as Vince Taylor. They have already said they'd be interested in hearing any other script ideas we've got. I've already started sketching out a few rough thoughts. The cash that we want to take now will be enough to live on for the next few months. I've put the barn conversion on the market this morning, and the estate agent is confident it will sell quickly, at the price I'm asking.'

'You seem to have it all worked out very nicely.'

'I'm thinking of giving it a go, this being an adult lark. See how it pans out.'

Actually, it seemed to pan out reasonably well. I spent Christmas Day with Jen and Charley. I'm not sure who was most excited, but one of us received an original copy of Electric Warrior. So Santa is a T. Rex fan. Who knew?

As winter moved towards spring, a dark cloud still hung overhead. I was due to give evidence at Robbie's trial. The prospect terrified and upset me in equal measures. Just the thought of having to stand up in court made my legs go weak. In truth, I still had mixed feelings where Robbie was concerned. I'd thought she was the one, the love of my life. Together forever, as the great Rick Astley said. Then again, she'd chosen her dad over me when everything went wrong. Anyway, at the start of March, I received a very official-looking letter. I was off the hook. Robbie had changed her plea to guilty, so I didn't need to give evidence. It was a tremendous relief, but it also confirmed that Robbie would face a lengthy prison sentence.

The Thursday morning storyline sessions continued. I loved those days, warm and cosy in Jen's kitchen, plotting, planning and laughing constantly. We'd also settled into a lovely Friday evening routine. I would turn up with a couple of bottles of wine, and Jen would cook something nice. I'd become an expert at story reading and even started to write my own. Charley seemed to love them, and Jen suggested I pull them together into a book. Not once had I thought I would become a children's author, but apparently, I am. I now have an agent, Flossie, who assures me a publishing deal is imminent. I felt like I would be found out any day now. They were just a bunch of silly stories I'd made up to send Charley to sleep.

Often, Friday evenings would continue well into Saturday morning, sitting on Jen's sofa and talking. In truth, we were both getting over a loss. Talking certainly helped me and, I'd like to think, helped Jen come to terms with losing Sean.

By the way, you can cut that out. I know what you're thinking. Obviously, one thing would lead to another and that sort of thing, but no, neither of us was ready for that. I'd sometimes stay over in the spare room and sometimes walk home. There'd be the occasional cuddle on the sofa in front of one of Jen's rom-coms, but both of us were quite content to let wounds heal.

Vince Taylor was working hard and starting to earn a reputation for quality script-writing. The production company had mentioned a possible trip to New York later in the summer. Perhaps Jen would get to see the Empire State Building after all. For now, Uncle Frankie was enjoying his new life as a writer and looking forward rather than back.

34

On the second Saturday in May, we held a wake for the writer that had been Frankie Dale. It seemed like the right time to do it. The final part of the serialisation of 'The Woman In The Yellow Raincoat' was published in a well-known Sunday paper that weekend. Gavin had sent a sizeable cheque to the local hospice, and the thank-you letter was framed on the wall above my desk. The website would be taken down at the end of June.

Vince Taylor had his first writing credit on the Netflix series due to start filming in September. There'd been a bit of a compromise there. The actress that Caroline had lined up announced she was pregnant. It caused a bit of a scandal, actually, as the father was a premier league footballer and married to somebody else. At least he was at the time. He's not now. Anyway, the upshot was that she couldn't do it, and as a result, Caroline withdrew the sponsorship. The role was recast, and an excellent but unknown American will now play the part. Daisy has become Daisy-Mae, and the series is set in Los Angeles.

The yellow raincoat was deemed unsuitable for the LA

setting because it never rained, so why would she always be wearing the coat? So, 'The Girl In The Red Tee-Shirt' is due to premiere next spring. Jen and I were very proud! Vince was more than happy with the fee.

The bar at The Crown was totally empty when I arrived. It was early, so I thought I would catch the football results for the last day of the season on the TV in the snug. I walked down the familiar corridor. I should've known, but the cheer as I walked in frightened the life out of me. Ambrose, as always, handed me a pint. Stella and Joe sat on either side of him. Ollie and Polly even got to meet each other in person for the first time. Spud was there with his new girlfriend, who I think is called Natasha (but could just as likely be Natalie). I played it safe and said a general hello to everybody. Spud spoke up.

'Frankie, I think you've met Nadia.'

'Yes, of course. Hi Nadia, thanks for coming.' That was close. Sitting on Jen's knee was Charley. Jen shuffled up on the bench to make room for me.

'Charley here wanted to show uncle Frankie her party dress before she goes to her Gran's for the night.'

'Very nice it is, too. Now don't go all shy on me.' Charley buried her head against Jen's shoulder. So much for my charm. Joe rummaged around under the table and produced a large, flat, gift-wrapped package.

'We had this made to commemorate the occasion.' He handed it over, and I made a show of holding it up and gently shaking it.

'Is it a book? A CD?' There was a chorus of 'Open it'. Somebody, I'm not sure who, added the word idiot at the end — no call for that. I asked Charley to help me open it. She climbed down from her mum's knee and helped me tear the paper off. I smiled, genuinely touched. It was a framed TWITYR tee-shirt with a gold-coloured plaque that read RIP

Frankie and Daisy with today's date. 'Thanks everybody, just what I always wanted.' I propped the frame up on the back of the bench, leaning against the wall. Charley got over her shyness and climbed onto my knee. Jen laughed.

'Wow. You're honoured. Only Gran and Santa get that sort of treatment.'

'Not bad company to be in, I suppose.' It was Jen's turn to hand over a package. 'This isn't fair. I haven't got anything for you guys. I didn't think it was that sort of do. In my defence, I haven't been to my own wake before.'

'I thought it may come in handy.' Charley opened this one for me and couldn't understand what was so funny. It was a big, green first-aid kit.

'Thank you very much, but I intend to avoid smacking my head on any hard surfaces this evening, but it's very thoughtful.' I took a long drink from my pint. As I put the glass down, I saw Jen shake her head at Charley and mouth what looked like the word later. 'What are you two up to?' I tickled Charley to try to get an answer out of her. She laughed hysterically, but didn't say anything. It was Jen that answered.

'Charley's got another surprise for you, but it's for later.'

'A surprise? For me? I want it now.'

'No. You have to wait. Do you want another pint?' Spud leapt to his feet.

'I'll get these. What does everybody want?'

'Cheers, Spud. I've always liked you. I'll have another pint of bitter.'

The drinks arrived just as a small, grey-haired woman popped her head around the door.

'Hi Mum. Everybody, this is my mum, Geraldine.' We all said hello, and Spud asked what she wanted to drink.

'Nothing for me, thanks. I've just come to collect Charley and take her for tea with Grandad and me. We're going for chicken nuggets.' Those were obviously the magic words, and Charley flung herself towards her gran. 'I think somebody's hungry. Say good night, Charley.'

Charley went and hugged her mum before demanding high fives from the rest of us in turn. I was last in line, and my high five was accompanied by 'Laters', and she took Geraldine's hand. I was proud that I'd taught her that.

Once Charley was out of the door, the noise levels started to rise, and drink was taken. As usual with this lot, the conversation was easy, and there was lots of laughter. It must've been an hour later when Ambrose held up a hand. The noise around the table subsided, and he spoke.

'I just wanted to say a few words to mark the occasion.'

'So do I, get 'em in' said Stella, holding her half-full glass up.

'In a minute, love. I'll keep it short. About eighteen months ago, this bloke here was a pitiful sight.'

'Cheers mate, none taken.'

'You were. No job, no woman and rarely a shower.' Lots of holding of noses and general abuse. 'But, he picked himself up, turned things around, and made a huge success of a project and made lots of new friends on the way.' There was a cheer and a round of applause. 'Yes, he put the work in, but I'm taking credit for all of it.' More laughter. 'I'm serious. I came up with the tweet challenges, and it worked. The challenges got him off his backside. Without them, he wouldn't have met Joe or Jen.' I raised my glass to both of them in turn. 'Granted, he wouldn't have met the woman who broke his heart again.'

Booing this time. 'But, he also wouldn't have come up with the success that was "The Woman In The Yellow Raincoat". So, let's drink a toast to the old Frankie Dale. RIP Frankie, long live Vince Taylor.' We all raised our glasses and drank a solemn toast. I was just about to reply when Ambrose raised a hand again. 'Just in case he thinks I've forgotten, the original challenge was in five parts. He only completed four.' Oh shit! 'Tonight we are going to complete the challenge; day five.' I began to protest, but it was no good.

'What if I want to go for the forfeit?'

'Trust me, you don't want to go for the forfeit. Phone out, come on.' I pulled my phone from my pocket. The time was 7.28. 'Right. You know how this works. Open Twitter, and refresh the timeline. When the time clicks to 7.30, you refresh again and have to act on one of the first five tweets.' Everybody leaned forward and stared at the phone. I suddenly needed to pee, but knew protest was futile.

The minute clicked over, and I refreshed the timeline. This was ridiculous. Why was I so nervous?

It was from the local paper.

'Man jailed for five years after a string of Post Office robberies.'

Oh dear, better luck next time, Billy. I scrolled to tweet two.

Detox your life with my fabulous new diet plan. Rid your body of toxins like alcohol, caffeine and sugar.

'That's a truly terrifying thought. Those are the three things that held my body together. Without them, I'd crumble to nothing.'

'I take it that's a no? Two down, three to go.'

I scrolled again. Next was an advert.

'Why the hell am I getting ads for incontinence pants?' Ambrose howled with laughter.

'Is there something you'd like to share with the group?'

'Ha bloody ha.'

'These things are based on your search history. What in the name of Bob Marley have you been searching for?'

'Can we move on?'

'Two to go. Squeaky bum time.' Ambrose was enjoying this far too much.

'Do you want to be famous? Channel 5 are looking for

contestants for their new reality show, Fame or Bust. Whatever happens, you will be famous!'

Everybody except me found this one hilarious. Ambrose almost choked.

'Why won't you go for that?'

'I've just gone to great lengths to become anonymous, thank you very much. That's a pass.'

'One to go. You have to take this, or it's the forfeit.'

'Is the forfeit really bad?' Ambrose nodded and patted me on the back. I took a deep breath and scrolled again. On the screen was a picture that looked like it had been drawn by a three-year-old. There was a man dressed in blue, with what looked like a guitar around his shoulder. Above his head was a sign that said "K. West". It was like the cover of Ziggy Stardust. The writing was suspiciously good, and I sensed that Mum had helped with that one. The text just said, *'I need to know what happened next to the spiders from Mars. Can I have a story tomorrow?'*

I looked at Jen. 'Is that by Charley?'

'She had a little help, but yes.'

'How the hell did you get that into my timeline at exactly the right time?'

'I have to thank Spud for that.'

Spud looked shifty.

'I doctored your phone when you went to the loo. I replaced the Twitter app with a dummy version that looks exactly like the real thing.'

'You do realise that's probably illegal? Then again, thanks, mate. That's a brilliant surprise.'

'Can I tell her that's a yes, then?'

'Course you can. Gets me off the forfeit at least.' Ambrose stood up and bowed.

'In that case, my work here is done. Challenge over. Who wants another drink?'

EPILOGUE

When I arrived at Jen's, the front door was ajar. I stepped inside and heard voices upstairs. After a minute, I called up.

'Come on, you're going to be late.' I turned, car keys in my hand, and my eye was drawn, once again, to the framed copy of the Ziggy album that Charley created. Much as I loved the original cover, it was the simple wax crayon version that always made me smile.

'How does she look?' It was Charley's first day at school. I'd never had to wear a school uniform, but had to admit it made an impression.

'She looks brilliant, as does her mum.'

'Charmer. You've scrubbed up quite well yourself.'

We stepped outside, and Charley climbed into the back seat of the Eos. After we'd dropped her at school, we met Gavin to formally sign the contract for our first film script. After that was a private screening of the first episode of the TV series.

Spud had taken over the lease of my old office, and I was a silent partner in his new software business. Joe had opened a club in Ibiza. It sounded like he was having a great time and was a regular in the gossip columns. Ambrose had bought the shop and spent his days surrounded by an outstanding selection of records. He and Stella were adopting a five-year-old daughter any day now. Charley was very excited at the prospect of a new friend.

Robbie was still in prison. A few weeks ago, she'd written to me, saying how sorry she was. She sounded very low, but determined to break away from the shadow of her dad. I believed her when she said her feelings for me had been genuine but, when it came to the crunch and the police started to take an interest, she backed her dad's emergency plan. Apparently, he'd even tried to claim his insurance to get back the deposit for the wedding venue. They told him to bugger off. Good.

Rupert had already been released from prison. Spud had offered him a job after he'd convinced us both that, he too, was finished with his dad. I'd met him in the Crown last week. He looked miserable, a bit scruffy. I bought him a pint and asked if he was up for a challenge.

'Right, get your phone out. Open Twitter.'

The End

Oh, hang on a minute, I almost forgot.

A few weeks later, we loaded up the car, and the three of us, me, Jen and Charley, set off towards the coast.

We'd been once before. Jen wanted to show Charley the sea for the first time, and I dealt with some of the guilt of not seeing my parents more often. I'd had to remind Mum that Jen and I were 'just good friends', and she didn't need to dash out and buy a new hat. We were business partners. That didn't stop her from making a real fuss of Charley, and they were now best friends.

Mum was bouncing on the spot again as I pulled up. Charley sprinted from the car and into her arms. The name Aunty Gran had stuck. Uncle Grandad appeared from inside and joined in. We were ushered into the kitchen, where a buffet was ready in its cling film wrapping.

'That looks nice,' said Jen, gently slapping my hand as it hovered towards a pork pie.

'Charley, would you like to come for a walk on the beach with Uncle Grandad and me? We thought it would work up an appetite.'

'What about Mum and Frankie?' She grabbed my hand. I squatted, so I was at eye level.

'Me and your mum have to dial into a meeting.'

'Not another meeting,' sighing like a pensioner.

'Tell you what. You set off, and we'll catch up. It won't take long.'

'How will you catch up?'

'Well, you and Aunty Gran only have little legs. We can take big strides and be with you by the time you've caught a fish.'

'How will I catch a fish? I don't have a net.' Just then, Uncle Grandad produced the net from behind his back, and there was a full-on charge towards the door.

Once we'd made sure they'd gone, Jen and I got to work. Mum had remembered to leave the garage open, and I soon retrieved the boxes marked as hi-fi. Everything had been neatly packed and labelled. Before long, the impressive speakers were in place, and the turntable and amp were in the stand next to Dad's armchair. I retrieved the two heavy record cases from the car and cued up Ziggy for a test drive. Everything worked perfectly. We locked up and set off for the beach.

Charley was in the middle of building a sandcastle. The four adults, I now included myself in that category, sat on the dunes and chatted. My parents had taken to Jen from the start and always carefully avoided the topic of Robbie. After a while, we heard the squeal from Charley as the incoming tide attacked the ramparts. At that point, we all decided we were hungry and headed home.

Jen took Charley off to the bathroom, and Mum attacked the cling film. I took the opportunity to pull Dad to one side.

'Come through here. I want to show you something.'

I opened the door of the back room, and Dad stepped in.

'Bugger me. So that's what you were up to, is it?'

'Why don't you sit in your chair and pick something to play?'

'But I don't have any records these days, after the f—' He stopped and looked at me and blinked back a tear.

'Have a look in the cases.' He took his seat and began to flick through the first case. He pulled out the copy of Ziggy. 'It's signed, look.' I pointed.

'How the hell did you get these?'

'Contacts. Look, I thought this might help. I know that you blamed me for the fire, and I'm really, really sorry.'

'What? Blame you? Nay lad. I don't blame you at all.'

'But you've been, you know, a bit…'

'Of a prick?' The word was a shock. 'I've been a complete prick for years, but I never blamed you for the fire — just the opposite. I feel guilty that you got so badly scarred. The fire was caused by the wiring that I did, nothing to do with you. The insurance company replaced the equipment. It just didn't feel right to replace the records. They all just reminded me of the pain you'd gone through. You could've been killed.'

'So, all these years, I thought you blamed me. I'm still really sorry I couldn't save more records. Can we just agree we've both been pricks and start again?'

'I'd like that.'

He turned and took the record from its sleeve before expertly cueing side one track four. By the time we got to the chorus Jen, Charley and Mum had joined me sitting on the floor.

'There's a star-man, waiting in the sky…'

The End (definitely)

Also by Roy M. Burgess

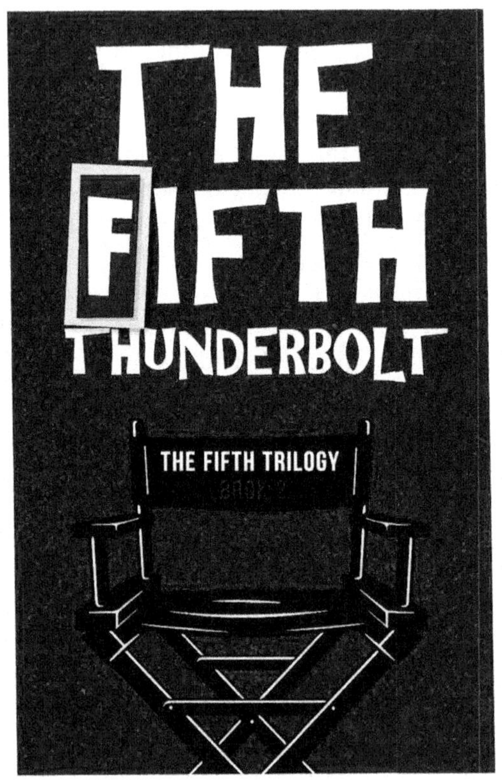

The Fifth Thunderbolt - The Fifth Trilogy Book 2

* * *

Frankie is in love with Jen but is afraid to tell her. Together, they are working on a film script about a kidnapping.

Roddy Lightning was a big star in the 60s, with his band, The Thunderbolts. A teen idol, with a habit of marrying his fellow Thunderbolts, he became a punk rebel in the 70s, a Hollywood star in the 80s, and a junkie in the 90s. At 78, he's a loveable senior with a twinkle in his eye, a lust for cake, and a failing memory.

Frankie risks everything to make him the star of the film, but when Roddy disappears, all seems lost. Is real life mimicking the film?

Can Frankie get the girl, find his errant star, make a success of his film and save his OEIC (whatever that is)?

Reviews on Amazon

"I love how these books are structured. I could read a little and potentially put it down for later. I could but I didn't as I wanted to see what happened next. Another book read in a couple of days as I couldn’t put it down ....just waiting for the next one Roy. Get writing!!!” - Jeanette ☆☆☆☆☆

“I love Roy M Burgess' witty writing style, and after reading his debut book last year, I was looking forward to Book 2. It did not disappoint at all. There are several cleverly woven threads running through this book: an adventure, a kidnapping, a love story, all told with the author's deft and humorous touch. I'm still smiling at our hero's adventures!” - Nifty Girl ☆☆☆☆☆

Buy now from Amazon - The Fifth Thunderbolt

THE
FIFTH

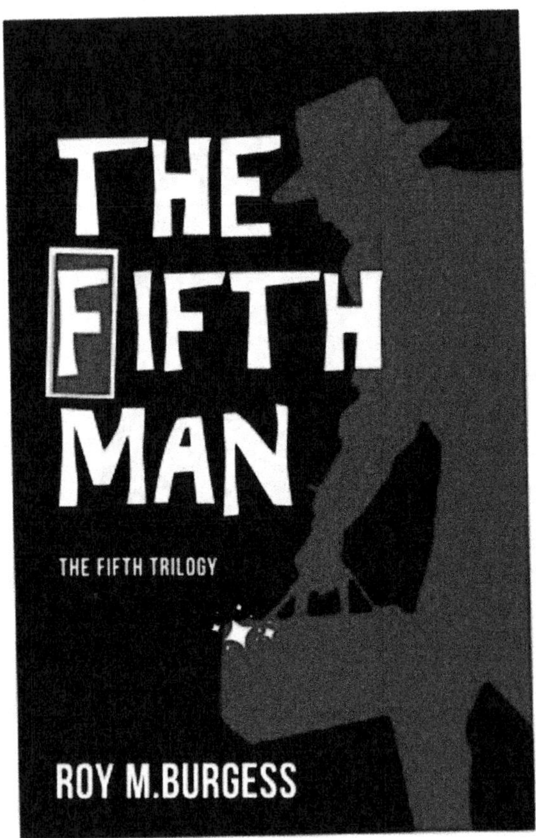

The Fifth Man - The Fifth Trilogy Book 3

Frankie's screwed up again — big time.

A stroke of luck, most often reserved for other people, offers a lifeline. Writing a TV script based on a true story could be his way out. Trouble is, he only knows half the facts behind a series of daring robberies that ended in murder. Turning detective, he teams up with a lapsed arsonist and sets out to reveal the truth. With his search threatening to put his loved ones in danger, he must uncover the mysterious Fifth Man.

But the clock is ticking, and the killer is ready to strike again.

Reviews on Amazon

An excellent third book in this funny, endearing and intriguing series

"So excited to read this third book in the series, and to find that Frankie is still on form, as is Roy M Burgess' witty writing style. The reader is taken along for the ride, with our hero hot on the heels of the Fifth Man, with jeopardy and intrigue amid the humour. Sometimes a series will lose momentum - not this one! Not to be missed by fans of Richard Osman."

Nifty Girl ☆☆☆☆☆

Like a good riff, this book will keep you hooked!

"I loved Roy's third book of the Fifth Trilogy. The narrative flows so easily, hilarious lines come out of nowhere and an ever evolving plot. I didn't want to put this book down."

Agostinho Lopes ☆☆☆☆☆

The Fifth Man is book three in **The Fifth Trilogy.** Buy now from Amazon

* * *

Printed in Great Britain
by Amazon

39756103R00169